PENNY

I was going to come. I shut my eyes, thinking of the unspeakable humiliation of being held over a short, squat old man's lap and told that my bottom and pussy were too fat. Then, having been so thoroughly humiliated, I'd be spanked . . . spanked . . . spanked . . .

I was saying it out loud as my orgasm built like a bubble in my head, then suddenly somebody spoke from directly behind me.

'You'd like that, wouldn't you?'

I jumped so hard that I bit my tongue, and turned to see a bulky man leering at me.

'Like a spanking, do you?' he asked.

Well, I could hardly deny it. He'd caught me masturbating over a spanking magazine and I'd been mumbling the word 'spanked' over and over when he'd come in. I could feel my face flushing as my embarrassment set in, but he took no notice.

'How about it, then?' he continued. It took a moment to register what he was saying. He was offering me a spanking.

Why not visit Penny's website at
www.pennybirch.com

By the same author:

A TASTE OF AMBER
BAD PENNY
BARE BEHIND
BRAT
DIRTY LAUNDRY
FIT TO BE TIED
IN DISGRACE
JODHPURS AND JEANS
NAUGHTY NAUGHTY
NURSE'S ORDERS
KNICKERS AND BOOTS
PEACH
PENNY IN HARNESS
PENNY PIECES
PETTING GIRLS
PLAYTHING
REGIME
TEMPER TANTRUMS
TICKLE TORTURE
TIGHT WHITE COTTON
UNIFORM DOLLS
WHEN SHE WAS BAD
TIE AND TEASE
WHAT HAPPENS TO BAD GIRLS
BRUSH STROKES

THE INDIGNITIES OF ISABELLE
THE INDISCRETIONS OF ISABELLE
THE INDECENCIES OF ISABELLE
(Writing as Cruella)

A NEXUS CLASSIC

IN FOR A PENNY

Penny Birch

This book is a work of fiction.
In real life, make sure you practise safe sex.

This Nexus Classic edition published in 2006

First published in 1999 by
Nexus
Thames Wharf Studios
Rainville Road
London W6 9HT

Typeset by TW Typesetting, Plymouth, Devon

Printed and bound by CPI Antony Rowe, Chippenham, Wiltshire

ISBN 978 0 352 34083 2

Contents

In for a Penny *is a collection of thirteen short stories, the first from me, the rest told by characters from my books,* Penny in Harness, A Taste of Amber, Bad Penny *and* Brat. *Anybody who has read my stories before will know that these are going to be pretty naughty; anybody who hasn't either has a treat in store or a big shock coming . . .*

A Perfect Example – Penny Birch

When I was at school, I had been nicknamed Little Miss Smarty Pants, and that was by the teachers. I was the girl who always had her head in a book, the one who was no good at games and never went out with boys. The teachers always complimented me, but with some I had a definite feeling of resentment. Looking back, I suppose they were simply uncomfortable with a pupil more intelligent than themselves. Only one was actually spiteful, and that was Miss Gower. She taught English Literature and always liked to have a little coterie of worshipful girls around her. When I joined the sixth form, she had done her best to persuade me to join her A level group, and had taken it as a personal insult when I chose to study sciences.

Given our past relationship, I was more than a little surprised to receive a letter from her inviting me to speak to the sixth form on careers in academia. Of course, to her, I was no longer Little Miss Smarty Pants: I was Dr Penny Birch BSc MSc PhD and the ideal old girl to inspire the current crop of senior girls to success in their careers. She was now Headmistress, and the tone of her letter was unctuous, to say the least. I was, she wrote, 'a perfect example of what a pupil might seek to achieve'.

I chose to accept, mainly because I hoped I might actually inspire some of the girls – even the boys – but also because it amused me to think of what the extraordinarily prim and proper Miss Gower would have thought if she had known what I was really like. At school, she'd been known to go into fits of moral indignation at girls and boys having a quick cuddle. If she'd known about my penchant for being spanked – let alone the pony-girl play, the watersports and the lesbian sex – she would have been nailing crosses to the front gates to keep me out, not inviting me in.

An even more obsequious letter of thanks arrived in response to my acceptance. I drove down the day before and stayed with my mother, intent on arriving early so that I could have a look round the school first. Lessons were in progress when I arrived and, rather than announce myself and be shown around formally, I decided to indulge in a bit of nostalgia and visit the places that had been special to me.

There were one or two new buildings and other smaller alterations, but essentially nothing had changed in the thirteen years since I'd left. The main building of red Victorian brick seemed identical, the playing fields had not changed one bit and the grounds were exactly as I remembered. I even managed to find the clump of rhododendrons beneath which my cousin Kate had lost her virginity. I smiled at the memory of how excited she'd been when she told me, and of her pride because she'd managed to seduce the junior groundsman. Not that it had been hard. Kate was gorgeous and he must have thought all his Christmases had come at once.

Gary Pugh had been his name, although we used to call him Ug. He was a big, swarthy lad who always went around with his shirt off. I'd thought he looked like an ape, with his hairy arms and his bulging muscles, but I find there's something sexy about the Neanderthal look. I had fancied him, if only from afar. Kate had been more practical, as always. At the time the head groundsman had been on the verge of retirement and did no work at all. Ug had ruled the place, buying cigarettes and beer for pupils – pornographic magazines for the boys, too, according to rumour. Possibly even cannabis, although I'd been far too good and shy to get involved with such things. I remembered that his centre of operations had been a red-brick hut. It was shaded by big old yew trees and well away from other buildings, and so had been ideal for his dubious behaviour.

That was where I turned my footsteps, feeling more nostalgic than ever. Gary himself would have been sacked years ago – nobody gets away with the sort of thing he'd done for too long. Still, I wanted to see, and there would be nobody about for a good hour and a half. I remembered the hut as a gloomy, rather sinister place where things happened that I dared not have anything to do with. It hadn't changed. In fact, if anything, the atmosphere was more intense than I remembered. The yews seemed to hang further down, the windows were more algae-encrusted and the huge heap of old leaves by the door smelt mustier than ever.

I stood there for a long moment with all the old memories flooding back. It had been a place of mystery to me, a place where daring things happened, where forbidden pleasures were indulged. I tried to tell myself not to be ridiculous and that some of the things I'd been up to since leaving would have shocked Ug himself. It didn't work, and I found myself taking a step towards the door with my stomach trembling as if I was once more an innocent school-girl.

All I wanted to do was look inside. Nobody appeared to be about and, even if the current groundsman appeared, I could easily explain who I was and make a joke of my interest in the hut. Telling myself to grow up, I stepped boldly forward and rapped on the door. Nothing happened – to my vast relief – but when I turned the handle it gave and the door came open with a low creak.

I had always pictured the inside as a sort of den of iniquity, with stacks of beer and cigarette cartons waiting to be sold on to the girls and boys, Ug sitting there counting his ill-gotten gains and perhaps a dirty magazine open on a table. Of course, it wasn't like that at all, but just a dusty old hut with pale sunlight slanting in through green and heavily cobwebbed windows, tools, flowerpots and other gardening paraphernalia and – of course – no Ug. My initial flush of disappointment was replaced by wry cynicism for my own over-active imagination and then by a mischievous feeling. Of course nothing was visible; staff might have looked into the hut at any time. Ug had been careful. He'd have had hiding places, maybe hiding places that still existed . . .

I began to look around, feeling wonderfully naughty and occasionally glancing out of the window to make sure nobody was approaching. Not that I expected to find anything, but it was such fun to search. Logically, any hiding place had to be sufficiently accessible for goods to be hidden and retrieved fast, yet obscure enough to avoid casual detection.

Being careful not to soil my dress, I started my search. Standing on the table allowed me to see in under the eaves but revealed nothing. The highest shelves had nothing interesting on them, either, while the chimney angle held only a pair of yellowing cigarette packets. It was as I climbed down that I spotted another possibility. In one corner, a huge earthenware flowerpot had been turned upside down on an old plastic sack. There was also a sack on top of it, and on that a small motor – filthy with oil and rotting grass.

It was probably innocent, but there was no harm in checking. I felt both excited and rather childish as I carefully lifted the sack with the motor on it, and then tilted back the flowerpot. I knew what I'd found the instant I saw the slim sheaves of paper and a flash of skintone. Nobody keeps their collection of motorsports magazines so carefully hidden.

Porn magazines aren't really my thing. Not because I object to seeing girls posing nude, but because they all seem to be aimed at half-witted Jack-the-lad types. This was different, and I recognised the style immediately. These were no ordinary dirty magazines, full of coarse observations on smiling girls in cheap lingerie. They were spanking magazines.

My hands were trembling as I took the top one. The

cover showed a girl – a ripe, young girl with full thighs and a plump peach of a bottom. You could tell that because all she had on was a pair of tight navy-blue knickers – knickers that were both far too small for her and half down over the crease of her bottom. She had her back to the camera but was peeping over her shoulder, as if at the reader. Her eyes showed alarm and trepidation, as well they might – on the table at her side lay a long, wicked school cane.

The other magazines were similar, each cover featuring a girl or girls in embarrassing postures and various states of exposure. Some were in knickers or shorts, some had their bottoms bare, a few had little skirts on, but every single one of them was quite clearly going to be getting her bottom whacked. Reasoning that it would be easiest to conceal if I heard anyone coming, I took the top one and carefully replaced the flowerpot.

Opening my selection I found more pictures of the girl from the cover – standing with her panties down at the front and her head hung in shame, kneeling in an armchair with her lovely plump bottom bare, ruefully clutching a bum-cheek across which a fat, grey-haired old man had just planted a long, red cane welt. There were others, too: a slim blonde on an exercise bike, a lovely full-bottomed woman in a traffic warden's outfit and a pretty dark-haired girl in her gymslip. In each case, the sequence of photos followed a predictable – but delightful – order. The first few would show the girl fully dressed, in attitudes of contrition or defiance. Then would come her exposure, sometimes of just her bottom, sometimes of her whole body, but always concentrating on her bottom. Next would be her punishment, with her bent into various rude and humiliating positions while she was beaten. Finally there were the corner shots, with the girls still bare-bottomed, but well-whacked and looking thoroughly sorry for themselves.

The pictures had their effect on me, but what I really wanted was a story. With trembling fingers, I flicked quickly through, hoping to find something that combined discipline with rudeness. The first was the gym discipline one, with a hard-faced young man making a girl strip to do exercises in the nude and then caning her. The second was about a girl shop assistant getting caught with her fingers in the till and being offered the choice of the sack or a spanking. It's the oldest plot of all, but I like it, and after another quick check out of the hut window I began to read.

It was presented as a reader's letter. That seemed unlikely, but I didn't care. First there was the description of the girl, Julie, a naïve young woman described as 'embarrassed over the size of her ample breasts and chubby buttocks'. That got to me. I may be petite, and my breasts are far from ample, but I've always felt my bottom to be disproportionately plump. Next came the description of the man, Mr Hodge. He was supposed to be the owner of a jewellers and 'short and squat, with a roll of fat above his tight collar and only a ruff of greying hair remaining on his head'. It was typical – the foul old man giving an intimate punishment to a pretty young girl – but I confess it brought home my sense of erotic humiliation. The story then went on to the theft and the actual spanking. I found myself speed-reading, eager to get to the place where the poor girl had her knickers pulled down before my nerve failed me.

For me, that is always the highlight of a spanking story, the moment when the girl has to endure the lowering of her panties in preparation for her punishment. This was a good one –

> 'Nonsense, Julie, of course your pants must come down. Do you really think a man of my age cares to see the bare bottom of a little snip of a girl like you? Good heavens, don't you think I've seen girls' bottoms bare before?'
>
> 'Yes, Mr Hodge, but not mine!'
>
> 'I'm sure you're no different from any other. Come on now, if you're going to be missish, I shall have to give you double, and it will be on the bare, believe me.'
>
> 'Mr Hodge! Please!'

'Come now, Julie, pop them down.'

'No! I won't! Not on the skin! It's . . . it's indecent!'

'Indecent? For a girl like you to have her pants taken down when she needs a spanking? By a man of my seniority? Nonsense: it's right and proper!'

'I shan't!'

'Oh, yes, you shall. Now, down they come!'

– and down they came, but only after Mr Hodge had pulled the frantically kicking Julie down over his knee. It described how she felt while her knickers were peeled down and how the filthy old bastard had a good feel and then told her that her pussy showed from the rear. Then she got her spanking.

I had just got to the point where he had decided that his hand wasn't having the proper effect and that he ought to be using a shoe, when I thought I heard a noise outside and quickly put the magazine under a flowerpot. I glanced out of the window and there was nothing, but it really brought home to me the appalling risk I was taking.

Yet I was shaking hard, and badly needed to masturbate. It was a hot day and I'd chosen a loose but smart dress, stay-up stockings and lightweight cotton undies. All I needed to do was slip a hand up my dress and down my knickers . . .

I didn't dare, not there, not in a hut where a groundsman read spanking magazines! God, he probably masturbated over them himself, sitting in the very chair I'd been in, his cock hard in his hand over the thought of Julie getting her spanking or the picture of the traffic warden having her panties pulled down. No, he was a man: he'd want to do it over the rudest picture, the big colour centre spread of the cover girl with her knickers around one ankle, her bottom lifted and her pussy and bumhole showing . . .

God, I needed it badly, but it was just too risky. Yet there was no sign of anybody, only birdsong and the distant sound of a mower. A mower meant a groundsman, and while he was using the mower, he couldn't be in his hut. What if there were two of them? No, there was only one chair, only one mug in the ancient china sink. As long as I could hear the mower, I was safe. Unless . . .

Unless a hundred things, but maybe if I was quick, maybe if I just rubbed myself through my panties. I didn't dare. I should wait until I got back to my mother's. No, I'd never be able to concentrate properly. I needed it now, anyway, and I needed to think about being spanked. To be spanked, just like Julie in the story. To be put over the dirty old bastard's knee and spanked and spanked and spanked; spanked until the tears ran down my face, spanked until I howled.

I was going to do it. My hand was up my dress. My finger was burrowing into the damp cotton of my knickers over my pussy, then going under the gusset. I found the wet, sensitive flesh between my lips, began to rub . . .

It was no good. I had to have my story. Quickly, I lifted the big flowerpot and pulled the magazine out from beneath it. Turning the pages with frantic haste, I found my place, the argument where Mr Hodge was trying to persuade the unfortunate Julie to pull down her own knickers in front of him.

I started a little earlier, at the interview where she chose to accept a spanking as punishment. The mower was still going in the distance, so I spread the magazine out on the table. I pulled my dress up and sat myself down back to front on the chair and slid a hand down the front of my panties. My bum was sticking out over the edge of the chair, which felt nice. It was the same position that the cover girl ended up sitting in, with her whipped bottom stuck out bare while her uncle and aunt took tea.

With my middle finger moving over my clit in my favourite little circular motions, I began to masturbate. My pussy was really soaking, and I soon began to feel the first stirrings of an orgasm. With my pelvic muscles clenching gently and my breathing rate growing, I let it build, twice going back to the story so that I could climax at the point I found rudest of all, when he told her that her bottom and pussy looked overweight.

As my climax approached, I focused hard on the story, forming the words of shame and ecstasy on my lips as I read –

'You see, Julie, one way or the other, they come down, and now you'll be getting double for your mulish behaviour.'

Julie gave a broken sob and then she felt Mr Hodge's hand in the waistband of her precious panties. Down they came, unhurriedly and without ceremony, as if the exposure of her bottom was really quite unimportant. Then they were around her thighs and she discovered the true meaning of shame.

'There we are,' Mr Hodge chortled, 'all bare. That really wasn't so bad, was it? Really, the fuss you girls make over your bodies, as if it could possibly matter that you're seen out of your pants!'

He had begun to feel her bottom, stroking and squeezing the cheeks as if testing the quality of a pair of ripe pumpkins.

'Please, Mr Hodge, if I must be punished, get it over with!' Julie pleaded.

'All in good time,' he replied. 'You really should lose a little weight, you know. It's just puppy-fat, I suppose, but your bottom is simply enormous and even your cunt mound looks fat. Oh, yes, I can see that, don't think I can't.'

That was too much. I was going to come. I shut my eyes, thinking of the unspeakable humiliation of being held over a short, squat old man's lap and told that my bottom and pussy were too fat. Then, having been so thoroughly humiliated, I'd be spanked . . . spanked . . . spanked . . .

I was saying it out loud as my orgasm built like a bubble in my head, then suddenly somebody spoke from directly behind me.

'You'd like that, wouldn't you?'

I jumped so hard that I bit my tongue. If it hadn't been for that, I think I'd have just run. As it was, I instinctively clutched at my mouth and found myself looking at a bulky man of about forty, now heavily bearded, but still with his hirsute chest and arms quite bare. It was Ug.

'Like a spanking, do you?' he asked, leering meaningfully at me.

Well, I could hardly deny it. He'd caught me masturbating over a spanking magazine and I'd been mumbling the word 'spanked' over and over when he'd come in. I could feel my face flushing as my embarrassment set in, but he took no notice.

'How about it, then?' he continued. 'I'll do it better than that old git, I can promise you.'

It took a moment to register what he was saying. He was offering me a spanking and the 'old git' was the supposed uncle in the photo on the page opposite my story. It showed him ordering the girl to take off her blouse, and she had two large, round breasts already on display.

I could have got up and walked away. I could have screamed the place down and accused him of assault. I could have kicked him in the balls. I didn't. If there's one thing I've learnt about sexual encounters, it's that when a chance comes, don't pass it by. This was Ug, the man who'd taken Kate's virginity. I hadn't lost mine for a further five years, and all because I'd been so timid.

'Yes, I would,' I answered, my jaw trembling hard, 'but you stop when I say.'

'Suits me,' he said and sat down on a pile of manure sacks.

He was grinning from ear to ear and eyeing me up and down, clearly impressed, which increased my confidence. Then he patted his lap in a gesture whose meaning was heart-stoppingly familiar to me. I went forward, bending my body over his legs until my fingers were touching the ground and my bottom was the highest part of my body.

'You're Katie James' little sister, aren't you?' he asked as he began to fondle my bottom through my dress.

'Cousin,' I answered.

'Wendy, isn't it, or Jenny?' he said, tracing a line up the crease of my bottom with one thick finger.

'Penny,' I corrected him, and swallowed the lump of tension in my throat.

'Oh, yes, that's right,' he went on. 'Who'd have thought it, Little Miss Smarty Pants a spanky girl?'

I was past replying, because he had started to pull up my dress and I could feel the material gliding slowly up the backs of my thighs, over the tops of my stay-ups and on to my bottom. Then it was tucked up under my belt and I was showing my panties, a little green pair in light cotton.

He kept talking and began to stroke my bottom through my knickers, asking what I was doing at the school and even what Kate was up to. He didn't seem too worried about having me bent over and willing for a spanking. Perhaps he just wanted to take his time, but it really added to my excitement as I waited for the supreme moment of indignity.

It came soon enough. He had a good feel of my bum, stroking my panty seat, weighing my cheeks in his hand, tickling the crease and even going down between my legs to feel over my pussy. I was soaking, and he gave a knowing chuckle when he found out, then prodded me as if to imply that my vagina would be easy to penetrate.

'Hot little bitch, aren't you?' he said. 'Well, I suppose we'd better have these down, then.'

He just reached up and jerked them down, but I almost came. One moment, I was covered, if only by my panties; the next, my bum was bare. I gasped at the sensation of exposure and he chuckled, a really dirty sound. With a couple of quick tugs, he pulled my knickers down around my knees and then laid a big, rough hand on the softness of my bottom.

I was whimpering and really shaking. I like being spanked, I really do, but that doesn't mean it's not humiliating and it certainly doesn't mean it doesn't hurt! Ug had been a strapping lad in his twenties; now he was a great brute.

Doubtless sensing my fear, he laughed and then caught me by the arm, twisting it up into the small of my back and locking my wrist in one massive hand. Now I was helpless, bare-bottomed over his knee and about to be spanked . . .

The first smack caught me hard across the crest of my bum and I yelped. It was really hard, not like the skilful stinging slaps that girlfriends give me, but a solid wallop that sent a shock right up my spine to my jaw. It left my bottom smarting terribly, but at my protest he just laughed and gave me another, even harder. As the pain hit me, I wondered how I could ever have been so stupid as to volunteer for a spanking from such a gross beast. I've been spanked by big men before. I've even been beaten with an oar, but this was worse!

After about five swats, I just lost control completely, kicking and squealing and wiggling my bottom about in a desperate response to my self-imposed punishment. Ug just laughed and carried on with my spanking, occasionally commenting on what a lewd display I was making of myself.

That was what turned it around for me. He used such crude words to describe my body as he beat me – 'cunt', 'fuck-hole', 'arse-slit' and even 'chocolate starfish' for my bum-hole. Certainly my endorphins were beginning to run, but on a conscious level it was his filthy language that got to me. Suddenly, I was once more desperately in need of my interrupted orgasm. I threw my knees across his nearer leg, stretching my panties taut against his shin and bringing my pussy into rude and intimate contact with the rough tweed of his trousers.

'Here, you'll get cunt-slime all over my trousers, you little bitch,' he protested as I started to rub myself on his leg.

He gave me a really hard swat, making my bum-cheeks bounce and slamming my pussy against his leg. His trousers were covered in oil and grass clippings anyway, so I didn't see it mattered to him if I rubbed myself off on them. It mattered more to me, but I was too far gone to care.

'Keep talking; tell me what you see,' I begged, 'and spank faster.'

'Dirty bitch,' he answered, but made no move to stop me rubbing.

He cocked his knee up suddenly, jamming his thigh hard into my pussy. Then the tempo of the slaps on my bottom changed, coming faster and lower, slapping the sweet spot where my bum-cheeks join my thighs. My clit was touching the coarse tweed of his trousers and rubbing with each smack on my bum. It was ecstasy and I knew I'd soon be coming. Then he started to talk.

'You love this, don't you? You love a good spanking. You love to have your pants down and your slit open. You love to show it all off, your little hairy cunt and your juicy fuck-hole. I can see it all, Penny, when my hand isn't in the way, 'cause I'm spanking your bare arse, that is. You've got a wet cunt, really sopping. Get your arse up higher, you little tart. Make the cheeks spread. Show us your dirty little ring. Yeah, that's right, you squeak like you hate it, but you keep rubbing your cunt on me, don't you? Yeah, up and down, up and down, smack, smack, smack. Oh, you want to see yourself, girl; every time your arse-slit opens, I can see your starfish . . .'

That was too much for me. On the word 'starfish', I started to come. I'd been holding back, but I could hold no more. Bucking my pelvis frantically, I got the full friction of his trousers on my clit. Every muscle in my body seemed to lock at once; my back arched and I screamed aloud. A smack caught me, squashing my bottom and giving me a new apex of pleasure. I kicked my legs and my downed panties strained between my knees as another smack and a third peak caught me, then a fourth and last and it was all dying quickly away.

'Stop! Ow! I've come,' I yelped as another smack landed on my cheeks.

He stopped and I slumped down. I felt limp, exhausted, thoroughly chastened, and happy in the way that only a really good spanking can make me. I was bare-bottomed over his lap with my reddened buttocks thrust high, my knees cocked wide, my panties stretched taut between them, my pussy and bumhole on plain show – a ridiculous, utterly shameful posture for me to be in and oh, so nice.

He tightened his grip on my arm and once more began

to explore my bottom. Maybe he expected me to try and get up because I'd come, but I'm not that selfish. Even without my arm twisted up, I'd have been totally compliant. I knew he'd want something out of me anyway, and I was happy to let it happen.

My bottom was burning: a hot, throbbing pain. He was soothing me by hand, stroking my sore cheeks and kneading gently, surprisingly gently, considering what a brute he'd been during my spanking. I lifted my bottom and gave a soft purr, pleased by the way he was handling me. He responded by sliding his hand between my thighs and cupping my pussy.

I had expected him to want his own pleasure and was surprised when he started to masturbate me. Not that I was going to stop him, and I relaxed as he put a big, callused finger along the length of my pussy-groove and began to rub at me. Before long, I felt a thumb inserted into my vagina and he began to fuck me with it and rub my clit at the same time. Soon, I was breathing hard and lifting my bum to his touch, then grunting and rubbing myself on him to get the contact with my clit just right. I came again, a long, drawn-out orgasm: not as intense as the first, but still lovely. He kept rubbing until I'd completely finished and then pulled his thumb out of my pussy with a sticky pop. I slumped down again, smiling happily to myself and quite off my guard.

'I do like a souvenir,' he said cheerfully and, with a sudden motion, he had whipped my panties down from knee-level and off.

'Hey, come on,' I protested, as I climbed off his lap. 'I've got to give a talk to the sixth form in half an hour.'

'Then you can do it knickerless.' He laughed and stuffed the little scrap of green cotton into his trouser pocket. 'It'll do you good; keep you in mind of Gary.'

'My bum will do that,' I answered. 'That was hard. It really smarts.'

'Liked it, though, didn't you?' he laughed. 'Now, how about a nice suck of my cock before you hurry off?'

'I . . . Only if you give me my panties back,' I answered.

I'd been spanked, well spanked, and I always like to give sex to someone who has spanked me, often oral sex. Sucking him was no problem, but I did want my panties back.

'Fair enough,' he answered. 'Go down between my legs, then. You can swallow and all. I don't like mess in my hut.'

He drew down his zip and flopped his penis into his hand. It was fat, a dull brownish pink, and already half turgid with blood. I knelt obediently – using a plastic sack to keep my knees clean – and took it into my mouth. It tasted intensely male and slightly of oil, as if he'd been using household lubricant to masturbate with. He probably had, but I was too turned on to make an issue of it and began to suck. His cock swelled quickly and, when it was fully hard, I put my fingers around the base of the shaft and began to masturbate him into my mouth. He was soon grunting with pleasure and calling me dirty names, which I knew meant he wouldn't take long to come. Sure enough, barely before I'd got into the rhythm of things, his erection jerked and my mouth was filled with slimy, salty male come. I gulped it down, no more wanting mess on my dress than he did on the floor.

Time was pressing and Miss Gower would be wondering what had happened to me, so I adjusted myself as best I could and asked Gary if there was anything about me that looked unusual.

'Only your red backside,' he laughed.

'Thanks,' I answered, ignoring his remark. 'Look, I've got to go, so can I have my knickers, please?'

''Fraid not,' he answered.

'You promised!' I retorted. 'I gave you your suck, didn't I?'

'And very nice it was, too,' he said. 'But I want a souvenir of this afternoon, and your panties are what I'll have.'

'Please!' I said. 'I can't go knickerless!'

'Don't see why not,' he stated flatly. 'I don't suppose you were exactly planning on showing the sixth formers your panties anyway, were you?'

'No, of course not, but . . .'

'Come on, Penny. I know you girls. You'll have three dozen pairs at home, all just as pretty. These are mine, now, so you'd best put up with it.'

'You're a bastard!' I snapped, but it was pointless. I couldn't get my knickers off him by force, so that was that. I'd be spending the rest of the day bare under my skirt.

I left, feeling thoroughly humiliated and intensely self-conscious. The worst of it was that being forced to go knickerless under a dress is just the sort of fantasy I like, and I knew that, by the time I got back to my mother's house and fresh clothes, I would be thoroughly turned on. That night, I'd masturbate over what Ug had done to me. I knew I'd do it, and that was the most humiliating thing of all.

Miss Gower greeted me in her study and I made some feeble excuse for being late. She suggested going straight to the hall, and chattered merrily all the way, talking about the school and asking politely ignorant questions about my work. I answered evasively, all the while thinking of my poor bare bottom and the way that bastard Pugh had pinched my panties.

I felt more self-conscious than ever as I walked down the length of the school hall. Externally I was immaculate, the very image of a successful young professional woman. Underneath, I had no knickers and a red bum.

I would have been nervous anyway, but having no panties on made it so much worse. Some three hundred sixth formers were looking at me: some intense, some rebellious, some just bored. I have lectured to larger audiences, I've delivered papers to hostile symposia, but nothing had prepared me for this. I'd expected it to be easy, a simple speech to an audience of sixth formers. It was anything but and, as the last of my confidence ebbed away, I found myself once more Little Miss Smarty Pants, going up to collect my Scholar's Ribbon with every single person in the audience hoping I'd fall flat on my face.

I wish I had. Instead I put my heel in one of the ventilator grates, just as Miss Gower ushered me towards the stage steps. I went over, hard: not on my face, but on to my knees. I tried to save myself, but it was a mistake. My bag caught my dress, pulling it up and leaving me kneeling on the steps with my bottom high and my dress over my back.

There were no knickers to cover my modesty, no tights, nothing. I was showing the full, naked moon of my bottom to all three hundred of them. Moreover, it was thrust more or less directly at Miss Gower's face. I didn't need a mirror to know what it looked like. My pussy would be well juiced and open from the spanking and his intrusive digit, all pink and wet and wide in her nest of black hair. My bumhole would be showing, a wrinkled knot of pinkish-brown flesh in the depths of a rather hairy crease. Worst of all, my bottom cheeks would not be their normal pale flesh tone, but a deep flushed pink, the colour of spanked bottom flesh, freshly spanked.

. . . oh, well, it could have been worse. No, on second thoughts, it probably couldn't have been.

Unlike me, Ginny Scott is one of those lucky few who never seem to worry. This must be partly because she is pretty and blonde with a figure that might have been taken from a naughty cartoon but, more importantly – I think – she was simply born with a playful personality. She takes an uncomplicated delight in life and particularly in sex, without any of the guilt and uncertainty that hinder so many of us. In Penny in Harness, *I described how she helped introduce me to the delights of pony-girl play, but her story takes place long before that, when she was Ginny Linslade and living on her parents' farm in Wiltshire . . .*

Sweet Charity – Ginny Linslade

There was a new man working in the High Forty who Arthur said was taller than Matthew. They're my brothers; Matthew's nice, but Arthur's a bit grumpy sometimes. Anyway, I like tall men, so I had to see this guy; and who knew, maybe he'd be worth luring into the long grass for a cuddle.

I knew I was supposed to be helping with the silly cheese-making project, so I threw on a skimpy blue summer dress over my knickers and escaped out the front. It was a lovely day, hot but with a breeze blowing from the downs so that I could smell the scent of hay. I felt great, and I knew I looked good. The blue dress complemented my golden hair, for a start, but that wouldn't be what the men were looking at. The dress was quite old, and I'd had a lot less boob when it had been new. Now they filled out the little pleated front until it looked fit to burst. The material was really tight, squashing them out and making me feel really conscious of them. As I had no bra, my nipples showed through underneath, and I know what that does to men.

Another good thing about the breeze was that, up on the downs, it would probably be strong enough to make my skirt blow up to flash my knickers. I love it when men see my knickers and think I'm all embarrassed about showing them, and it's a sure way of getting attention. I'd chosen a pale blue pair to match my dress, skimpy enough to show my bum off properly. I'm afraid I do rather tend to grow out of my clothes and, like my dress, my knickers were tight and made my bottom bulge out rather around the sides. I knew it made my bum look pretty big, but men like girls to have big bums, or at least that's what they're always telling me.

I ran most of the way up to the ridge and then walked, ever so demurely, when I reached the lane that leads to the High Forty. He was there, and he was gorgeous. I suppose he must have been about six foot four, and he was working with his shirt off so that all the big, golden-brown muscles of his chest showed. Matthew was there, too. He knows what a little flirt I am and doesn't mind but, after greeting me with a knowing grin, he warned me not to break up their work.

The rest of the morning was really frustrating but also really exciting. Knowing that it was best not to cheek Matthew, I chose to wait until their lunch break. The top end of the field made a lovely place to sunbathe, so I lay down and spent my time giving my man a tease-show that there was no way he was going to resist.

First it was my legs, with my dress rucked up to show their full length as I lay on my front. An 'accidental' movement left the bit of my knickers showing where they tuck under my bottom, and I stayed like that until I was sure he'd had a good stare. After a while, I rolled over and pulled my dress even higher, right up until it was tucked up under my boobs. I closed my eyes and lay back, feeling incredibly horny. The sun felt hot on my body and I could feel the tight material of the little blue knickers that were all that shielded my pussy from his gaze. My boobs felt huge – they are pretty huge, I suppose, embarrassingly so sometimes: but not now, not when the man of my dreams was eyeing them and wondering how they'd feel in his hands. I began to think of how he would hold them, weighing them in his hands as if he couldn't believe how big they were, stroking my nipples until they were all hard and tingly, sucking them until I was melting in his arms . . .

It was too much; I had to do it. With what was supposed

to look like an impatient shrug, I pulled my dress up over my head and lay back down. I was topless, with only my knickers to hide me and my nipples stiffening in the light breeze. It felt so good, and if he'd just come over, ripped my knickers off and mounted me, I'd not have put up the smallest fight. My eyes were closed but I knew he'd be looking at me. I mean, what else could he do?

Of course, it worked two ways, because his body was well worth looking at, too. After a while, I rolled back over to give him a view of my bum and sneaked a look. He was working on the bales, looking so good. He had really tight jeans on and I could see the shape of his bum and the outline of what looked like a really good-sized cock and balls. Come lunchtime, I was going to have that cock out, in my hand, in my mouth, up my pussy . . .

By the time lunch came, I was really in a sweat. Finally, Matthew brought the baler to a halt and signalled a break. I stood up and put my dress on slowly, making sure my man got plenty of chance to watch. Matthew was dishing out beers as I walked over to them, and I took one, then smiled and asked who the new man was.

It was dreadful. He was introduced to me as Luke, but in reply he addressed Matthew and referred to me as 'baby sister', as if I was a little girl! Then he asked if I'd just come up, as if he could possibly have missed me sunbathing! Finally, he wandered off to talk to the man who'd come with the dray!

I was so cross, I stamped my foot, which made Matthew laugh.

'I wouldn't get your hopes up, Tartlet,' he chuckled. 'Luke's as gay as they come.'

'Gay?' I answered.

'Gay,' Matthew assured me.

Well, it made sense. I mean, if a man ignores me sunbathing topless, he more or less has to be gay. I was so cross – with Luke for not being what I wanted, with Matthew for not telling me earlier, but most of all with myself for looking a right little idiot! It just wasn't fair, anyway. I mean, I'd never met a gay field-hand before, never. Now I had, and it just had to be the best-looking guy we'd ever hired!

I stormed off, red in the face and close to tears. Matthew laughed and then called after me with real sympathy in his voice, but I carried on. By the time I got to the lane, I felt a bit calmer but had realised that there was another problem. I was urgently, desperately horny. My pussy was soaking and my nipples were so stiff that they hurt. I could feel a flush right across my chest and even the motion of my hair against the nape of my neck was maddening. If things had gone right, Luke and I might have already been kissing – more, even. Maybe he'd be stroking my breasts through my dress. Maybe he'd have let a hand stray down my knickers. Maybe I'd have been holding his big, stiff cock . . .

It was agony; I had to have a man. In fact, I was so horny that when Barry – Toby Burrel's big black retriever – came past, I had a really dirty thought. I mean a really, really dirty thought. Barry had these big balls, all covered with sleek black hair, and a cock at least as big as some men's. For one dreadfully shameful moment, I wondered whether he would mount me if I knelt down and showed him my bare bum; then I realised exactly what I was thinking of doing and felt my cheeks suffuse with the hot blood of a really burning blush.

Anyway, a moment later, Toby himself appeared and probably saved me from doing the most disgraceful act of my life. Still, I'd given myself a shock and so decided that the best thing to do was go and play with myself. A good rub at my pussy always makes me feel better when I get too horny, at least for a while.

The sensible place to go was Haddows Wood, which started only a little further along the lane. It's our land and there was no work going on in it, so I knew I could get the privacy I'd need. Not that I really wanted privacy. What I wanted was for half a dozen big, strong lads to come and take turns with me down in the grass. When I play with myself outdoors, I often imagine what a man would do if he caught me. I like to think he'd fuck me on the spot, and that's always a nice thing to think about while I play with myself.

I tried that this time. There's a deep gully in Haddows Wood, and at one point a big beech has fallen across it, making the perfect little place for me to be naughty. I stripped – not just partly, to let me get to my pussy and boobs, but completely, so that I could feel the fresh, tingly air all over my naked body. After walking up and down a bit, to enjoy the feeling of being in the nude, I sat with my bare bum against the lovely smooth bark of the beech trunk.

With one arm holding my boobs up and the flat of my hand pressed to my pussy, I started to play. It felt nice, really open and sexy, naked, playing with myself in the big beech wood with the breeze rustling the leaves overhead and the air warm and scented with earth and things. As I closed my eyes, I started to rub, bumping my fingers back and forth over my bud. I imagined a man catching me as I was: getting himself all hard over the sight of me and then grabbing me and pulling me down among the leaves. He'd throw my legs high and stuff his big, hard cock right into me, pumping and grunting as he enjoyed me, then pulling out and telling me he couldn't do it because I was a girl . . . He had turned to Luke in my mind, spoiling my dirty thoughts and leaving me just short of my climax.

I opened my eyes and took a couple of deep breaths, then tried again, only this time thinking of the man who'd taken my virginity. He'd come to install the new milking machines, and Arthur had told me to help him in any way he wanted. He'd wanted to fuck me, and I'd let him, in a stall with my dungarees down around the tops of my wellies and my jumper up over my boobs. He'd rolled my legs up and held my thighs, then poked his cock up my pussy. It hadn't hurt at all, probably because of all the times I'd used those handy little deodorant bottles. He hadn't rejected me . . .

My mind had gone back to Luke again, just as I was getting there. It was no good: every man I thought of turned to Luke. Yet I was well steamed-up and needed to make it more badly than ever. I felt so dirty that I tried Barry, thinking of how I'd been tempted to kneel, knickers down, in the soft grass by the lane and see if he'd mount me. Just the thought made me shiver, of how his fur would have felt against my bare bum, of how his cock would have prodded at my pussy, my willing, wet pussy, willing to let . . .

No, it was just too dirty. That left one thing: other girls, and especially my best friend, Amber. There was something about her, something strong, something that made me want to be cuddled by her, to be naked in her bed, to have her weight on top of me, to have her rub her boobs in my face, to lick her pussy for her, to make her come . . .

I got there, moaning and then giving out the little grunts that I always think make me sound like a pig but which I can't help. It was nice: perhaps nicer, for the effort it had taken to get there and, as I let my weight settle back against the beech trunk, all my bad feelings seemed to drain away.

I felt better after playing with myself, but in no mood to go back to the farm. Matthew would tease me for one thing and, anyway, I'd just get roped into the cheese-making. My head felt a lot clearer as well and I found I could think sensibly about my little problem. It was easy, actually, because there was a boy over at Broadheath who'd been trying desperately to get into my knickers ever since I'd been home. He was young and skinny, and I knew he'd fumble around, which was why I hadn't gone for him. But at least he wasn't gay and, by the time I'd climbed back up to the lane, I'd decided that it was going to be his lucky day.

I needed a pee, quite badly, and was going to nip back into the bushes, when I realised that there was a better choice. There's a cottage where the wood ends that used to belong to old Mrs King. Unfortunately, she'd been taken into a rest home and I knew it was empty and also had an outside loo, possibly even with some paper.

I was right, but the seat was all green with algae, so I

pulled my knickers down, lifted my dress and squatted over the bowl. As I let go, I got that lovely feeling of release and closed my eyes to enjoy it. I hadn't shut the door properly, and the breeze blew it open. I heard a rusty squeak and felt the cool air on my body, making the feeling even nicer because I was showing off to the garden. Feeling lovely and naughty, I pulled my dress up over my boobs, showing them off too. Only when my pee had dried to a trickle and I needed to get some paper did I open my eyes.

There was a man standing outside the door, staring right at me!

I couldn't drop my dress because I'd have got pee all over it, but I did cover my boobs. He was staring open-mouthed, but suddenly turned away and started to apologise, mumbling out how sorry he was, while I quickly made myself decent.

My first instinct was to run, but he was standing right in the way. Anyway, he was obviously the new owner of the cottage, so it really should have been me who was apologising to him. He wasn't threatening, either, and not just because he was so apologetic. He was old, and small, and fat; rather like Tweedledum or Tweedledee but with a big, red beard and a bald head.

I was blushing hard, but my initial shock started to wear off as soon as my knickers were up. He was still apologising and seemed to be getting really emotional, so it seemed to be up to me to say something.

'I thought the cottage was empty,' I tried. 'You must be the new owner.'

'Yes,' he answered. 'I am. Look, I really am sorry about that, and I really don't want to get a bad name locally or anything. It really was an accident.'

'I know. Don't worry.'

'Do you mean that? I mean, you're not going to tell everyone that there's a dirty old man up at Pinchloaf Cottage?'

'No, I promise. It was an accident.'

He seemed really worried, far more worried than he had any reason to be. Most of the men I know would have had a good peek at my boobs and pussy and then either tried to chat me up or thrown me out by my ear.

'You're a very considerate young lady,' he answered. 'I'm Rufus, by the way.'

'Virginia Linslade – Ginny.'

'Do you live locally?'

'Down at Whitemead Farm.'

'Whitemead? Of course: Linslade. I recognise the name now. Your family own most of the land around here, don't you?'

'A fair bit. We own Haddows Wood. I was walking there when I realised I needed a pee. I always used to visit old Mrs King so . . .'

'Of course, and I would be delighted if you continued to drop in whenever you please.'

It was a nice thing to say, but saying it made him bashful again, as if he had made a rude suggestion. Having heard everything from really tricky schemes to make me do something naughty to straight-out orders to drop my knickers, I found his shyness rather sweet.

We chatted for a while and, when he suggested a glass of cold orange juice, I accepted. It was baking in his garden, with the sun full on us. I was feeling a little drowsy and just in the mood for a relaxed chat, so I sat down in one of the big iron chairs that had always been there and sipped my juice, the boy in Broadheath all but forgotten.

Rufus was easy to talk to, shy but full of knowledge and ideas, and our conversation became increasingly open. After a long while, there was a pause, and I saw that his cheerful expression had changed to a sad little frown.

'What's the matter?' I asked, wondering at the sudden change in him.

'I shouldn't really say this,' he sighed, 'but I have to. Thank you.'

'Thank you?'

'Yes, for allowing me – albeit unintentionally – a glimpse at something that to you is mundane, everyday, but to me represents a world always denied me.'

'How do you mean?'

'May I tell you a story?'

'A story? OK, but . . .'

'My life,' he began, without either allowing me to finish, or explaining himself, 'has been what many would consider at least moderately successful. I attained reasonable status in my chosen profession, I am comfortably off, and I live in a cottage that looks out over some of what I consider the world's most beautiful country.

'No, I'm not unlucky, nor a failure: not by the way men are judged. I'd give all of it, and more, if once, just once in my life, I had known what it means to have a woman love me – even want me.'

He paused to look out over the trees of Haddows Wood, and I thought I'd never seen such sad eyes. I felt embarrassed by the intimacy of what he was saying, but I simply hadn't the heart to leave, as to have me for an audience obviously meant so much to him.

'I don't suppose I got much of a start, really,' he continued. 'Red-haired, short, with a tendency to run to fat. My father was a reformer, forever angry over some injustice done to the poor, but with no time for his son. My mother's only real concern was for her status in the eyes of her social peers. Oh, they gave me a good education, all right. I wish they hadn't – ten years of single-sex boarding school in Scotland left me with a fluent command of Latin and a total lack of social skills to add to my unfortunate looks.

'It was no better during the war. None of the services wanted me and I spent the duration pushing paper in the ministry. I lacked looks, glamour, money, charm – no woman showed the least interest. My self-confidence dropped and dropped and, as it did so, I put up a barrier. God, I was pompous.

'The fifties came and went, and then came the swinging sixties, by which time I was a balding forty-year-old civil servant and the epitome of the boring, stuffy establishment. By the time I realised that I was wasting my life, it was too late, as what had been disadvantages as a youth had now become an insuperable barrier. So here I am, sixty-one years old, and never been . . .

'It's all too late, now, of course: which is why I feel so pathetically grateful to have so briefly glimpsed your beauty.'

He stopped and spread his hands in a gesture of weary resignation. He'd had pretty bad luck, but I could see his problem. I mean, you don't exactly see many pin-ups of fat boys with red hair, do you? Still, men are always trying to get into my knickers, and I usually let them. It seemed hard to believe that in all his life he'd never once managed to get a girl. Yet there was something dreadfully honest about him as he sat there, looking miserable.

'Seriously,' I asked, 'do you mean you've never done it; never, in all that time?'

'My dear girl, until a few minutes ago, I had never even seen between a woman's thighs, never mind been privileged to any greater intimacy.'

He sighed and pulled a wry face, then shrugged. I couldn't really think of anything to say, so I just smiled.

'And now I don't suppose I ever shall,' he continued.

He lapsed into silence, his plump face set into a look of utter misery only made more hopeless by the false smile on his lips. I felt really sorry for him, but I was embarrassed, too, and could think of nothing to say that would do the least good.

We fell silent, both looking out over the trees of Haddows Wood, and thinking our own thoughts. I tried to imagine how he must feel, but couldn't: it was just too different from my experience of life. People like me. They say I'm easy-going, but it's not something I try to be, it's just me. Yet, that morning, with Luke, I'd felt perhaps just the tiniest moment of the pain he must have gone through for his whole life. It had made me feel bad, really bad.

'Would you . . . I mean, could I . . .' he suddenly stammered. 'No, of course not. How could I even think such a thing?'

'What?'

'Nothing; it was just a stupid old man's dream.'

'No, tell me.'

'No, I mustn't. You'd just run screaming to the police, and then God alone knows what would happen.'

'I won't, I promise. Why should I, anyway?'

'Wouldn't you? I mean, I know I don't really understand women, but I'm a bit surprised you haven't already. I mean, I saw you peeing, I saw . . . well, everything.'

'That was an accident! What is it? Do you want another look at my boobs or something?'

He looked at me and blushed, bright red. I'd known it was something like that, from the way he was talking; it always is with men – except gay ones.

'Would you?' he stammered. 'I mean, it's very secluded round the back. You could sunbathe or something, nude if you like. I'd just look.'

I hesitated. I would have given him a flash of my boobs, because, well, I don't know, really. I just felt I'd like to. To be nice. To make him feel better. Besides, I was still cross about getting snubbed earlier. I needed to be appreciated. But sunbathing topless, or even nude, for a fat, red-faced, balding old man who wanted to get his kicks by peeping at me sunbathing? Sure, I like to go nude, and I know people ogle me, but he'd asked for it, and that made him a dirty old man.

I'd known worse. At least Rufus was clean and well dressed, and he had asked nicely . . .

'OK,' I answered. 'I'll go in just my knickers, if you promise not to do anything tricky.'

We went into the back, which was the sweetest little walled garden, full of lupins and hollyhocks and butterflies and things. Old Mrs King had often given her granddaughter Katie and me tea there. It was a special place for me, and one I'd expected to lose. Now I'd made friends with the new owner, I might not have to, and that actually meant a lot. If I was rude with him, I certainly wouldn't have to, so I peeled my dress off and bared my breasts to old Rufus.

He sat down on the iron bench beneath the parlour window. There was a blanket already there, which he pulled over his knees, despite the heat of the day. He was watching as I hung my pretty blue dress up on a trellis where it wouldn't get dirty. I could feel his eyes on me, lingering on my legs and bum and hair, then riveted to my boobs as I knelt down and made myself comfortable on the warm grass of the lawn.

I'm not stupid, whatever people say. What Rufus wanted was obvious. He wanted to pull himself off over the sight of me in my knickers. I could feel the tension in him – the need to get his cock out straining against his promise not to be rude with me. He wouldn't do it, I was sure; not in front of me. He'd sneak off upstairs after I'd gone and do it in the bathroom or something. At most, he'd make an excuse to go in and do it while he watched me through the window. Unless . . .

I had gone front down, not because I didn't want him to see my boobs, but because I needed a bit of time to feel OK about it. Closing my eyes, I relaxed, enjoying the warm sun on my legs and back. I could feel my hair stirring in the light breeze, tickling my shoulders and the nape of my neck. The only sounds were bees and a distant engine: soothing sounds – homely, safe sounds.

My face was turned towards him and my eyes were almost shut. I did feel drowsy – it was that type of afternoon – but there was no way I was going to sleep. That was just what I wanted him to think, to see what he'd do if he thought I was sleeping. Naughty, I know – risky, even – but fun.

I let my eyes close completely and thought about what I was doing. Teasing is such fun, and I knew his cock would be hard in his pants, just from looking at me. He'd never seen a girl even half-naked before, let alone in nothing but a pair of over-tight blue knickers. For him, I would be the sweetest dream girl, but also torture, because he couldn't touch.

Once I was sure he had had a good stare at my bum, I rolled over, sleepily, trying to give the impression of indifference to his burning eyes. My boobs were tingling where they had been pressed on the grass and, as the breeze caught my nipples, they began to stiffen. I stretched, pushing my chest up, then laid my head on my arm and once more closed my eyes.

I started to think about what I had done in the wood, and how lovely it felt to be naked in the open air, stripped with my fingers on my pussy, playing with myself, stark naked and full of dirty thoughts. For a long while I lay like that, not moving, but constantly aware of his gaze on my body. My boobs felt huge, really prominent. My pussy-mound seemed ripe and swollen, almost ready to burst my knickers.

Then I became aware of a new sound – a furtive, fleshy slapping. The dirty old sod was doing it! He was pulling on his cock under the blanket! I hadn't thought he'd have the guts, but I'd been wrong! I felt a shiver run down my spine, halfway between excitement and disgust. Not ten feet away, a dirty old man was wanking over me. His horrid little cock would be all stiff and long, the head swollen and red, poking in and out of his foreskin and slapping on his fat belly.

It was such a filthy thought that I allowed a little moan to escape my lips. Abruptly, the slapping noise stopped. I suppressed a giggle. He would be burning with desire for me, I knew it: ready to burst, just over the sight of my bare boobs. Suddenly I wanted him to come over the sight of me. Not to touch me or anything, but to come in his hand out of sheer lust. I wanted him to know I knew as well. I wanted him to be full of gratitude to me. I wanted him to come and to know that I knew all about his dirty little game.

'Why don't you pull your little cock?' I suggested. 'I don't mind, really. Just keep it in under your blanket.'

He said nothing. Maybe he guessed that I already knew, maybe not, but the slapping noise started again. That was the end of the pretence. I'd said I wanted him to pull his cock and he was doing it.

I opened my eyes and rolled on to one elbow, keeping the other back to keep my boobs stuck out. He was red in the face and his blanket was jerking up and down, a really dirty sight. I stuck my boobs out even more and smiled at him. He swallowed hard, and the jerking motion under his blanket became frantic.

'God, you're beautiful, Ginny,' he grunted. 'Pose for me, come on, pose for me.'

'I am,' I answered.

'Your bottom,' he gasped. 'Please, your beautiful bottom . . . bare . . . please, Ginny.'

'I said knickers,' I answered, all at once rather cross because he'd gone back on what we'd said.

'Please, darling,' he went on, really begging. 'Please! Or just kneel for me and stick it out. Please?'

'Look, I . . .' I started, then broke off as he stopped masturbating.

'Surely it's a little thing for you,' he said, pleading yet somehow resentful. 'I mean, just to stay in a kneeling position, just for a couple of minutes. Surely it's nothing to you, but to me, it would be the world, believe me. Please, Ginny?'

I felt pushed, and a bit used, but it obviously meant so much to him. Did I really mind, just kneeling up to show him my bum for a bit? Yes, I did. Well, sort of. But sixty-one years old, and he'd never even kissed a girl . . .

As I knelt up and pushed my bottom out, I heard my own sigh of resignation. He was going to wank off over my bum, in a much ruder position than I'd bargained for, but at least I had my knickers to cover me. Not that they hid much, being so tight that the material was caught up between my pussy-lips, and not really large enough to properly cover what I admit is a rather big bottom. I felt dirty and rather put upon as I parted my knees to show him my panty gusset. But I'd teased him, so it was only fair to go through with it.

I heard the slapping sound again as he started to pull at himself under his blanket again. It disgusted me, but I felt good as well. After all, I was giving him something he'd never had. I've stripped for boys lots of times, but always more or less as equals. For Rufus, I was something special, something unique.

He quickly started to get excited again, panting and grunting as he tugged furiously at his willy. I kept thinking he'd come and, the longer I stayed there with my bottom stuck up in the air, the more resentful I felt about having my bum used for a dirty old man to wank over. The thing was, I'd been in charge before. Now, he was.

'Oh, God, you're lovely,' he grunted.

'Do it, then,' I answered.

'I am,' he gasped. 'I just need more. Pull your sweet little knickers down! Show me it, Ginny: show me it all.'

'No!'

'Please, Ginny. I need it bare. I need to see your hole. Pull your knickers down, please!'

'No!'

'Oh, God, please pull them down. Please!'

'Oh, OK! But you're a dirty old sod!'

I snapped the words out and promptly whipped my knickers down at the back, feeling really cross even as I put my bare bum on show for him.

'Oh, my darling,' he groaned. 'You're gorgeous. You have the most beautiful bottom in the world!'

I could see him over my shoulder. His face was dark red and he was pumping like mad at his cock. The blanket was jumping up and down like crazy, and then suddenly it was off and I was faced with his naked cock, really hard and jerking in his hand. I'm no stranger to men's cocks, but this really looked obscene – not so much the cock as what he was doing with it. I suppose it showed in my face, because he suddenly stopped wanking and slumped miserably in the seat and covered himself with the blanket.

'I can't do it,' he puffed. 'I don't know why, but I just can't. I do know actually: it's because I know you're only doing it to be nice to me. Really, you can't stand the sight of me, especially my cock. I'm sorry. I should never . . .'

He trailed off and hung his head. For a moment, I really thought he was going to cry. My anger just melted away and, before I really knew what I was doing, I had come over to him and taken his hand.

'You've got a nice cock,' I told him.

'You're just saying that,' he sighed.

'No, really.'

'Oh, come on, Ginny. You can hardly bear to look at it.

The idea of touching it must make you sick. I'd better put it away.'

'No, really. I promise. I mean ... Look, Rufus, I'm going to pull you off, but you must promise never ever to tell anyone. OK?'

He nodded dumbly.

I had to do it. I felt so sorry for him. I mean, what was it to me? A cock in my hand – big deal, it wasn't like it would be the first time. I'd even done two men at once.

Neither of us said a word as I pulled the blanket away. His cock was still hard and his balls were poking out of his fly. I'd been truthful about him having a nice cock. It was big and white and all silky-smooth. I'd imagined a miserable little thing, all wrinkled and veiny, but it was as nice as any I'd seen on younger men and perhaps the third, or maybe fourth largest. I know they say size doesn't matter, but it does to me, if only to look at. It was really meaty, too, with lots of flesh round the shaft. I like cocks that way, rock hard in the middle and a bit rubbery when I squeeze.

I sat down next to him and he pulled his jumper and shirt up, exposing his big, heavy belly, which was thickly grown with coarse red hair. Then I reached out, gingerly took his cock in my hand and began to jerk it up and down. I'm good at pulling men off and I soon had the rhythm of it, with his foreskin rolling up and down over his knob while I felt his balls. His sac was really hairy and his balls felt huge inside it, like two hard-boiled eggs wrapped in sheepskin. I squeezed gently and felt them squirm in my hand. He sighed in response and put his hand on the back of my head, starting to stroke my hair as I wanked him faster and faster.

Most men come in moments when they're in my hand. Rufus didn't, but just lay back groaning softly and stroking my hair. Then I felt a gentle pressure on the back of my head and knew that he was going to try and push me further.

I was wanking his cock as a favour, honestly, just out of charity. But I was also sitting outdoors, all but in the buff and with a big cock and a pair of plump balls in my hands. I know I shouldn't have done it. I know I should have told him not to push his luck. I didn't, but I did tell him that he was a dirty old sod, as he started to push my face down towards his erection.

Anyway, I like cock-sucking. I know some girls find it a bit of a chore. I love it, and really all I had to do was forget whose cock I was having to suck. I closed my eyes and followed the pressure of his hand, finding the rich, male smell of his erection faint in my nose. He smelt nice, of man mixed with some sort of aftershave or perhaps soap, not nasty at all. That was what finally decided me.

I opened my mouth and let him push me down before I could change my mind. Suddenly my mouth was full of cock: thick, salty, fleshy cock, as big and hard as any of the young men I'd had. I began to suck, closing my lips gently on his shaft and moving my head up and down as if he was fucking in my mouth. He gave a long moan and started to stroke my hair, then to tickle my neck. I love that when I'm sucking cock, and it really turned me on to it. My head was on his big fat tummy, and my cheek would bump on it with each sucking movement. His belly-hair tickled, making me want to giggle, so I pulled his cock forward a bit and changed the way I was sucking.

Taking the knob between my lips, I began to nibble, all the while wanking his shaft up and down. He groaned, really loudly, and put his hand on mine, squeezed and began to help me tug. The hand on my neck moved up, took my head, pressed me down and his knob popped in between my puckered lips. His spare hand closed on one of my boobs and he gave a really loud grunt as he squeezed me.

I tried to pull back, but too late. His cock jerked and suddenly my mouth was full of spunk. He can't have come for a year, because there was gallons of it, spurting up in my mouth until I started to gag and then bursting out around his prick as I finally managed to pull back a little. That was a mistake, because the next spurt caught me right in the face and the one after that went in my hair. I was covered in it. There was even some up my nose.

Not that I cared any more. I had to come myself. Ignoring his sudden flurry of apologies, I stood up and pulled my knickers off my legs. I'd have fucked him willingly if he'd been able to get hard again, but it didn't look likely. Instead, I sat down on the lawn and began to frig myself. He watched, his eyes big and round and his hand stroking his slimy cock. He'd been weeding earlier, and there was a trug on the path with a trowel in it, one of those old-fashioned ones with a big wooden handle and a round end. It looked perfect for my pussy and I grabbed it and began to rub myself with the handle and then slid it up my hole. I was really showing off, naked with my legs wide apart and the big trowel sticking out of my pussy. The handle was big, far bigger than any cock, and really stretched me open, which was lovely.

My boobs were aching and needed to be touched, but I also wanted to feed the trowel handle in and out while I rubbed myself. He saw my problem and very sweetly came to help, taking the end of the trowel and starting to slide it in and out of me. I took a boob in one hand and started to play with a nipple, meanwhile rubbing my bump harder and harder.

It was glorious when it happened. He had the trowel right up me and I felt my pussy clamp on to it. I started to grunt and suddenly there was a finger touching my bumhole, then in it! The dirty old bastard had fingered my bum, but I was coming and I didn't care. I heard myself squeal and felt both my holes tighten on what was in them, again and again while I grunted and screamed in helpless pleasure. He kept me full, right until I'd finished coming, by which time I was lying, panting, on the ground.

He pulled his finger gently free of my bum, then eased the trowel handle out of my pussy. I felt really ashamed, but he said nothing and the feeling quickly died away. I waited while he washed his hands and cock at an outdoor tap, then washed myself before getting dressed.

Afterwards he was ever so nice, saying sorry and thanking me, and then saying sorry again. I told him not to be silly and to look on it as my good deed for the day.

He made us tea after that, which we drank on his lawn, quite calmly, as if nothing had happened. Then I left.

Walking back home, I felt good, really good. I'd been right when I said to look on it as my good deed for the day. What I had done had been an act of a charity, a gift to a poor, friendless old man. I know that to most of the men I've been with I'm a bit of a dream girl, but to old Rufus I was *the* dream girl.

It was like the difference between spending money on chocolate and putting money in a charity box. I enjoy chocolate the same way I enjoy sex – lots of it and often. If I give to charity, I don't feel I've wasted my money, because it feels nice to know I've helped someone in need. It had been the same with old Rufus. He'd been in need, and I'd helped him.

For the rest of the week, I had a warm glow of satisfaction inside me. I visited the boy in Broadheath and let him fuck me, doggy-style. He did fumble and he came before he'd really got it in me, but I wasn't cross about it. I gave one of the older farmhands a suck in the barn, and felt good about that, too. He'd wanted me for ages. If neither made me come, then I was still left with that sweet glow of charity. Besides, there's nothing wrong with a quick frig: one in my bedroom, one behind the dairy.

On Sunday, I got dragged along to church in Broadheath as usual. Afterwards Katie King and I slipped off together, intending to go up to the old park and swim in the lake. We wanted to avoid the others, and so took a back lane that has a ford. As we were both in frocks, we had to take our shoes and socks off and hitch up our skirts. There was some old guy sitting in a car on the far side and, not surprisingly, he had a good peek, doubtless hoping he might get a flash of our knickers. I didn't care, but I could see Katie was embarrassed. When we were safely past, she turned back and stuck her tongue out in his general direction.

'The dirty old bastard! He was really staring at our legs!' she said, sounding really outraged.

'Who cares?' I answered.

'Ginny! He's a dirty old man!'

'So? He didn't hurt us, did he?'

'No, but . . .'

'Think of it as a good deed, then. He got a nice buzz out of seeing us like that, and it didn't do anyone any harm.'

'You're talking nonsense, Ginny!'

'No, I'm not: I'm just being nice. It's not his fault that he's old and not attractive any more, so give him a break.'

'Ginny!'

'No, really. Look, do you know the old guy who bought your Granny's cottage? A fat guy, bald with a big red beard? '

'Yes.'

'Well, he shows what I mean. He . . . he accidentally saw me peeing last week, and . . . and anyway, we got talking, and do you know, he'd never even seen a girl's pussy before, never!'

'Ginny! That is nonsense! That's my uncle Rufus. Granny left him the cottage. He's been married twice and he's got seven kids!'

. . . and serve her right, the great tart! Actually I wish it had been me: being tricked like that would have really turned me on.

Next comes a story of revenge – the revenge taken on me by Anna Vale. We met Anna in Penny in Harness, *when I gave her her first ever spanking. It had taken a good deal of scheming to get her over my lap, and it had taken a lot of soul-searching for her to accept the punishment. I'd done it out of simple mischief – and because I was attracted to her. So when she asked if she might turn the tables on me, I could hardly refuse. Perhaps revenge is not really the right word: justice might be more accurate.*

Anna had created something really special, just for me . . .

Justice 1950 – Anna Vale

For an alpha-dominant woman to demand respect from those to whom she gives discipline is one thing; to truly deserve that respect is quite another. In preparing myself for my appointment with Miss Birch, I had neglected no detail of apparel, environment or temperament. I was, after all, WAAF Section Officer Vale, and I expected her to accept the authority of my rank. My sole concern, as I waited, was that she might lack the wit and imagination to do so.

My uniform was of fine wool, the weight chosen for the warmth of the day. The skirt was tight without being impractical, and the tunic cut to my figure. As I have the good fortune to be a brunette, the official grey-blue colour suits my hair and my complexion. My blouse was of crisp cotton and made to the regulation cut. Beneath, my underwear was exclusively silk and of a delicate ivory tone, which I favour as being both feminine and demure. I had selected camiknickers with a broad fringe of pretty lace, a long corset which contributed to the natural elegance of my figure, a brief slip and fully fashioned stockings. Given that I enjoy a natural advantage in height when compared to Miss Birch, I had chosen shoes with only three and a half inches of heel. A neat little hat and a woollen neck-tie to match completed my ensemble, with two broad bands on each sleeve of my tunic and other relevant insignia proclaiming my rank.

Austerity was the key-note in my surroundings. The walls were the same grey-blue as my uniform, and decorated only with sanctioned informational posters. A clock hung above the door, its steady ticking clearly audible in the silence of the room. The furniture comprised a filing cabinet, two plain chairs and my desk: nothing more. On the desk stood ink, a pen, two neat piles of paper – and a cane.

It was a fine malacca cane, dark, glossy brown in colour and ridged at intervals of some six inches. That its bite was one of exquisite pain, I had no doubt, its weight and flexibility providing proof to my experience. Nor was Miss Birch a stranger to its kiss, a fact I knew would add to her fear and trepidation when she saw it on my desk. Indeed, I had purchased it from her close friend Miss Oakley, the subtle irony of which I was sure the former would appreciate to the full while it was being applied to her bare nates.

Allowing myself a brief moment of frivolity, I ran my finger along the smooth, cool surface. As I did so, I felt my mouth curve into a smile – a response to the knowledge that here was an object designed specifically for the application of discipline to soft, female bottoms.

No other instrument of correction matches the cane. A good cane is a thing of beauty – elegant, balanced, a source of pride to the wielder and of terror to the miscreant. Hairbrushes, rulers, belts, may all be pressed into service when a girl needs swift and impromptu discipline, yet in all such cases the smacking of bottoms is only a secondary function. A cane is designed for chastisement, and only that.

While caning girls is a serious and very necessary task, I cannot deny my pleasure in it. It is bliss to watch some pretty little mouse expose her most intimate parts, to see her naked buttocks twitch in anticipation of discipline, to see her flesh quiver and to hear her cry of pain at the impact, to watch the long welt of rich pink rise on her fresh bottom skin . . .

The distant sound of a motor-car engine cut through my

reverie. I controlled an unworthy shiver of anticipation – an emotion more suitable for the girl who is to receive justice than she who is to administer it. The engine sound stopped abruptly and I put back my shoulders to perfect my posture. A door slammed and I heard Miss Oakley's voice, then a laugh that contained all the nervous quality one might expect from a girl who is about to be caned. I waited, listening to the click of dainty heels approaching my door and then a gentle knock.

'You may come in,' I responded.

The door opened to reveal my assistant.

'Cadet Birch, ma'am,' she announced and then stood smartly to attention.

My victim entered the room, a petite woman, strikingly pretty and with her dark hair worn in a neat, practical bob. She stood and saluted, then lowered her hand to her side, coming to attention with only a slight trembling of her lower lip to betray her nervousness. I said nothing, but cast my eyes over her uniform. This was of the same grey-blue cloth as my own and identical in every respect, save for the lack of insignia on her shoulder tabs and sleeves. She was, I realised, a mere second-grade cadet, as junior as it was possible to be. Beyond her, my assistant had the expectant look of one who is hoping for the pleasure of watching another girl caned. I did not intend to allow her the privilege.

'Thank you, Poppy; you may leave,' I informed her. 'Be sure to keep Miss Oakley entertained.'

Her big eyes opened in alarm and she cast an apprehensive glance back to the corridor. Entertainment for Miss Oakley, I had little doubt, would be at the expense of Poppy's bottom. I had said Poppy could watch the punishment, but it amused me to change her immediate prospects from the pleasant stimulation of watching a whacking to the rather more direct, and vigorous, stimulation of receiving one.

I put her out of my mind as the door shut, turning my attention back to Miss Birch. She and Poppy were sufficiently similar in appearance to have passed for sisters.

Her hair was straight, where Poppy's was curly, and her features conveyed rather less insolence and more sensitivity. There was also rather more flesh on Poppy's hips and buttocks and a great deal more on her breasts. Height, hair colour and general build were all the same, yet where Poppy was petite with a subtle accent of the voluptuous, Penny – Miss Birch – was both petite and pert.

Her apprehension was growing under my casual inspection. I could sense it in her body, the way she poised her head and the slight movement of muscles in her hands as she held herself back from nervous fiddling. Also, the trembling of her lip had increased and her eyes were wide – and locked on the cane that lay between us on the desk. I let her wait, observing her response and allowing the tension to build in her mind. Finally, she could endure it no longer.

'I . . . I was sent to see you, Miss Vale,' she blurted out.

'Ma'am will do,' I responded, 'or Section Officer Vale. Yes, Miss Birch, you were sent to see me, and do you know why you were sent to see me?'

'I am to be caned,' she replied quietly.

'Speak up, girl! Address me correctly!'

'I am to be caned – ma'am.'

'Yes, to be caned. To be caned on your naked buttocks. It is hardly a dignified procedure, is it?'

'No, ma'am.'

'Yet you – a grown, responsible young woman – will shortly be kneeling over a chair with your skirt up and your knickers pulled down, to be beaten with a stick. Doubtless you will mewl or even blubber, and there is no doubt whatever that you will be making a most indecent display of your private parts.'

'Yes, ma'am.'

'Do you think it wrong that you should be made to endure this? Inappropriate? Improper, perhaps?'

'No, ma'am.'

'No, ma'am? Why is that? Do you think it is suitable to flaunt your naked bottom? Do you think I want to see the disgusting details between your buttocks and thighs?'

'No, ma'am!'

'So why are you going to do it? Why are you going to kneel obediently with your fat little rump stuck out bare for the cane? Do tell me.'

'I have forfeited the right to dignity, ma'am.'

'Yes, you have, haven't you? Dignity, and with it self-respect, is not something to which a woman has an automatic right, Miss Birch. To the contrary, it must be earned. By your actions, you have forfeited what little of such right you had earned, so you will be beaten on the bare skin, both to improve the value of your punishment and because you have no right to expect it to be otherwise. Furthermore, at your rank, it would be a presumption to expect to be allowed to keep your knickers up. Do you understand?'

'Yes, ma'am.'

'Good. I always feel that is so important for a girl to understand why her bottom needs to be naked during a beating. Come on then, do it! What are you waiting for?'

She began to inch her skirt up with every evidence of reluctance, taking the slip with it. First she exposed the upper parts of her stocking-clad thighs and then the narrow band of bare skin above them. The softness of her thighs was evident, with her flesh bulging slightly above her stocking tops and especially around the places where her suspender straps were anchored. Her face was a picture, showing worry and a shame that became ever more acute as the tight V between her legs came on show and then the full expanse of her undergarment as she rucked the uniform skirt up around her waist. She wore American-style 'panties', a garment I consider as evidence of vulgarity, especially when it seemed likely that she had performed some 'favour' for a US serviceman in order to obtain them.

These were plain white cotton and large, covering her hips and bulging out to gentle swells over her belly and pudenda.

Her richly grown pubic hair showed as an unevenness and a trace of darker colour beneath the white panties, while a slight furrow with a trace of dampness in it betrayed the involuntary excitement brought on by her humiliation and the prospect of worse.

'Turn around,' I instructed. 'Slowly.'

She obeyed, revealing first her side view with the panties stretching out over her chubby bottom and the more subtle bulge of her belly, and then the full width of her bottom. Her cheeks were peeping out from beneath the hem of her blouse, chubby and exquisitely feminine in their case of taut white cotton. Most of the delicate groove where her buttocks met her thighs was showing, squeezed somewhat together by the upward pull of her suspender straps and disappearing beneath the gusset of her panties.

'Lift your tails,' I ordered, keeping my voice firm and dispassionate.

Her hands went to the tails of her tunic, also catching the hem of her blouse. Hesitantly, she pulled both up, revealing the full expanse of her panty seat. The material was taut, leaving a shallow groove between her buttocks, to give the impression of a fat peach wrapped in cotton. The garment also fully covered the upper slopes of her bottom, ending in a thick band at the level of her waist, where her hands held up her clothing. Here her suspender belt also showed, a confection of lace and white cotton that I felt a little pretentious for her station. I had to admit that she had made a sensible choice of underwear. Although indecently tight, the panties were sufficiently demure to ease the shame of showing them and also thick enough to provide a measure of protection for the tender bottom beneath. That, of course, assumed that she would be allowed to keep them up, which we both knew was ridiculous.

She was trembling, creating a delightful quivering in the two creamy slices of bottom-flesh that showed beneath the rim of her panties. The urge to take her across my knee and spank her in her knickers was strong but out of place, so I resisted it. Instead, I took my time in admiration of the panty-clad bottom she was so reluctantly revealing – stretching out the moment until she was obliged to subject herself to the further indignity of pulling down her panties in front of me. I knew just how strong the moment would be for her and intended to make her feel every agonising nuance of the experience.

'Kneel on the chair,' I said suddenly, after waiting until her fingers had begun to fidget with her upraised skirt.

She had been expecting to be told to pull her panties down and bracing herself to have to do it. With the unexpected order, she immediately became flustered, losing a little more of her precious control as she scampered over to the chair and quickly knelt on its hard wooden seat.

If her bottom had been enticing before, it was now so stimulating that I had to remind myself who I was, to keep my natural instincts in check. Kneeling, with her tunic, blouse and skirt thrown up on to her back, her panty-clad bottom was on display in full magnificence. So taut was the material of her panties that I could only surmise that the garment had originally been designed for a girl of about eleven. Certainly, it had difficulty in constraining Miss Birch's small, but mature, curves. The seat was stretched absolutely tight across her out-thrust bottom, while the hem cut into her soft flesh deeply enough to leave low, meaty bulges where her buttocks spilt from their restraining influence. Her new position had also put her rear suspender straps under greater stress, providing two taut lines of white elastic that ran from the exposed part of her suspender belt to the tops of her stockings. The urge to grab her bottom or to cuddle her to me and kiss her shamed and miserable face was close to overwhelming, and only by closing my eyes and counting slowly to ten did I resist what would have been a quite improper act.

She needed her panties taken down, of course, and I was only too aware of how trying this would be for my senses. Steeling myself for the task, I stepped up smartly behind her and took hold of her waistband. She gave a whimper of utter shame as she felt the elastic lifted from her skin: then another, more plaintive still, as I slowly began to peel the panties down over the small of her back. A faint red mark remained where her knicker elastic had been tight against her flesh, with the pattern and the outline of the label visible as a tracery of lines in subtly varied shades of pink. Immediately below were revealed the twin dimples that so enhance the female rear, set on either side of the last inch or so of the gentle valley that marked her spine. Lower – as I stretched out the agonising shame I knew she would be feeling at having her bottom stripped – was the low bulge of her coccyx and then the fan-shaped depression that marked the beginning of her bottom-cleft, with the upper slopes of her cheeks swelling out to either side.

She had begun to shiver as I eased the panties down over her bottom, inch by dreadful inch, exposing her glorious, pale cream nates and the valley between that led down to her very rudest details. I could feel the texture of her buttocks under my knuckles as well, the flesh firm and resilient, the skin creamy smooth but roughening quickly as the goose-pimples rose in response to her exposure.

With the panties down to the level of the crests of her buttocks, I began to see a little hair, dark and crinkled between her shivering cheeks, a sight at once dirty and undeniably stimulating. More hair came on view as the panties continued their inexorable downward progress, with a suspicion of pink deep beneath to hint at the yet dirtier secrets of her anus. I gave a sudden little tug and the tuck of her cheeks popped up over her panty elastic, wobbling for an instant and then calming. This meant that her pussy was showing, completing the shameful and vulgar display of her rear. She knew it, too, because, as the panty elastic snapped home against the soft flesh of her rear thighs, she gave a broken sob of pure humiliation.

I settled her panties just below the level of her stocking-tops, leaving myself an unobstructed view of her bottom and upper thighs, the full expanse of which I intended to use as a target for my malacca. The pale, rounded surfaces of her nates were soft and inviting, the skin smooth and unblemished, with no more texture than the goose-bumps that so often rise on the bottom skin of a girl about to be disciplined. From my vantage, her pussy was clearly visible, an oval of plump flesh a shade darker than the thighs from between which it pouted out. A thick growth of crinkly black hair on her outer labia hid much of the detail, although the hood of her clitoris and the swollen, bright pink flesh of her inner labia were clearly visible. These were small, and actually rather sweet: twin ridges of wet, succulent flesh running down to frame the damp hole that gave access to her body. A bead of white fluid had formed at the entrance to her vagina, again marking her instinctive excitement at what was being done to her. There was also an unreasonable amount of hair between her buttocks and even a little on her inner thighs.

'Your rear view,' I remarked, 'is actually quite vulgar. You should shave, particularly around your bottom-hole. Now, stick it out further, and pull your back in.'

She gave a little mew of shame but said nothing, simply obeying my order so that her buttocks parted and I was presented with a yet more glorious display of her bottom. Not only did her cheeks seemed to fatten and swell, but her bottom-hole was now clearly visible, bare and rude in a nest of dark hair. It was the inner curve of her nates that was really hairy, with her perineum spick and glossy and with a naked area roughly the shape of a candle flame above it, centred on the actual hole into her bottom. The anus was a puckered, pinkish-brown ring, with little humps of dun-coloured flesh separated by yet darker valleys which crowded together into the tightly shut hole at the very centre. Her sphincter was pulsing slightly under my scrutiny – perhaps in anticipation of the cane, perhaps from the shame of having her most intimate details so minutely studied – most probably from both, and from arousal as well.

'That is better,' I continued as I rose from my inspection. 'Now, you make a frankly disgusting sight, which I shall describe to you as I wish to bring home to you fully the shame of your position, and something of how ridiculous you look.'

'Yes, ma'am,' she whimpered.

'Firstly,' I pointed out, 'for a girl so slender, your

buttocks are remarkably fat, a characteristic which I consider common in the extreme. A lady should be elegant, slender, svelte: not built as if intended for the carnal amusement of the lower orders of male society. You must be aware that, in your pose, the rear of your cunt shows – yes, let us call it what it is: a rude, vulgar name for the sex of a rude, vulgar girl – and that you are all too clearly in a quite disgusting state of sexual arousal. Your pubic hair is rank, and damp with your own fluid. And finally – while I fully realise that you are probably incapable of controlling the lewd way in which your anus appears to wink at me, it is quite the most crudely immodest sight I have ever had the misfortune to witness.'

She hung her head in shame, doubtless thinking of what I had just described to her. I stepped back, wondering if my words had caused her sufficient humiliation to make her receptive to her beating. Certainly, the nudity of her buttocks and thighs allowed no avoidance of the proper measure of pain, while I could only trust that her mental state was suitable for the effective reception of chastisement.

Of course, all of this was necessary. Punishment serves two functions: to chastise a girl for her sin and to ensure that the sin is not repeated. In so thoroughly humiliating Miss Birch before her beating, I had ensured that the memory of the punishment would linger far longer than if I had merely stripped her impertinent bottom of its protective woollen skirt and whacked her across the seat of the demure white panties. To leave her skirt unraised would have been a travesty, allowing her not only the protection of the wool but a quite inappropriate level of modesty. Now, in the unfortunate – and unlikely – event of myself needing to be beaten, it would be quite proper for me to be allowed to retain my skirt and unthinkable that my knickers should be taken down.

I confess that I felt a little sorry for her as she began to snivel at the effect of my treatment. It is always a pity to have to chastise a woman, especially such a sweet and pretty young thing as Miss Birch. Nevertheless, it was my duty to both beat her and to ensure that her punishment was entirely efficacious, and duty – however onerous – is something that I never shirk. With a deep sigh of regret, I stepped back and picked up the malacca from my desk. I felt its weight and adjusted my grip, then gave it an experimental swish through the air that had Miss Birch clenching her buttocks and coming up on to her toes as if I had actually hit her.

Despite my sympathy, I was unable to restrain a light chuckle at the sight of her so evident consternation. Until then, she had kept her head obediently down in a properly shamefaced way, but at the sound of my amusement she raised it and looked back at me. Her eyes were peeping out beneath the neat fringe of her hair and looked huge, with the wide brown irises staring pleadingly at me and the hint of a tear in one corner. Her lower lip was pushed out and trembling violently, showing her fear without the least attempt at restraint.

Feeling sympathy is one thing, showing it is quite another: and I returned her fearful glance with a cold look. She turned her eyes quickly back to the floor. I lowered the cane and reached out to touch her bottom, stroking and then pressing gently with my fingers. Her skin felt smooth and warm, while her flesh was resilient, with the firmness of her muscle evident beneath a soft layer of puppy fat. She gave a little whimper at the feel of my exploring fingers, then a little squeak as one of my nails brushed the skin in between her bottom cheeks.

'Don't mewl, Birch,' I snapped, as I stood back and lifted the cane. 'And stick that fat bottom up properly!'

I could sense her fear and shame as she thrust her naked buttocks higher still. For a moment, I waited, watching the muscles of her bottom and thighs tense, relax, then tense once more. I tapped her bottom with the cane, laying it across the crest of her plump cheeks to judge my aim. She flinched and gave a low, agonised sob. I raised the cane once more, held for a second, and then brought it whistling down across her bottom. There was a loud smack and she squealed out as her bottom flesh jumped, wobbled briefly and returned to shape, only now with a long, white welt crossing the fat hemispheres. As I leant forward to inspect my work, she began to sob.

The welt was an arrow-straight line of raised flesh, crossing her bottom from side to side. Its colour was turning to a livid pink, while two thin tramlines of angry scarlet marked the entire length. It began gently, rising from nothing until the hurt flesh stood perhaps one twelfth of an inch proud of her cheek at the point where the tramlines began. Two points, somewhat broader and of a deeper, blushing hue, marked where the ridges of the malacca had struck. At the point where the welt crossed the divide of her buttocks, it broke off briefly, with two shapes like the tips of pink pencils pointing together over the furry, inviolate cleft, directly down to the rude puckering of her bumhole at their centre. I had seen the way her buttocks squashed together at the instant of impact and knew that her cheeks must have been forced together by the blow, with only the girlish fullness of her bottom protecting her anus from the sting of the malacca. The cane tip had struck at the point where her right buttock blended into her thigh, leaving a mark a tone pinker and a little wider than the rest, like a teardrop that has trickled halfway down a woman's cheek, taking with it the darker pink of running make-up.

I touched it, feeling the roughened surface under my finger, and drawing a low whimper from the girl whose bottom it decorated so prettily. With my face close, I could smell her arousal and the faint, fresh tang from where her pain and fear had raised a speckling of sweat on her milky skin. She was trembling, a normal reaction to being beaten with a cane – and one that was making her chubby bottom quiver in the most delightful way.

It was beautiful, and I wanted to kiss it, setting my lips to the roughened skin of the welt and planting gentle, soothing pecks along its length to ease her pain and lessen her anguish at her beating. I could even have pressed my face between her sweet cheeks and kissed her anus, in a gesture of womanly affection designed to balance the indignity which she was enduring at my hands, but not – of course – the pain. I would have licked the little hole until her moans signalled that I had been forgiven, only then transferring my attention to her vulva and, ultimately, to the hard bud of her clitoris.

Unfortunately, such indulgences were impossible. She was my inferior and in the process of being given discipline, a process that I would have to complete, regardless of how sorry I felt for my victim – or how much I wanted to take her in my arms. I shook my head to rid myself of such disturbing thoughts and returned to the task at hand.

She had stayed in position while I inspected her bottom, snivelling slightly but no more. I have known beaten girls who blubber at the first stroke, while others can accept a round dozen without a whimper. I cannot say that I approve of howlers, as such behaviour shows a lack of fortitude. Nevertheless, I do find their reaction to the cane arousing. Miss Birch, I was sure, would prove to be a howler by the time I had finished.

I applied the second stroke a little below the first, again tapping her bottom first to take my aim and increase her sense of anticipation. As with the first, she whimpered beforehand and then squealed like a stuck pig when the cane found its mark. Her bottom then gave a little shimmying dance of pain, which quietened to reveal the second welt exactly parallel with the first and an inch lower.

She was sobbing quite loudly now and fighting back the tears, but managed to keep her bottom stuck out with proper acquiescence. With two cane weals decorating the pale surface, her peach looked more beautiful than ever, and both the lewd winking of her anus and the dampness of her cunny had become more pronounced. She was aroused, of that there could be no doubt. As I tapped her bottom to place my third stroke, I began seriously to consider taking my pleasure of her when the beating was over. It is hard to resist the temptation offered by a well-chastened girl, and the harder they have been caned, the more tractable they are. I determined to deliver the remaining four strokes with the full power of my arm.

I raised the cane behind my head and then let go. The malacca whistled down and landed plumb across her bottom; she yelled out as her cheeks bounced in response. She began to kick her feet in a pathetic effort to lessen the pain and let out a series of lesser yelps, which then turned to sobs. I waited for her wriggling to subside, meanwhile admiring the new welt that ran across the very fattest part of her bottom, where the cheeks began to tuck down to meet her thighs. It was a touch darker than the others, with the tramlines and nodes rather more pronounced.

By the time she had managed to regain enough control over her body to stop wriggling, she had started to cry. One heavy tear had traced a mascara-darkened line down her face, while another hung, balanced, in the corner of her eye. We exchanged a look that contained the first hint of that curious intimacy that builds between a beaten girl and the one who administers the punishment. She sniffed and hung her head, then raised her posterior more.

I gave her the fourth one high, not so high as to risk striking her coccyx, but above the first where the flesh is tauter and there is less fat to cushion the impact. She cried out as the malacca bit into her naked buttocks, so loudly now that she had clearly given up all intent not to be heard during her caning. She began to blubber openly as I raised the cane once more, but still managed to hump her bottom up into the exposed position I had demanded.

The application of a cane to a girl's bottom causes sexual arousal. A girl who is a newcomer to physical discipline will often be horrified as she feels her vagina start to juice during punishment, and the shame of becoming excited in such circumstances never quite goes. Sometimes I will deliver the last two or three strokes of a caning across a girl's thighs, which lessens her arousal and – so I am told – hurts even more. The effect is to reduce their need to play with themselves when they go and cry in the lavatories afterwards. It also serves to improve their posture and makes them think twice before indulging in the sort of immoral dancing that deliberately allows them to show off their knickers – even the most incorrigible flirt is unlikely to want a man to know that she has recently had to be whacked.

In Miss Birch's case I had intended to do this, but now the last thing I wanted was to diminish her arousal. The beauty of her body, and her response to the beating, were both affecting me deeply, while the air was thick with the rich scent of her sex. Rather than apply my fifth stroke to her thighs, I laid it hard across the lower part of her buttocks, directly over the pouted lips of her vulva. Her crying was broken by a yelp of pain and then resumed, harder than before and accompanied by another flurry of frantic leg-kicking.

When a girl is to be given six and has taken five, it is inevitable that she will be thinking that there is just one to go, and then it will all be over. That is why I make an invariable rule of allowing a substantial pause before giving that merciful last stroke. Miss Birch had quickly resumed her position, and had her bottom stuck up as if positively eager for the final stroke of her punishment. I raised the cane and she flinched and clenched her buttocks. They came apart slowly as she relaxed, the inner surfaces sticky with the sweat of fear and arousal.

I looked up to the clock, finding the second hand a little short of the vertical. Its ticking was loud in the room, the only sound other than Miss Birch's broken sobbing. Fifteen seconds later, she looked up at me – perhaps wondering if she had miscounted the strokes – then looked hastily away as she found the malacca poised high above her naked rump. By the time the second hand had reached the half she was shivering visibly; then she began to shake her head in an agony of anticipation and I finally took mercy on her.

The sixth stroke whistled down to impact her bottom directly on top of the weal that was still swelling from the previous one. She screamed and went into a frantic, bucking dance, jumping from knee to knee on the chair, kicking her legs about and jiggling her bottom in a desperate effort to lessen the pain. As soon as the immediate pain was gone, she really started to bawl, and I waited patiently for her to regain at least the minimum of self-control. She knew better than to rise without permission and, when she was finally ready, she once more stuck her bottom up. Six welts covered her beautiful pink globes, while her skin was slick with sweat and heavily goose-pimpled. Her vulva was gaping and sodden with juice, her vagina an open black hole big enough for a finger. The flesh of her anus was swollen and somewhat pouted: a typically vulgar response to punishment. I could smell her excitement, as I was sure she could and, in a sudden spirit of malicious humour, I dipped the tip of the cane into her open vagina. She gave a squeak of alarm and then a low, involuntary moan of pleasure as I drew it slowly out. I wanted to have her then and there, but forced myself to hold back, knowing that if I was to do it, I would have to wait for her arousal to exceed her pain.

Her crying had lessened to a loud sobbing noise and her breathing regained its regularity. She was waiting, not daring to move unless I should decide to add to the official six strokes she had been awarded for her offence. I had no intention of doing so, as she was so obviously repentant; yet I deemed it proper to make her wait. I stood there a full minute, admiring her bottom and trying to control the warm, open feeling in my own sex.

'That will suffice,' I finally announced. 'You may rise, and I trust you will think twice in future before appearing on parade with your shoes improperly polished.'

She dismounted the chair and turned her tear streaked face to me.

'Yes, ma'am,' she said, in a barely audible whisper.

'Well,' I demanded, 'aren't you going to thank me, or do I have to give you another six for impudence?'

'Yes, ma'am. Thank you, ma'am: thank you for beating me, ma'am,' she blurted out hurriedly and then bent to retrieve her panties.

'What do you think you are doing?' I asked.

'Pulling up my knickers, please, ma'am,' she stammered.

'Well, you can stop pulling up your knickers, can't you, Birch?' I answered her. 'Your beating may have provided redemption for your misbehaviour, but do you suppose that immediately restores your right to dignity? Do you?'

'No, ma'am,' she responded, hastily taking her hands away from her panties.

'Then go to the corner, face the wall and tuck your skirt and tails up so that your bottom remains bare. Then you will place your hands on your head and take some time to reflect on your behaviour.'

'What if somebody comes in?' she quavered.

'Then they will see you,' I answered. 'Really, girl, do you think it matters to anybody that you've been caned?'

'But ...' she answered miserably, 'but what if it's a man?'

'Then he will see your well-whipped bottom, and perhaps pass a remark on the benefits of corporal punishment for female members of the service. Now, do as you are told: unless you would care for another half-dozen?'

Her reaction was instantaneous. She scurried across the room in a flurry of loose tails and lowered panties. In the corner, she hastily readjusted her clothes to leave the whole of her bottom showing and then placed her hands meekly on her head. Her buttocks seemed heavier in this new, standing position, the cheeks hanging to make a fat pear of girl-flesh, both showing a general red flush and marked with the six darker cane welts.

I walked to my desk, seated myself and folded my hands in my lap, breathing deeply in an attempt to regain my composure. Outside I could hear the familiar drone of an aeroplane and distant voices, but both noises might as well have been in another world. It was no good. Miss Birch was still snivelling gently and occasionally her well-whacked little bottom would clench with the throbbing pain of her caning. She had her legs tight together, which kept her panties trapped at the level of her stocking-tops – a quite enchanting image. The material of my cami-knickers was wet between my legs, very wet indeed, and I could feel the warmth of my own excitement in my sex. My nipples felt stiff against the silk that restrained my breasts and my pulse was hammering, despite my best efforts to remain calm. Miss Birch gave a little wriggle of discomfort, making her bottom shiver and providing me with a brief glimpse of the hair between her legs.

I could no longer resist my need. With a less attractive girl, I might have quietly played with myself over the sight of her well-beaten nates while she fondly supposed that the long corner time was merely an added humiliation. They never dare to turn round, and besides, my lower body would have been hidden behind the desk, so that she would not have seen the surreptitious hand working against the front of my camiknicker gusset. Penny was simply too beautiful for such a fleeting and stolen pleasure. I needed her tongue applied between my legs, where it would do the most good, and I needed it then and there.

This, of course, was a little difficult. I had every right to cane her, and I had seen the way her vulva had juiced during her exposure and beating. That she was ripe for sex, I had no doubt, but she was certainly under no obligation to submit herself to me. Yet I had heard rumours, rumours to the effect that each night she warmed the bed for Miss Oakley: and that, more often than not, she stayed in it. After being well beaten to put her in her place and with her pussy running juice, it seemed unlikely that she had the will to refuse me.

'I confess to a slight discomfort,' I remarked. 'I think you understand me?'

'Yes, ma'am,' she stuttered, clearly aware of exactly what she was going to have to do.

I smiled. It is not easy to accept the ministrations of a girl's tongue with anything approaching poise. One cannot simply lie down and throw one's legs apart, like some common slut eager for the clumsy attentions of her brash boyfriend; nor do I feel that it is at all ladylike to kneel and allow a tongue to be applied from behind. Seated, with the girl kneeling on the floor, is more appropriate: but the truly elegant way, I feel, is to drop a neat curtsy on to her face while she lies prone, thus avoiding unseemly display while retaining full control of the situation.

Queening, it is called, the act of sitting on a girl's face. Not only is it elegant and practical for the dominant, but it is highly appropriate for the submissive. The position leaves her firmly under the control of her rider, but is intensely humiliating – not that I know from personal experience, needless to say. Thus the contrast between dominant and submissive may truly be said to be regal, the one seated in comfort, the other prone with a naked bottom sat squarely in her face. To do it correctly, the rider must face her mount's body, thus ensuring the added sensation that comes from the girl's nose being pressed into her queen's bottom-hole.

This was what I did with Miss Birch, after locking the door of my office to prevent untimely intrusions and then ordering her to lie on the floor. She obeyed without question, even showing a glimmer of intelligence by positioning herself so that there was no chance that we might be observed through the window. I turned my back to her and made a brief adjustment to my camiknickers, opening the buttons and tucking the front and rear tags up to leave me naked under my skirt and slip.

I found her looking up at me as I turned, her eyes big and round as they followed me across the office. I wanted her to get a clear look at what she was going to have to lick, and so went to stand with one foot on either side of her head, allowing her to see directly up my skirt.

'Take a good look, Miss Birch,' I said, 'and think how this will feel in your face.'

As I spoke, I began to squat, tugging my uniform skirt and slip up as I went down, until I was kneeling across her head with her face only inches from my vulva. I knew she could see every detail of my sex: and not just that, but also in between my bottom-cheeks. A pause allowed her to really savour the thought of what was going to happen, and then I sat down, plumb on top of her, so that my pussy was pressed to her mouth and her pert little nose was poking a little way into my anus. I wiggled to make myself comfortable and to settle my bottom evenly across her features.

'You will lick now,' I instructed, 'but not you know where – I intend to take my full pleasure of your dirty little mouth.'

She obeyed, starting to lick at my vulva with a timidity that, while charming in its way, was intensely frustrating.

'Harder,' I ordered, 'and put your tongue in.'

For a moment, she made no response; but as I settled a little more of my weight on to her face, her tongue began to probe at the opening of my vagina. I could not resist a sigh as it opened me and she began to lick around the entrance of the hole. The sensation was exquisite, as was that of her pretty nose in my anus and the wet, slippery feeling between us. Before me, her body was laid out, with the lifted skirt and lowered panties leaving the thick puff of hair between her legs on show and her breasts poking up impudently under her blouse. I wanted them bare, and could see no reason why they should not be.

I took a firm grip on the front of her blouse and pulled hard. The material strained around the buttons and then tore, exposing the most darling little pair of titties held snug in the cups of a white lace bra. I popped them out with a single motion and took the teats between my fingers and thumbs. The urgency of her licking increased as I began to play with her breasts, twisting and pulling at the nipples until they felt like a pair of under-ripe mulberries in my hands.

It was clear that she was becoming ever more excited – unreasonably so, in fact. Not only had she relaxed her thighs and opened them a little, but she had put a hand on her belly, where her fingers were stroking her skin only an inch or two clear of her pubic hair. I could see that she wanted to masturbate while she licked me. It would have been a pretty sight, and for a moment I considered permitting it. Then again, given our respective ranks, it was hardly suitable.

'Stop it,' I ordered. 'Put your hands by your sides, you dirty child!'

She obeyed instantly, yet I still felt she needed something to remind her who was in charge. It was obvious what I needed to do. A girl who is being queened may think she is suffering the last word in indignity, with her tongue in her rider's vagina and her nose to the anus, but she would be wrong. I moved a little forward, no more than two inches, but enough to place my bottom-hole directly against Miss Birch's mouth.

Her immediate reaction was one of confusion. She tried to move her mouth forward and once more on to my vagina, but I simply pressed my bottom more firmly into her face, squashing her soft lips directly on to the hole. I felt her suck in air and give a desperate little wriggle beneath me, but she kept her tongue obstinately withdrawn. I shimmied my bottom into her face, to show what I wanted, but her only response was an oddly muffled noise that I took for a protest.

'Do not be pert, Miss Birch,' I remarked, enjoying her evident distaste for the task but determined that she should do as she was told.

Still she refused to oblige.

'Come on!' I urged. 'You know it's all you're good for!'

She gave another muffled squeak.

'Lick it, you common little tramp!' I snapped. 'Else I'll take you out to the parade ground and add another two dozen stripes to your fat behind!'

That did the trick. Slowly, with every evidence of reluctance, she poked her tongue out. I felt her lips part and something muscular touch my anus. It was drawn quickly back, then once more applied, licking at the sensitive flesh of my bottom-hole, tentatively, and then more firmly as she surrendered herself to the enjoyment of the degrading act of licking another woman's bottom clean. The sensation was exquisite both at a simple, physical level, and because of my delight in her absolute capitulation to my will.

'That's good,' I told her, not wanting her efforts to go entirely unrewarded.

She began to lick more earnestly at my praise.

'You may get your tongue well in,' I added, as I relaxed my sphincter.

Her tongue burrowed into my anus, creating a sensation so sweet that my resolve to hold myself aloof broke down completely. I was struggling with my blouse, all thought of decorum forgotten as I tore it in my urgency to get at my breasts. They came free, firm and large beneath my camisole, the nipples pushing up the silk into little mounds beneath my thumbs. With a breast cupped in each hand, I began to stimulate myself as Penny licked out my bottom-hole. I was about to order her to touch my pussy, but she seemed to sense my need and curled her arms up between my thighs.

Her fingers found my vulva, two opening the lips and a third starting little circular motions over my clitoris. A thumb slipped into my vagina and began to wiggle in time to the frigging of my clitty. I closed my eyes and let myself go, allowing the exquisite sensations of my body to build up, piling one on another until I could stand it no more and the dam burst. I know I screamed when I came, and was vaguely aware of making the most unladylike grunting noises, but with a tongue up my bottom, a thumb in my cunt, fingers on my pussy and my breasts in my hands, I simply didn't care. Only when she took her hands away from my pussy and the agonising rubbing stopped did I even begin to regain control.

When I came down far enough from my orgasm to open my eyes, it was to discover that she had started to masturbate. I judged it only fair to allow her the pleasure and made no move to stop her, nor to get her to take her tongue out of my anus. Indeed, while the sensitivity of my ring was close to unbearable, being tongued up the bottom was not a sensation I had any desire to bring to an end.

Penny's thighs were as far apart as the half-lowered panties would permit, and her hands were down between them. I could see that she was diddling herself, and using the same circular motions of her fingers that she had on me. Quickly, the muscles of her thighs and belly began to contract, and I knew that she would soon come. The licking of my anus had become really quite demented, as if she was determined to ream out the full depth of my sphincter. It was more than I could resist not to put a finger to my own clitty and, as she started to push her hips up, I too felt a climax approaching.

We came almost together, with my vision going momentarily red at the sheer intensity of my feelings. I could hear her buttocks slapping on the floor as she bucked frantically up and down, and thought of how it must hurt from her caning, even as my orgasm welled up inside me. I yelled out her name and called her a slut, as my thighs locked hard around her head. She thrashed beneath me and kicked out, once, twice, and then she was going limp as her tongue withdrew slowly from my bumhole.

I sank down, exhausted on top of her, kissed the sweat-damp skin of her belly and then rolled off to collapse on the floor. For perhaps a minute we lay still, slowly recovering ourselves. Finally, determined to retain at least some vestige of my dignity, I got to my feet and ordered her to do likewise.

She rose slowly, then rocked back onto her knees. Her thighs were well apart, with the big white panties stretched taut between them. The tails of her blouse failed to obscure her pussy, which was dripping with her juices. The torn blouse had stayed open, caught as it was into the sides of her bra, and I could see her little breasts clearly, thrust up by the lowered cups, the nipples still stiff with reaction. Her face was a mess, the hat gone, the hair dishevelled, the cheeks stained with lines where her mascara had run with her tears. Worse still was her mouth, with the once carefully applied lipstick smudged irreparably, and a good deal of white juice around her lips, and even on her chin and nose.

Her degradation was complete – her bottom sore, her face soiled, her expression set in a petulant moue that showed the most extraordinary depths of shame and misery. Never had I seen a punished girl look so sorry for herself, nor one who has been taken advantage of look so chagrined – it was simply pitiful. Then, as she looked up at me, her expression changed, her eyes opening wide, her cheeks dimpling and her mouth breaking into a wide, mischievous smile.

. . . a delicious experience, and one that repaid my impertinence with interest.

Susan Wren appears in A Taste of Amber *as the small, shy girl who first brought out Amber Oakley's feelings of lesbianism and sexual dominance. I confess to being a little jealous of Susan, for whom Amber still has a special affection. Yet while Amber's taste for other girls developed into nearly pure lesbianism, Susan's need proved to be more for security, authority and above all protection. She also introduced Amber to Anderson Croom, who became Vicky Belstone's boyfriend and has given us all a great deal of fun.*

Susan's story is from her time at Oxford and, as it shows, her need to be surrounded by protective types sometimes gets her a little more than she bargains for . . .

Orsino – Susan Wren

Jesus was well behind us and that was all I needed to know. We had done it. Two row-overs, one over-bump, one bump, and we were Head of the River!

That also meant that I was shortly going to be very wet indeed. Sure enough, in time-honoured tradition, the boys picked me up as soon as we had pulled alongside the bank and threw me into the Isis. I emerged with weed in my hair but without taking in any water, which was just as well, considering what gets into the river. What I didn't realise for some minutes was that my sodden top had gone completely see-through and was clinging to my braless breasts. By then, everyone who wanted to had already had a good look at them. I was simply too excited to care anyway, and nobody seemed to think any the worse of me for flashing.

The traditional method of celebrating such a glorious win is to burn the boat and oars. Unfortunately, this had been banned on pain of being sent down and, although some of the boys thought we should do it anyway, the rest of us managed to talk them out of it. In the end they contented themselves with pinching the oars and we marched back to college in mock-solemn procession.

If it hadn't been a victory party, there would have been some serious drowning of sorrows, so the JCR common room was already booked and well stocked with champagne and Cognac. I made myself comfortable while the boys broached bottles and made champagne cocktails in half-pint beer glasses. We planned to make the party last all night, and I was the only girl invited. I was bound to get teased, maybe molested, or even spanked, and that was just fine.

I don't like to ask for sex. I like it done to me: but, of course, by the right person and in the right way. Most of all, I don't like to ask for the sort of sex I like best – being tied, having my pussy and bottom-hole attended to simultaneously and especially having punishment spankings. That was the great thing about being with the boys. Of the eight of them, five – Guy, Angus, Justin, Tom and Charles – had been to public school and had a childishly humorous approach to sex that suited me perfectly. Tying girls up was 'a bit of a laugh', spanking 'a spot of fun'. Buggery was a bit more serious, but definitely on the menu. Bruce was a Scot with an unusual background and the most reserved of them. Josh was much more ordinary and was the only one who didn't seem to regard girls as a different species. Mehmet was half-Turkish, half-Egyptian, and claimed that he'd put his cock in anything that didn't run away.

It hadn't been long after my appointment as cox to the first boat that they discovered just how pliable I was for that sort of thing. Guy had been the first, jokingly tugging my shorts down when I'd been bending to tie off the painter. I'd been bare underneath and so had flashed my bottom to all of them and several others who'd happened to be on the towpath. I'd squealed and quickly covered myself but my attempt to show anger had failed miserably. Since then, teasing me sexually had become part of the camaraderie of the team.

Modern women are supposed to hate that sort of thing. I don't. You see, there's a cost and a reward. The cost is smacks and pinches, and the occasional humiliating experience. The reward is to be close to eight of the biggest, strongest lads in the University and to have their protection and friendship. The naughty bits turn me on anyway, so I win both ways.

Things got rowdy fairly rapidly. We chalked the full

details of our victory over the arch of the JCR door and raised toasts to the teams we'd bumped. Each toast was a half-pint of champagne cocktail, which the boys downed with enthusiasm. I tried to hold back, but got spotted. Guy – who's usually the most forward of them – suggested spankings as penalties for failing to keep up with the drinking.

All the others had finished their glasses, so that left me with a stark choice – drink up or get spanked. I could already feel my bottom tingling in anticipation. They'd do it on the bare: I knew they would. It wasn't the first time, and they always stripped my bottom, just as a matter of course. It was going to hurt; it always did. Yet with my frame, a pint of Cognac and champagne downed in one would leave me in the gutter. I chose the spanking.

Anyway, it was only fair. All term, I'd been bullying them and shouting at them during training, and throwing me in the water was simply not an adequate revenge. So over the table I went, and down came my pants.

They had hold of me by the arms and Angus lifted my skirt to show my bare bum off. Then they whacked me, eight hard ones with the blade of an oar. Every smack made me yell and drew a laugh from them until, by the eighth, my bottom was on fire and I had tears in my eyes. When they'd finished laughing, they showed me my bum in the mirror. Both cheeks were a flaming red. Just eight swats and I looked as if I'd been over someone's knee for an hour!

I stuck my bottom out and gave my sore cheeks a good rub before pulling my knickers up, making sure they all got a good view. They were a big, dark blue pair of sports knickers which I knew the boys liked and which I hoped would be coming back down before too long. I'd put a sports bra on, too, and a loose blouse and skirt, all in the hope of providing easy access if they chose to molest me.

They did. Things got smutty quickly after my spanking and, as always, I became public property. I'd always been careful to keep my favours even, because I didn't want to be girlfriend to just one of them. All my first year I'd been with my tutor, Francis, and now I wanted freedom.

I was pulled down on Josh's lap first and he made a big show of feeling me through my blouse. Soon he was undoing my buttons, and then he whipped my bra up to flash my boobs to everyone. I giggled and pretended to try and stop him, but he just pulled my blouse back to trap my arms and left me with my bare chest sticking out for all to see. In my fake efforts to get away, I was squirming my bum in his lap and I could feel his cock, which was more than a bit hard. All he'd have had to do was pull it out and mount me on it, but he pushed me up and sent me staggering towards Guy with a hard slap on my bottom.

Guy grabbed my hands and threw me across his armchair. This left my bottom sticking up in the air and he held me while Justin's hands went up my skirt. I kicked and wriggled while my bottom was touched up, telling them to stop but praying they'd pull my pants down and take it further. One thing they always joked about was buggering me, and I thought that maybe, just maybe, this was my night.

Instead, I was put through an intensely humiliating exercise. Guy held me for some time while my bottom was fondled. My boobs were dangling bare as well, and it was Mehmet who decided he wanted a feel of them. It was also him who started to get positively rude.

'Her nips are like bullets,' he said, tweaking them between his fingers and sounding well pleased with himself. 'Let's give her what she wants.'

'You tie her hands; I'll pull down her pants,' Justin declared cheerfully as he found my knickers' waistband.

I struggled, just for the form of it, but it got me nowhere. They pulled me up and lashed my hands together, then strung me up from a beam so that I could only just touch the floor with my toes. Guy put his hands up under my skirt and took hold of my pants, and then down they came again, over my bum, down my legs and off. I was wriggling and helpless, bare-breasted and bare-bottomed.

They stood back, their faces set in lewd, childish grins or calculating smirks, each wondering just what he could get away with. I knew they would take advantage of me, maybe even take turns with me. There was no reason why they shouldn't, after all. I was knickerless under my skirt, and too drunk and turned on to stop them, even if I hadn't been tied up.

They shaved me. Josh suggested it and Charles was despatched for a razor. My skirt and blouse were taken off to leave me naked but for my boots. They sprayed foam on my pussy-mound and up between my legs. Charles and Guy held my legs apart and Josh shaved my pubes, not just on the mound but on my lips and down between my bum-cheeks. It stung, especially down in the crevices of my pussy, and my whole sex was throbbing before they put the razor to me.

I felt every scrape of that razor, every probing, intrusive finger, until my mound was as bald as an egg. Josh even put two fingers up my pussy to stretch my flesh out, and spread my anus between his finger and thumb to clear the last of my hair from around it. To get between my cheeks, they had to lift my legs up to my chest. I was held like that, completely open to them, while they denuded my sex.

By the end, I was faint with pleasure and the rude feeling of exposure and of being bald on my pussy. They cleaned the foam off with champagne, shaking the bottle and spraying my crotch. Some of it went up my pussy and they finished by doing my boobs as well. I could feel it, cold and fizzy, as the bubbles prickled around the entrance to my vagina, making me desperate for a cock. For all the teasing sex-play, I hadn't been fucked in months and, at that moment, I needed it more than anything else.

I think I'd have got it, too, if someone hadn't hammered on the door and told us to keep the noise down. Fortunately, Charles had had the sense to lock it when he came in with the razor, or I'd have been caught with my pants down in no uncertain terms. Worse, in fact, because Mehmet had started to lick the Champagne off my boobs and had a finger up me.

A hasty conference was held and we decided to find somewhere more private. This clearly implied the desire to do more rude things to me, so I agreed without hesitation.

I was untied and let down, even permitted to dress, except for my knickers, which I was told were now rowing club property, as Guy stuffed them in his pocket. Angus had the best room in college and he suggested we go there, but I pointed out that it was on the ground floor and likely to attract attention.

Grinning at what was in effect an offer to continue molesting me, Guy suggested that we should visit Anderson Croom, who could always be relied upon for a free drink and a cheerful welcome. Croom was one of those people who are either lucky or sneaky, because he had a whole set of rooms sandwiched between his college's two best guest suites. They were on the ground floor but overlooked a meadow.

So we abandoned the JCR and trooped off through college with all eight oars and my sports knickers as a flag. Out in the High, plenty of people were milling about and I felt immensely self-conscious, walking with the knowledge that I had a short skirt on with no knickers underneath. All it would have taken was a puff of wind and my bare bum would have been exposed to students, locals and tourists alike. The thought made me giggle, especially as some people noticed the knickers on Guy's oar and then gave me a shocked look as they wondered if they were mine.

Opposite All Souls, one hard-faced old lady gave me such a dirty and knowing look that I seriously wondered if she wasn't going to pull my skirt up to check if I was the owner of the offending knickers and bare underneath. I whispered this to Angus as soon as she was past and, the next moment, my skirt had been hoisted and my bum was bare to the world.

They paraded me like that all the way to the Longwall Street junction, with my little pink bum, all coloured up from my spanking, showing to everyone! It felt so rude and, what was best, was that everyone who saw must have thought it was being done against my will. Angus and Guy had their arms tight around me, and it was obvious that I could do nothing to cover myself. I could just imagine them all thinking of me as the poor little innocent having her skirt held up by the horrid, rough boys. As to why I was knickerless and had a red bum, goodness only knows what they thought! What was certain was that they'd guess I'd been spanked, and that got to me.

We got to Croom's college to find the side gate locked for the night. As there was little chance of the porters allowing in a group of nine drunken rowers from another college, we were forced to get in by the old-fashioned method – scaling the wall. This was all very well for the boys, few of whom stood under six foot, but for me – small, drunk, pantiless and wearing high-heeled boots – it was a different matter. They laughed uproariously over the display I made of myself as I tried to climb over, telling me they could see up my skirt and comparing my shaved pussy with ones they'd seen in dirty magazines.

I made it, despite everything, and dropped to the far side. Only then did they let me have my knickers back, and I scrambled into them in the shadow of an ornamental bush, even though I was pretty sure they'd be coming off again before long. We made it to Croom's room without attracting undue attention and were welcomed by him with enthusiasm.

Croom was reading philosophy and French so he went to some of the same lectures as I did. Not that he was there often, and the impression of him I had was of languor, elegance, humour, high intelligence, and not the slightest inclination to work. Most students nowadays are both hard-working and impoverished; Croom was neither and did his best to live in the same style as his forebears had at the same college for several generations. His rooms certainly looked the part: a fine double suite with a bathroom, antique furniture, rich, dark colours, while a smell of age and fine brandy all added to the atmosphere, which I had always enjoyed, and envied.

Ever since *Brideshead Revisited* had become popular, a few of the more pretentious undergraduates could always be guaranteed to own teddy bears with vaguely louche names. Croom, being Croom, had gone one better and had managed to buy a full-sized stuffed grizzly. This stood in the corner of his room on a heavy wooden base. By careful manipulation, he had adapted the expression of ferocity which the taxidermist had left the beast with to an inane grin. Some wag had suggested that this made the bear appear as if it had just finished a strenuous but satisfying masturbation session, and had presented Croom with a huge, and lovingly carved, phallus, testicles and all, which he had attached to the bear. Normally, it wore a pair of fifty-six-inch waist London Transport bus driver's uniform trousers, for the sake of decency. When Croom gave parties, the phallus would invariably be protruding from the fly, or the trousers would be off completely, which never failed to break the ice.

That was how it was now, with a good ten inches of highly polished and improbably thick wooden penis projecting from its crotch. Croom had a decanter in his hand and, as we trooped into the room, he began to wave it cheerfully and to recite a seriously perverted version of one of Lewis Carroll's poems:

'You are old, Father William,' the young girl said,
'And frequently rise in the night;
Yet you insist that my friend goes nude to her bed –
Do you think, at your age, this is right?'

'In my youth,' Father William replied,
'I feared lewdness might ruin my standing
But now I am eighty I will not be denied,
And plan to watch when she crosses the landing.'

'You are old,' said the girl, 'as I mentioned before,
And have grown most uncommonly fat;
Yet you rogered the parlour-maid and she came back
for more – Pray what is the reason of that?'

'In my youth,' sighed the sage, as he took out his
cock,
'I could manage a hard-on all day;

But your breasts are quite fine and they show through
  your frock –
Perhaps you would care for a lay?'

'You are old,' said the girl, 'and your cock is as soft
As a condom that's filled up with suet;
Yet you buggered the girl who was lagging the loft –
Pray, how do you manage to do it?'

'In my youth,' said the seer, 'I worked in a lab,
To formulate bonder and glue;
Just one shot in the glans makes it easy to stab.
Here, is this hard enough, maybe, for you?'

'You are old,' said the girl, 'and clearly quite mad
If you think I would lower my drawers;
But I'll give you a suck if you don't tell my Dad
And promise to give up the whores.'

'In my youth,' he replied, 'I'd have pulled up your
  dress,
And given your bottom a slap;
But I haven't the strength to do more than caress,
So come over and sit in my lap.'

We listened in silence until he had finished. He then took a bow and made a sweeping gesture to indicate that we might make ourselves at home. I was keen to get back into the naughty spirit of things and so gave Croom a big kiss and sat down on his lap. He put an arm around me and then brushed a nipple through my blouse, casually, gently, but sending a ripple of pleasure right through me.

Drinks were handed round and the conversation quickly picked up. They started to tease me again, telling Croom how they'd spanked me and shaved me. Of course, I had to show off my bottom and pussy, so I got off his lap and made a big deal of peeling down my knickers under my skirt with mock reluctance and then giving him the briefest of flashes, first of my red bottom, then of my shaven pussy.

As I'd known full well it would, that led to demands for a better show. Again I pretended not to want to, and suffered the exquisite indignity of being grabbed and stripped naked on the floor. Once down and nude, my legs were held apart to show off my hairless pussy, then I was turned over and made to kneel in a position that left not just my red bum showing but also every rude detail between my cheeks.

Croom made appreciative noises and gave my bum a friendly slap. I sank down, putting my face to the floor. I was naked, dizzy with drink and the need for sex. I had nine men to myself – nine young, virile men – who thought nothing of pulling down my knickers and spanking me with an oar or even of parading me bare-bottomed down the High. I was theirs and all they had to do was take me.

It wasn't enough. Nobody came forward; nobody pushed me down on the carpet and used me as I wanted to be used. I wasn't going to give up so easily and I determined to show that I was willing, and enough of a slut to take it. The bear was nearby, a gross, hairy thing rearing above me with its obscene phallus sticking out blatantly, shiny and intensely male. I crawled over and knelt up, facing the bear's crotch, the bulbous tip of its cock an inch from my face. The glans was a huge thing: impossibly huge for a man, perhaps not for a bear. It was glossy with varnish, perfectly smooth to my touch as I ran a finger over it.

'The little tart's going to suck it!' Justin declared.

He was right. I opened my mouth and took the knob in, gaping around the fat wooden end. It completely filled my mouth, and was smooth and cool, but with the shape of a real cock. They began to laugh and cheer as I sucked on the bear's cock.

Guy came over and began to slap at my bottom with a shoe. I stuck it out, hoping for more, hoping for his cock in my pussy – even up my bottom. He continued to spank me, calling me a dirty tart, and worse, as I sucked on the bear's penis. I was wishing it was real, even wishing it was a real bear, anything to satisfy my need. I was being as rude as I knew, offering myself as obviously as I could, but still they wouldn't . . .

'Let's row her,' Charles called. 'All nine of us!'

I pulled back from the bear's cock and spread my thighs to them, offering my open, wet pussy.

'Come on, then: do it,' I gasped. 'I bet you wouldn't dare.'

There was an immediate hubbub of contradiction, but only one of them actually had the guts to do anything. This was Mehmet, who didn't join in the smutty remarks but just drew down his zip and pulled out his balls and fully erect cock.

I swallowed as I found my eyes locked on it, a big, dark-fleshed penis sticking up over a big, rough-skinned scrotum. He was awfully hairy, too, with a thick tangle of pubes around his shaft and all over his balls. Everyone went silent when they saw what he'd done.

He stood up, sporting his cock, and the ball was firmly in my court. I glanced round, wanting to do it and seeking approval in the watching faces. Most were goggled-eyed, stunned by my rudeness and Mehmet's blatant response. This was further than we'd gone before, far further, but there wasn't a cock in the room that wasn't hard in its owner's pants. Bruce looked stern – aggressive, even – and his knuckles were white on the stem of his glass. Tom had his hand on his crotch and was squeezing a rather obvious bulge. Guy had his head to one side, calculating my response: perhaps hoping I was drunk enough and dirty enough. Only one face was calm – Anderson Croom, whose mouth was turned up into the slightest of smiles, as if he'd seen it all before.

That was what decided me. The rest of them wanted me, hoped I'd dare to do it. Even Mehmet I could turn down and leave with a raging erection. Not Anderson Croom: he would watch and enjoy the view. Maybe his cock would be stiff, but he'd stay calm. Then, at the end, he'd have me and maybe he'd do what his dirty Father William had done to the girl in the loft – maybe he'd bugger me.

Before I knew what I was doing, I had shuffled forward

on my knees and taken Mehmet's hairy ball-sac in my mouth. He tasted salty, and strongly male, as I rolled his balls back and forth over my tongue, revelling in my own filthy behaviour. I took his cock and began to masturbate him, then turned my eyes up. He was stood over me, his hands placed boldly on his hips, his face showing triumph and pleasure.

'I always knew you were a tart, Susan,' he grunted, and then abruptly pushed me backward.

I went over on my back with my legs up and he was straight on me. His weight settled on me and my face was against his neck. I felt his cock bumping against my bum-cheeks and thought he was going to do what he had so often threatened and bugger me. Instead, it went up my pussy and I was soon panting and clinging to him as he gave me what I had been angling for. It was fast, and rough, a hard fucking with no gentleness, or concern for my needs. Again and again he rammed himself home inside me, using my body, using my vagina, using me just as a receptacle for his come. He soon came up me and I felt the sperm squash out around the mouth of my pussy; then he was off and I found myself surrounded by a ring of erect cocks.

They had me, all nine of them, one at a time. Guy went after Mehmet, mounting me and plunging in so roughly that I cried out in pain. I put my arms around him, but his sole concern was to fuck me and he came even faster than Mehmet. With my pussy dribbling two men's come, I was mounted by Josh. He seemed bigger than the others, filling my pussy and making my head swim with the feel of him inside me. He had shaved me and, as if to celebrate his action, he pulled out and came all over my sleek pubic mound. Angus was next, red-faced with lust, as he took my ankles and spread my legs wide. He did me like that, upright with my legs held up and apart. It took longer, too, and let me get at my breasts, which I squeezed and stroked as I was rowed. Like Josh, he came on my belly, spraying his come right up to where my hands were working my nipples.

Bruce came forward as Angus stepped back. He looked

down at me, his face registering disgust at the state of my front. Grabbing my hips, he turned me roughly over, then pushed my legs apart and entered me bum-up. His thrusts jammed me again and again into the floor, leaving me breathless and gasping when he came, deep up me. Tom, always the quietest, followed, pulling me up on to my knees. I knew how sloppy my anus was and stuck my bottom out, hoping he would take the hint and use my tight bum-hole instead of my soaking vagina. He didn't, but gave me a fast, hard ride from the rear and came up me, only to wipe his cock on my thigh.

By then, Justin already had his cock in my mouth and Tom was quickly replaced. He had trouble, gripping my hips and slamming himself against my bottom. It felt much like being spanked with the oar and left me gagging for breath. When he finally came, it was deep up me; and as his cock left my vagina, I felt a thick wad of semen start to ooze down my pussy.

Charles rolled me face-up again and took off at a frantic pace, fucking me with a desperate need. Perhaps he was small – perhaps I was just too open and sloppy – but I could barely feel him. Nor could he feel me because, try as he might, he couldn't come and he had soon begun to gasp and curse while his face was the colour of a beetroot.

'I can't! You're too slimy!' he hissed through gritted teeth. 'I just can't get . . .'

'Then use my bum,' I grunted.

I had to say it. I wasn't going to be used by nine men and escape buggery: the experience just wouldn't have been complete without at least one cock up my bottom. Charles pulled his cock from my pussy and I rolled my legs up to accept it in my anus.

'The filthy little whore!' Josh exclaimed. 'She wants it up the dirtbox!'

Charles stopped, his prick an inch from my bum-hole. I grabbed the insides of my knees, more turned on by Josh's comment than put off. Charles wasn't so independent. Scrambling round to my head, he put his cock in my mouth and began to masturbate himself. I sucked obligingly and swallowed what he did in my mouth about ten seconds later, but I was full of disappointment.

One man was left: Anderson Croom. Unlike the others, he had undressed and was standing by a bookcase, nursing an impressive erection. He was less muscular than the rowers, but elegant and strong.

'Anderson?' I asked, spreading my thighs in invitation.

Anderson smiled and sank down on the floor. He took his time, using each orifice of my body with careful deliberation. First he made me pull at his cock, then suck him. Only when I thought he was sure to come in my mouth did he stop and straddle me, to make use of the valley between my breasts. When he mounted me, it was on top, and he alone kissed me. He took his weight on his arms too, and nibbled my neck and an ear as we fucked.

I knew what I wanted, his cock up my bottom, and was looking forward to the reactions of shock and jealousy from the others when Croom did it in front of them. No longer caring about pretending innocence or unwillingness, I whispered into his ear.

'Would you like it up my bum, Anderson?'

'Yes,' he answered. 'I would. I'd adore it up your bum.'

'Bloody show-off!' Guy remarked loudly from above us. 'Come on, Croom. You've fucked the little doxy; now finish it off!'

'Another time,' Anderson whispered to me and kissed me hard on the mouth.

He began to pump faster as our tongues met and I actually felt we were making love as he held me, but only briefly, and then he'd come deep inside my pussy.

The others were already sitting back with drinks in their hands and their cocks put away. I was shaking hard and had difficulty getting up, but Anderson helped me and was about to take me to the bathroom when Guy whispered something to Angus, who burst out laughing.

'I demand fair play!' Angus roared. 'We have all nine had her, but what of the tenth person present? Is it fair that he should go without his share of pussy? Look at the poor fellow: he is clearly beside himself with lust!'

He pointed at the bear.

'Dammed right!' Guy declared. 'One for all and all for one. Let the bear fuck her!'

'Come on, boys,' I tried, but it was a feeble protest and they knew it.

'Let him have the little prick-tease,' Justin called out. 'She sucked his cock and now she won't go through with it! Shame!'

'Typical girl!' Charles added. 'Likes to see a man desperate for it, but won't put out! Come on, Susan, give the poor fellow a break!'

'It's a bear!' I protested, unleashing a whole volley of remonstration.

'Bloody animalist! That's disgusting!'

'How could you be so prejudiced?'

'Tie her to him, with his cock up her cunt! That'll teach her a lesson!'

'A valuable lesson! There's no room for prejudice here!'

'Mount her on the bear!'

'Mount her on the bear!'

'He does have a name, you know.'

The last was Croom, and spoken quite calmly. For a moment, I thought I was going to be spared the ignominy of having the bear's cock put up me, but he rose and strolled over to the hideous thing.

'Care for a spot of pussy, Orsino?' he asked.

'Is it fresh?' the bear appeared to respond in a low, gravelly voice.

'Perhaps not entirely,' Croom admitted diffidently, as my cheeks suffused with blushes, and everybody else burst out laughing.

'Sloppy seconds, eh?' the bear grumbled.

'More like sloppy tenths,' Croom replied.

'Little tart, eh? Oh, what the hell: pop her on.'

Strong male hands grabbed my arms and thighs. I could only squeak in vain protest as I was lifted and hustled over to the bear. Angus and Guy had my legs, and spread them open. I felt the beast's coarse fur on the insides of my thighs, then on my chest as I was pushed on to it. Something bumped on my pussy – its cock.

I felt my pussy open as my weight drove me down on to the cock. I was so wet with semen that I could do nothing but gasp out my surprise as I slid down the huge thing. One second the knob was stretching my hole: then it had filled me and stopped, the rounded end pressed hard against my cervix. My mouth was wide with shock. I didn't know whether to scream or groan. My vagina felt full to bursting, so full that the sensation seemed to pervade every part of my body. Even my brain felt full of cock, an experience I had only known before when being buggered.

They took my legs and arms and crossed them behind the beast's back, lashing my ankles and wrists with ties. That destroyed my last chance of getting off the bear's cock without help. With the knowledge that I was truly and utterly helpless, my dizzy feeling of pleasure rose yet higher. I was sure they would use me again, but my pussy was full, which meant my bum-hole was the only suitable orifice for their cocks. I'm no virgin anally – Francis used to bugger me all the time – but there were nine of them!

I nearly fainted just at the thought, then opened my eyes suddenly at a noise. Angus was holding my bundled sports pants up in front of my face.

'Open wide, Susan,' he quipped,

I gaped obediently and he stuffed them in, making me gag on the dry cotton and filling my mouth with the taste of my own pussy. A tie was used to hold them in place, gagging me and robbing me of my last chance of protest. Then my blouse was wrapped around my head and tied off, leaving me blind as well as dumb.

I was breathing hard, expecting the feel of a cock-head between my buttocks at any moment. Nothing happened, but I could hear them laughing at me and saying how ridiculous I looked, which just turned me on even more. Then Angus's voice cut through the others.

'Let's take her out in the quad! The two of them'd make a damn fine statue!'

I could do nothing to protest. The bear and I were picked up and carried out of Croom's room. They bumped me down a step, laughing, and occasionally feeling my bottom, then outside. I felt the cool night air on my naked body and renewed my protests, managing muffled squeaks thought my panty-gag. Nobody took any notice and I was dumped somewhere well out in the quad. Then they just left me.

I immediately felt myself start to panic. I was mounted, naked, on a bear's cock in the middle of a quad, absolutely helpless. I couldn't move, except to wriggle my poor, straining vagina on that enormous wooden penis. I couldn't call out, even if I'd wanted to! I couldn't even see!

It was like that for what seemed an age. Nothing was happening, but my brain was whirling in an agony of embarrassment and anger. The worst of it was, I hadn't come, and underneath there was a desperate need to be well and truly abused before I was released. It was the better option anyway. If I was found, there would be hell to pay, unless – just unless – some randy undergraduate or dirty old goat of a don found me and couldn't resist the open invitation of my spread bottom-cheeks. Then it would be a cock up the bum for me and release, after which I could demand some attention to my pussy. Of course, it was hopeless. However excited my rescuer was, he would hardly bugger me in the middle of the quad.

I felt a pang of despair, then a sudden, stronger panic as I heard a noise. It had to be the boys coming back – or at least I hoped it was – and, for all my anger with them, I'd have been grateful. Then I felt a hand slip between the bear's belly fur and my pussy. Fingers opened my lips, found my clit and started to rub. I couldn't fight: I just melted and began to sob and gasp into my mouthful of wet cotton. Something touched my neck: lips, kissing, gently exploring the sensitive places behind my ears and on my nape. Then he was kissing my ear and a hand had slid down between my bum-cheeks and found my anus. A finger popped inside and I was lost, my need rising to a crazy level as he masturbated me and fingered my bum.

'I'm going to bugger you, Susan,' he whispered.

I didn't reply. I couldn't: my mouth was stuffed full of my knickers. I wouldn't have done, anyway. I didn't want to talk about it; I just wanted him to do it. I wanted to be buggered with the bear's cock still in me, buggered while I was tied, and gagged, and naked.

I didn't care about where I was any more, just as long as I got that long, hard, eager cock up my bottom. He pressed himself to me, pushing me into the fur of the bear. His cock was between my buttocks, a hard rod of hot flesh. I knew it would shortly be going up the tight little hole at the centre, rewarding my sexy behaviour with anal sex. No: punishing my dirty behaviour with buggery.

A sudden flurry of hard rubs on my clit made me gasp, then choke as I swallowed a fold of my knickers. His hand slid under my bottom, opening my cheeks. I felt his cock slide down between them, moving slowly, the tip tracing a line down towards my anus, prodding just above it, then on it and I knew that this was no tease. He was actually going to bugger me. I felt a sharp pain in my anus and tried to cry out, but he gave another sudden burst of dabs to my clitoris.

'Gently, easily,' he whispered, placing his lips against my ear. 'Push out. Don't fight it, let it slide in.'

'Mmmh,' I managed, and tried to obey, letting my sphincter relax as he once more pushed the head of his cock against it.

I gasped as I felt myself open and the head of his cock slid into my rectum. Up it went, eased inch by inch into the depths of my bottom, filling me out, stretching me, until my bum felt as full of his cock as my pussy did of the bear's. It was quickly up, right to the hilt, wedged into my bottom. He was up me. I was being buggered, used up the bottom as I'd so badly wanted.

The sensation was beyond anything I'd experienced before. I was mounted on a bear, its hair rough on my naked front, its cock pushed right up into me, filling me until I felt I would burst. A man's cock was up my bottom, rutting up and down in the wet tube of my rectum, straining my anus, which had been greased with the come of nine men. His lips were on my neck, his front was against my well-spanked, well shown-off bottom, and his hand was on my bald, swollen pussy, rubbing my clit.

He diddled me off with an expertise I'd felt only once before, and that from a girl. I could do nothing about it, but just came under his fingers. Everything became centred on my sex as I started to climax, the warm erection up my bottom, the bear's cock in my pussy, my sloppy wet labia, the fiery bud of my clitoris, my throbbing buttocks. I felt my straining bumhole contract on his shaft, again and again, just as my pussy was squirming on Orsino's gross phallus.

It all just exploded in my head, the teasing, the touching, the spankings, being stripped, being humiliated, sucking the bear's cock, being mounted and fucked again and again, being put on Orsino's cock, being tied, and gagged with my own knickers. Then, best of all, being entered up the bottom by a strange man, frigged and buggered in the open quad while I came, and came and came. Then he came, too, spurting hot semen deep in my bowels as he jammed his prick hard up my rectum and my ring clenched his invading cock . . .

I must have lost my senses briefly because, the next thing I knew, I was alone. I could feel the semen dribbling down the inside of my bum-cheeks, warm and wet on my sore flesh. Then I heard Anderson Croom's oh, so welcome voice and, as my blouse was pulled up, I found myself standing in his bedroom with the lights on and the window open to let in the air.

. . . and she thought she was a lesbian! Having said that, I suppose the bear might originally have been female. So, with grovelling apologies to Lewis Carroll, I will move on to the next story.

Amber would like me to picture Morris Rathwell as an arrogant, scheming, villainous control freak with a penchant for dominating girls and, in particular, virgins – not that they stay virgins for long, if he has any say in the matter. That is how I have pictured him in A Taste of Amber, *and it is pretty accurate. Nonetheless, I find he exerts a certain horrid fascination for me. I adore erotic humiliation and, at the end of the day, nobody does it better, nor more naturally. He is a predator but, as every tiger-skin rug shows, it is all too easy for even the fiercest of predators to become prey . . .*

Cindy – Morris Rathwell

The key to women, the real key, is that to have sex they need an excuse. Men like sex: they know they like sex. Women like sex, but they kid themselves it has to be for a reason – like 'he was Mr Right', or 'I was a bit tipsy', or even 'I only did it to make him shut up'. OK, there are exceptions – like the wife, Melody, and her twin sister, Harmony, both of whom are as randy as polecats and fuck like it was going out of fashion.

Old Charlie Oakley's daughter, Amber, shows what I mean. She wants it, like they all do, but she can only let go if the offer is put in the form of a bet: that's just nuts to me. I first fucked her when she was eighteen. Normally, she's a hoity-toity piece but, once she's lost her bet, she has her excuse and shows what a tart she is underneath. The first time, I put a few stripes across her arse for fun and then had her suck me, in the middle of a pony-girl club meet. The second time, I put her in a yoke and fucked her doggy fashion. She loves it: but, without that bet, she's not even good for a quick wank.

I met Sophie the first time I ran the club at this big warehouse in Silver Town. Things had been getting bigger and better since I'd added new attractions, as well as the pony-girl stuff, and there were pushing eight hundred people in. I had the girls with no pants and little tunics that left their tits bare, Mel running the dungeon and Harmony on the door. That left me free and, with all the bum and tit that was on view, I was beginning to wonder if I couldn't find a girl to squeeze a blow job out of.

That was when Anderson Croom and Vicky Belstone turned up with this ruddy great box and asked if they could do a cabaret. He's a right smart-arse and she's well stuck-up, but then he's a dirty bastard and she's a slut, so I knew it would be good.

They had fixed this really neat game. The thing they'd brought was a basic bondage stool with a superstructure built on to it to support this crazy enema device. There was a tube to go up the victim's backside and a glass reservoir which they had filled with orange squash. This was positioned so that the victim could see it, and it had a fancy affair with a valve and funnel attached to it. To stop the squash going up her arse, she would have to hold a sort of counterweight, with her teeth.

Vicky was going to go in it, just for the thrill of torturing herself, but I had a better idea. I don't normally get on with Anderson, but when I suggested offering a hundred quid to any girl who could hold off getting her enema for five minutes, he went for it like a shot. So they rigged the thing up in the middle of a tarpaulin and I announced the game – for girls only.

We had the greedy little tarts queuing up for it, so we had to draw lots to see who went on first. Sophie won. She was a cute little package, about five foot tall with a blonde bob and a nice set of curves. She was in a schoolgirl outfit – pleated tartan skirt, crisp white blouse, tight white pants, little tie, the works – and really looked the part.

It was a great laugh. They strapped her up so that she could barely wriggle, lifted her skirt and pulled her pants down. Then they put a the tube up her arse. I could see what was going to happen. It looked really easy, but that bastard Anderson had fixed a lever of sorts so that it was much harder than it seemed at first glance. Sophie hadn't bothered to check it out, or maybe she wanted two pints of orange squash up her back passage: anyway, she wasn't going to be getting the hundred quid.

Most people had gone to stand behind her to get the best

view of her arse. Not me. Don't get me wrong, she had a great arse – meaty, without being fat – but I can see great bums any time: all I have to do is tell the girls to get their pants off. No, when a girl's going to go through a heavy SM experience, it's not her arse you want to see – it's her face.

Sophie's was a picture. She started off confident – cocky, even – with a cheeky smile for the crowd, until Vicky put the toggle in her teeth. Then she looked determined, holding on bravely against the strain. Anderson was standing next to me, counting down the time from a big silver half-hunter and, as the seconds ticked by, her determination grew and grew.

She has such a sweet little face, and it was great to see her confidence ebb away, to see the determination turn to strain and then desperation as she realised she couldn't hold it. She actually started to panic just before the end came, kicking her legs in her bonds and trying desperately to get free. Then it happened. She let go of the toggle and let out the sweetest little sob of pure misery and then a gasp as she felt the cold squash start to flow up her arse. As her dirtbox filled, she screwed her face up in disgust, and then started to make little mewling noises when the pressure began to tell. When her belly started to stretch, her eyes came open wide, then her mouth. I could tell she'd never had an enema before, from the look of amazement and horror on her face as her bowels filled and stretched, and then the look of panic grew once more as she realised what was going to happen – there was too much for her to hold in.

It was something else. Her mewls turned to gasps as the pain in her rectum built, and then to even, regular pants – like a hot puppy – as she struggled to keep herself under control. Then she began to mumble, saying 'it's going to happen' over and over, louder and louder as her panic grew.

And it did happen. With a final yell, she let go, forcing the tube out of her bumhole and sending a spray of squash out in a great arc of glistening liquid. Her breath came out as the squash did, a long sigh of consternation and self-disgust that failed to entirely hide her relief. Her fountain was squirting a good seven feet behind her – which was another good reason for being at the head end – and splashing on the tarpaulin. It started to die and, as it did so, the sounds she was making trailed off into broken sobs and finally silence, leaving her mouth still wide open in shock and her eyes tightly closed.

She had volunteered, but I've known girls to freak after heavy scenes. Not Sophie. While everybody clapped and cheered, she said nothing. As the last of the squash dribbled out of her bum-hole into her lowered panties, she turned her head, made eye-contact with her friend and spoke three words very quietly:

'Bring me off.'

The friend was a skinny piece with great legs and a pert little arse, dressed in a tarty French maid's outfit. Without a word, she slid her hand under Sophie's tummy, found the clit and started to frig. It took seconds, Sophie starting to gasp immediately and then coming with a sweet little cry of pleasure.

That was when I knew I just had to have her. A girl needs to be a dirty bitch to take an enema in public. To ask to be frigged off afterwards, that takes a truly filthy mind. Now, sometimes, I like them innocent, and the old happy stick's taken five virgin cunts, but there's something special about a really filthy slut as well.

I tried to play it straight, waiting until she had cleaned up and then suggesting a blow-job in advance of a proper date. She turned me down, which didn't surprise me. It wasn't that she didn't want it. She needed her excuse. My problem was to find it.

This was no big deal. When she'd volunteered to go on the enema machine, she'd known the risks, but had loved it when it had all gone wrong. So there it was: she liked to think that getting sex was an accident. I don't mean something she didn't want, but something that just happened, something that she didn't see coming. That way, she could get off without admitting to herself that she had wanted it all along. Sure, it's illogical, but then that's girls all through.

The next bit was to set it up. She'd been a big hit on the enema machine and everyone was saying how great she was. Like any other girl, she was a sucker for flattery, so I got Mel to tell her she was the best and ask if she'd like to go in next month's cabaret. She agreed. Then my dirty tart of a wife took the little bitch into the ladies to have her cunt licked! I put Mel up on stage and gave her two dozen of the cane for that, right across her bare, black arse – which shows what a nice guy I am, because it would have been four dozen if Sophie had licked her but not gone for the cabaret.

At the next month's club I got out the old Devil's Wheel. It's an oldie but a goodie. There's this thumping great wheel which the girl has to spin. Depending on where it stops, she either gets a prize or gets punished. The audience love it and I guessed it'd be right up Sophie's street. Of course, it's fixed.

We put Vicky up first and she won a hundred. The money came straight out of Anderson's pocket, and it got the crowd going, so I didn't care. Next we had this gay guy up. It was hilarious when he lost and had to take six whacks from Mel. Afterwards, she made him kiss her big, girly arse and the look on his face was something else. I'm no homophobe – a lot of my friends are gay – and I'd have got as big a laugh out of seeing some straight bloke get made to suck cock – as long as it wasn't me.

I had Mel go next, so I could show Sophie that when it comes to dominating girls, nobody does it better than the Maestro. The wheel stopped on 'Hand Spanking', so the instant it was certain, I grabbed Mel by the ear and pulled her across my lap. We made a great show of it. She had on one of those little dresses with a flared skirt like a tutu so that her frilly knickers showed. Mel hates it because she always gets her bum pinched, but she looks great. Her arse was to the audience and I peeled the knickers down really slowly, giving everyone a good look at her. She really is a peach. Her bum sticks out the way only a black girl's can, and the cheeks are big and muscly but not too hard. There were cheers and claps as her cunt came on view, all wet, with the pink centre showing, because she was so turned on.

She got her spanking the way she likes it – stinging slaps with my fingers and a rub at her clit every now and then. The knack is to slap her as if you were clipping somebody around the ear, a glancing blow that makes the skin sting. I got harder as she got more randy, and then cocked my leg up between her thighs so that she could rub her cunt on it. She started to rub and the crowd went wild. Then I changed my spanking style, giving her hard swats right on the underside of her cheeks, as if I were trying to ram something up her arse. I could feel her cunt on my leg, pushed in really hard, with the lips spread out. She came like that, calling my name as she climaxed, and then calling me a bastard. She always does that, and I don't care, but there was enough cunt-cream on my suit trousers to keep a supermarket in stock, which was a pain.

We put Sophie up next and the wheel awarded her a shaved pussy. That was no accident, because a few weeks before I'd tried one of those menthol shaving creams and discovered something really neat. The stuff makes flesh swell and warm, like muscle relaxant but not so strong. On my chin, it was no big deal, but on the girls' cunts it was nearly enough to make them come without anything extra. This was what Mel used on Sophie

I wanted to play it cool and hung back, allowing Mel to strip Sophie naked and spread her out on a frame. Her legs were wide and her cunt was showing to the whole room, neat and pink, just the thing for the happy stick. She had a lot of hair, too, a dark blonde bush a few shades darker than the hair on her head. It was thick on her mound and lips, with a good-sized tuft down in her crack.

Mel sprayed the foam on to Sophie's pussy mound and rubbed it well in. Sophie liked this, and was moaning as Mel touched her up – then the stuff started to work. Her eyes went round and her mouth came open, just like they had when she'd been on the enema machine and the water started to flow up her arse. This time it was less painful and not quite so humiliating, but it took longer, and I reckon gave her the bigger turn-on. Mel really took her time, starting at the top and shaving a couple of strokes before dipping the razor back into her bowl of hot water. It took a good ten minutes to get Sophie's mound shaved, by which time she was writhing slowly from side to side and obviously only needed a few touches on her clit to bring her off.

By the time Sophie's cunt-lips were bare, she was begging to be brought off. Mel ignored her, but adjusted the frame to bring Sophie's legs up and spread her out even more. Sophie hadn't been expecting this, and gave the cutest little gasp of alarm when she suddenly found her arsehole stretched out bare in front of a good four hundred people. Mel put more foam on, then shaved around Sophie's arsehole and the lower parts of her cunt-lips.

Of course, the foam had got in among all the little folds of Sophie's cunt, not to mention up the hole and in her arsehole. By the time she was spick and span between her legs, she was absolutely gagging for it, begging Mel to touch her and sticking her cunt up in the air in desperation. With her hands and feet tied, she could do nothing, and that was when I made my first move. Mel washed Sophie's cunt down and pretended to start on the knots, to the poor little tart's all too obvious disappointment.

'Finish her off, Mel: she deserves it,' I chimed in.

Mel gave me one of her fake dirty looks and then sank to her knees and buried her face between Sophie's thighs. It was like an explosion. Sophie came in seconds, crying out and slapping her fat little arse up and down on the frame in a way that had the crowd yelling and cheering like nothing else. It was all Mel could do to keep licking, and when she came up she had a little moustache of Sophie's cunt-cream.

From there on, it was plain sailing. Mel invited Sophie home after the club and was accepted. I drove, and Mel and Harmony molested our new little friend in the back of the Roller – nothing heavy, just feeling her tits and cunt to keep her hot. Back at the house, she was well up for it, giggling and posing around. She had changed into jeans, which were well over-tight, and showed off the outline of her cunt-lips a treat. She kept talking about the shaving and, after she had downed a few glasses of pink Dom, I knew for sure I'd cracked it.

Soon she was crawling along the ground with her jeans and panties down to show off her lovely round arse and shaven pussy. The smell of her fat little cunt had the old happy stick twitching but I still held back. Then Mel whacked her with a slipper, turning her arse a nice rich pink and making her squeal and moan. She loved it and started flaunting her beaten arse for us.

The girls stripped her and held her down for me to get a good look at. She was giggling, but she'd got her excuse – she wasn't doing it for me: the girls were doing it to her. If I got turned on to her, then it was an accident.

She looked great nude – fat little bum, tight waist and pert titties, all spread out on the carpet. My girls knew what to do, and started to torment her by saying they were going to let me have her. She loved it and I could see her getting randier and randier. Now was my moment, and I whipped out the happy stick and stuck it right up close to her face.

Mel ordered her to suck it and that was that. She opened her mouth and leant forward, then her lips were around my shaft and I was up to my balls in wet, warm, girly flesh. The girls were feeling her cunt and tits while she sucked me and, after a while, I gave them the signal to spin her around. They did it with one smooth motion. Sophie squeaked as she was turned and then gave a little choking gasp when she found her newly shaved cunt spread and bare in front of my cock.

It went in easily and she was soon lying back, loving it, while I fucked her. Her legs were right up and well open, which is always a sure sign that a girl's actually having fun. Mark you, why not? After all, she had my cock in her cunt, Mel's tits in her face and Harmony was feeling up my balls and her arsehole.

I had her on her knees next, with her buns spread so I could see her arsehole and the join between the happy stick and her cunt. I love the way that little ring of flesh goes in and out when you fuck a girl and I love to see their arseholes while I'm in them, mainly because that's where the happy stick's going next.

Sophie didn't know that and, if there's one thing girls get more precious about than their cunts, it's their tight little arseholes. For her butt-fucking, she needed to be really high, but I had that all worked out.

Once I'd tired of Sophie's cunt, I got up Mel, and left Harmony to it. She got in a sixty-nine with Sophie on top, and started to explore Sophie's bum while they licked each other. I could see everything, and watched Harmony at work. First, she let her licking get really wild, so that her tongue went right up Sophie's crack and some saliva went on her bumhole. Then she settled down to licking cunt and started to tease Sophie's bum.

It was a treat to see it done. First, Sophie's arse-cheeks were fondled and smacked, then it was fingernails in the crack and on the shaven areas. Only then did Harmony go for Sophie's arsehole, touching it, tickling it, then putting a finger in. Sophie was far too high to care, and let Harmony bugger her without any hassle. She squeaked when a second finger went in, and again, more loudly with the third. By then, her arsehole was well stretched and looked ready for me.

Harmony left Sophie's bum and reached up to fold her in her arms, holding her tightly. I'd been keeping the happy stick nicely hard in Mel's cunt and now pulled out. Sophie gasped when she felt my knob against her arsehole and wriggled a bit as I stuffed her. Then it was up, the full length embedded in her box.

She called me a bastard as I began to bugger her, but that was all and she was soon panting and squealing like the best of them. I love the feel of the happy stick in a girl's arsehole – the tight, hot sheath of her tube, the ring tighter still and pulling in and out as I fuck. Their reaction's great, too, all the grunts and pants, squeaks and groans, and then that lovely breathless panting when I take them by the hips and go for my orgasm.

The best bit is when they come themselves, because their rings clench: and to feel that around your cock-shaft is something else. Sophie still had Harmony's tongue on her clit and I measured my pace, watching the join between cock and arsehole and waiting for that glorious moment. It came quickly, Sophie suddenly screaming out and then going silent as she buried her face in Harmony's cunt. I felt Sophie's arsehole contract and I rammed home, knowing I was going to come myself. She clenched on me again and I felt the happy stick jerk. Then Harmony had taken my balls in her mouth, like the good girl she is, and I was coming, pumping three days' worth of spunk up Sophie's bum while she clutched frantically at the carpet.

She sucked my cock after I'd pulled out, which really shows what a slut she is. Then we sat back and I poured more champagne, while the girls got in a tangle on the floor to bring each other off. For the rest of the night, she was quite happy with me, and I fucked her again and came in her mouth. She didn't need to be prissy any more: she had her excuse.

I explained all that to her in the morning – not that I expected her to understand. Sure enough, she didn't, and got fairly pissed off because I knew how her mind worked. She said she did as she pleased and didn't need an excuse for anything, but that was bollocks and we both knew it.

Well, Sophie was nice, but at the end of the day she had been too easy to be really satisfying. Don't get me wrong – I like to hear them beg, but I prefer a bit of reluctance. Besides, if I show too much attention to one girl, Mel and Harmony get pissed off, and that would never do. Sometimes it's a bit tricky after a one-nighter like we'd had, but at the next club she went off with Vicky and Anderson, so there was no problem. What that did mean was that her friend Cindy was at a loose end and I was quickly beginning to wonder if she might not provide an equally worthwhile sheath for the old happy stick. She was a bit skinny for my normal taste, without much of what you might actually call tit, but she had nice legs, and was a natural show-off.

She was a little flirt, too, because when I suggested a quick fuck in one of the back rooms she went all coy. It wasn't a rejection, not by a long way, but she made two things pretty clear. One was that it had to be just the two of us, the other that she needed a big fuss made over her before she'd put out.

That was all right by me. I like a chase and if her excuse was the sense of obligation that comes from being taken to expensive restaurants and generally shown a good time then, what the heck, I can afford it. So I fixed a date for the following Friday evening, and the cheeky tart asked if I'd send the Roller round to pick her up, just so she could show off to her mates.

So that's how it went. On the Friday, I dolled Harmony up in a chauffeuse outfit – peaked cap, little tight skirt, the lot – and sent her off to some drossy part of the East End to collect Cindy. The Roller must have impressed the mates, because Cindy was in great form when they arrived at my place, giggling and chatting with Harmony. She looked good, too, dressed in some fancy white kit halfway between harem pants and a sailor suit. It was just nicely daring without being the sort of thing to get us barred from the restaurant, showing off her bum and what tit she had without being blatant. I complimented her and got a smile and a peck, which boded well for the evening ahead.

I took her to Raoul's, which I reckoned was posh enough to get her little cunt hot. It's sometimes a risk taking a slut to a fancy restaurant, but Cindy actually knew how to behave. She ordered in French and didn't guzzle her wine, or laugh loudly, or make funny remarks about the other customers, or do any of the hundred and one embarrassing things she might have done. We had *hors d'oeuvres*, then some fancy fish thing, then lobster, all washed down with pink Dom, which was the most expensive champagne on the wine list and impressed the hell out of her. By the end, I was well impressed myself, mellow with good food and wine, and with the old happy stick rock-hard in my trousers because the little minx had been subtly flirting with me ever since the fish course. We finished with a leisurely Cognac and then left.

As we climbed into the taxi, I got a glance from her and I just knew she was up for it. She was stroking my legs and crotch all the way back, but she wouldn't let me return the favour, which put me in a fine sweat by the time we got back. She didn't want to go in: she wanted it in the back of the Roller. It was the old excuse again – she could justify being a slut, by telling herself she was doing it for the experience of sex in the back of a Roller.

Once in the garage, she was pretty straight about what she wanted. She was going to give me a blow-job, and that was it. I can bide my time, so I didn't push it. After all, being offered a blow-job is a lot better than some girls who want this, want that and want the other but don't want to put out in return. So we went in the back seat and I pulled out the happy stick. She lay sideways and took it in her hand. I put mine on her arse and she didn't object, so I began to feel while she began to suck. Her arse was small and tight and I could feel her panties through the seat of her harem pants. Just that would have been enough to get me hard again.

Not that I needed it. Cindy was an ace cock-sucker, and I mean an ace. I get my cock sucked like most men smoke cigarettes or drink pints – when I want it, how I want it. In the office, all I have to do is bell Harmony and down she goes. OK, so I have to fit it in between appointments, but that's easy enough. At home, I've got both of them, and it's damn seldom that neither are in the mood. Now, they know how to suck cock, and they do a great double act, but Cindy was in a class of her own.

For a start, she knew all the right moves. She quickly had my balls out and gave them plenty of attention, sucking and licking and popping them in and out of her mouth until I was going crazy. She had a hand down the front of my pants as well, tickling my arse, touching and fingering like she was taking an exam in it. The other hand was on my cock, teasing with her nails, ringing me, stretching the foreskin down, everything, and always firmly but never too hard.

Fortunately, I know how to hold back, or I'd have done it in her mouth within the first minute. As it was, I held off for what must have been a quarter of an hour, and never once did she complain or try and hurry me up. By then, she had a finger well up my arse and prodding my G-spot. She was jiggling my balls about with a thumb as well, and moving her whole hand like she was playing an instrument. The other hand was ringing the base of my cock and moving up and down with little jerking motions while she sucked on my knob. Then, suddenly, she just jammed her mouth down on me, taking me right in her throat. I felt the tube of her throat around my knob, just like a big, firm cunt. She kept it there, moving just a little, and began to jerk me into her mouth, hard. I knew I was coming and then she jabbed her fingernail right into my G-spot.

It fucking hurt, but it was like an explosion. I was coming, gushing it down her throat while she wanked me furiously. How she didn't gag is a mystery, because there was a lot of spunk and my knob was jammed right between her tonsils. She didn't, but drained every last drop and swallowed the lot. Girls ought to swallow spunk, but they don't always like to. Cindy did, gulping it down like it was banana cream, and then cleaning me up with her tongue afterwards.

When I'd got my breath back I offered her a lick. After all, fair's fair and she'd given me the best blow-job I'd had, which is saying something. To my surprise, she refused and just gave my knob a last kiss before asking to clean up and then be taken home. I was in no state to drive, so I knocked Harmony up and sent Cindy back with her. Of course, Mel wanted her share, the randy little tart, and I managed to fuck her, only for her to demand a tonguing. So I ended up licking cunt anyway.

After Sophie, I felt I'd had her and didn't care when she went off with Anderson and Vicky. With Cindy, it was different. She'd gone with me, as I'd known she would, just as soon as she had her excuse. She hadn't gone all the way, though, and I'd let her call the shots. Now, I don't mind humouring their whims, just as long as I get my way in the end: so for me young Cindy very definitely came under the heading of unfinished business.

I didn't feel like waiting for the next club, either, so I pulled her name off the mailing list and gave her a ring. She sounded a little surprised at first, but accepted a date willingly enough. The routine was much like before, only this time she was bored with the Roller and wanted to come out to my place in Essex. I played along, and took her to a quaint old pub near Saffron Walden that was a sight cheaper than Raoul's. Then we went to my place. Now I like my sex and I like to be in control, but Morris Rathwell never forced a girl yet. So when she declined my offer to strip off and climb in the Jacuzzi for some wet sex, I let it go and settled for another top-class blow-job.

She did this one kneeling between my knees while I smoked a twenty-pound cigar and sipped a glass of old Remy. I've always liked that – to be seated in comfort with a glass and a smoke while a girl kneels on the floor with the happy stick in her gob. Ideally, I like the girl to be naked and with a well-whipped arse, or at least with her tits out. It was a great blow-job, maybe even better than before, but I wanted more and, even immediately after I'd spunked up in her mouth, I felt dissatisfied.

As before, I offered her a lick, or a frig while I beat her, or the use of a vibrator, any fucking thing as long as it had her grunting! Jesus, I'd have let her piss in my mouth if she'd said that was what she needed to get her rocks off. She thanked me but turned me down, so I poured a couple of large measures of Remy and sat her down in the armchair opposite me. When a girl's got half a pint of your spunk in her tummy it's no time to be coy, so I came right out with it.

'You're a great cock-sucker, Cindy,' I said (always start with a bit of flattery when you want something from a tart), 'but I want more out of this, and not just for me. I want to make you come. I want to see the look on your face when you hit your orgasm. Sure, I'd like to shag you, who wouldn't? But there's more to it than that. I want you, all of you.'

She didn't reply immediately, and looked down at the floor, as if making a big decision.

'Look, Morris,' she finally chirped up, really quiet and timid, which wasn't normal for her at all. 'You may not believe this, but I've never done it with a man.'

'You're a virgin?' I asked, pretty taken aback, because if there's one thing you don't get many of in my club, it's virgins.

She nodded.

Well, that took the biscuit: a fucking virgin! I didn't know whether to believe it, and one thing seemed seriously wrong.

'So if you're so innocent,' I demanded, 'where did you learn to suck cock like that?'

'Oh, I'm not inexperienced,' she answered. 'It's just that I've never done it properly.'

Now, if there's one thing I love, it's a virgin cunt. Just to know that the old happy stick is the first cock to go in gives me a hit like nothing else. But you've got to be careful with virgins, tactful, even with one who sucked cock like an angel.

'Is there something wrong?' I asked, really gently. 'A problem? A nasty experience?'

'No,' she answered. 'Nothing like that.'

'Are you waiting for the right moment, then?'

'Something like that.'

'Well, love, why not make it now? I'm no teenage kid who's going to stuff it up hard and hurt you. I know what to do, how to go easy. Come on, love: when are you going to get a better chance?'

'I couldn't,' she answered, 'not that. But I don't know – maybe the other.'

Well, it was well coy for the sort of girl who comes to my club, but I knew what she meant at once. She couldn't hack getting her cunt filled – probably for some soppy reason about keeping it until she got married – but she wanted the happy stick in her and was prepared to try it up her arse. Well, that was just nuts to me, because if there's one thing better than being the first to fill a girl's cunt, it's being the first to stretch her arsehole.

I played it easy, letting her call the shots. She was a fussy cow but then, that's virgins for you. She didn't want to strip off, and it had to be in the bedroom. She didn't want the lights off, but they had to be real dim. She didn't want the stereo in the bedroom on, but she wanted the one in the lounge playing softly. She didn't want her panties off, but she wanted it doggy-style.

She got it, all of it, and I was actually quite grateful because it gave the old happy stick a chance to get going again. Once she was on the bed, I knew there would be no problem: it was as stiff as a board. It was really dim in the room, with just the dark golden light from the big Chinese lantern. She was kneeling on the four-poster with her tight little arse up high. Her legs looked great, long and slender with her suspender straps straining her stockings up around her thighs and vanishing under the hem of her skirt. Her legs were together, but I could see a little bulge where what looked like a remarkably plump little cunt was wrapped in white cotton. I suppose it's because my nannies used to wear clothes like that back in the forties and fifties, but I just love stockings, suspenders and big white panties. No nanny of mine ever wore a skirt like Cindy's, though: it was so short that, in her kneeling position, I could see the tuck of her arse-cheeks.

Then she flipped it up and I got the full moon, a tight, round little tush encased in panties that came right up to her waist and really hugged her bum. She looked good enough to eat and, as she began to slide those gorgeous panties down, I was clutching my cock and thinking: What a lucky bastard I am. It came on show slowly, her panties sliding down inch by inch to expose one of the sweetest little arses I've ever seen. It was a shame about the light because, while her cheeks showed as two balls of pale gold, all the detail in between was hidden, including the tight little virgin arse-hole I was about to fuck.

I could smell her perfume, something strong and floral. The music was faint in the distance, the air cool but not cold. Conditions were perfect, perfect for a first bum-shag for the cute little piece kneeling in front of me with her arse bare and expectant.

She settled her knickers just below her tuck, making her arse bulge up sweetly but protecting her cunt so I couldn't just shag her unexpectedly – not that I'd have done it, but I could see her point. It looked good, too, with her bum a nice target framed by lowered panties, suspender straps and the frill of her dress. What's more, she had found the Analube in the bathroom and laid it on the bed behind her, and that's an invitation that Morris Rathwell does not ignore.

I climbed up on the bed and took the tube of lubricant. It felt cool in my hand and she gasped as I squeezed some of it out in between her bum-cheeks. I did it just above the hole, so that she could feel it run down her crack and would get the sudden cold sensation on her anus. Being lubricated is a good reminder to a girl who is about to be buggered of exactly what is about to happen to her, and so I let the stuff run down her crack and saw to greasing the happy stick. It was cold, but warmed quickly on the hot skin of my cock as I rubbed it in. I kept the other hand dry so that I could spread her cheeks easily, only for her to reach back and take me by the cock.

As I shuffled forward on my knees, she placed my knob in her crack and started to smear the lube onto her own arsehole. Her cheeks felt hard around my knob and the tip kept bumping on the fleshy bits of her arsehole, which was nearly enough to make me come then and there. I didn't, but let her open herself with my knob, gradually exciting her greasy little hole until it began to open under the subtle pressure of her hand. The first half inch or so slipped in and I could feel her ring, taut but easy, opening and closing as she slowly buggered herself.

I let her do it, waiting until her arsehole had opened far enough to take my knob before beginning to push. She seemed pretty skilled for an anal virgin, which gave me a stab of disappointment. Then my knob was up her bum and I didn't care if I was the fiftieth. She started to grunt as I forced myself up her, inch by inch, until my front was pressed to the firm mounds of her arse-cheeks and the full length of the happy stick was up her arse, clamped in a hot tube of wet girl.

When I began to bugger her, she started to pant like a bitch on heat. I could easily have come in the first few strokes, but didn't want to waste it and so paced myself, easing it in and out and feeling her buns for her.

'Why not come?' I suggested, eager for the feel of her hole clenching on my shaft before I took my own orgasm inside her.

She shook her head, but reached back between her legs and began to play with herself. I slowed my pace and started to slap her cheeks gently, waiting for her orgasm. It didn't come and, after a while, she took her hand away from her crotch.

'This is nice, Morris,' she said, 'but I want a suck for a bit before you come. So pull out, please.'

'Dirty bitch,' I answered, but I liked the idea and began to ease myself free of her bum.

As my cock pulled free she rolled over and, with one swift motion, pulled her panties off her legs. Then she spread her thighs and I was left staring open-mouthed. There, nestled in a bed of thick hair, was a tiny cock and a diminutive set of balls, minute but, beyond doubt, male and well excited.

She, or rather he, pointed to my straining erection.

'There's your excuse, Morris: now get sucking.'

. . . and I hope he did. As you can see, Morris has a pretty high opinion of himself, which is not universally shared – especially not by Vicky Belstone.

Vicky appeared in Penny in Harness, A Taste of Amber *and* Bad Penny. *She's great, a tall athletic girl with just enough flesh in the right places to make her sexy for me. Looking at her, you'd think her sexual preference might be for dominating, especially with her long black hair and slightly stern expression. Actually, what she likes best is to go flashing and then have her bottom beaten to punish her for being such a slut. She is the best of all racing pony-girls and, when it comes to naughty sports, she does like to excel . . .*

Mucky III – Vicky Belstone

It was that time of year again, the season for Morris Rathwell's 'Dirty Bitches Wrestling Extravaganza'. 'Dirty Old Bastards' would have been more appropriate as, under Rathwell's rules, the winner was the first to have her opponent stripped naked, while the ring was a pool of whatever foul substance he decided would be amusing to watch two girls writhing around in. It tended to get pretty humiliating for the losers too, and it wasn't unknown for unfortunate girls to get public spankings, or to be made to lick their victors clean.

That wasn't going to stop me entering. Just the opposite, in fact, although the chances of my being subjected to some deliciously degrading fate weren't too high – I'd won for the last two years, and Rathwell's book had me at three to two and second favourite. The favourite was his own wife, Melody, a strapping black girl for whom I had a lot of respect. I'd beaten her in the final, two years previously, but not before she'd had me down to a pair of torn panties and covered every square inch of my flesh with a revolting mixture of cold porridge and raspberry syrup. In fact, if she hadn't shown off by trying to make me eat some of it . . .

But no matter, I'd won, and once I'd had her knickers off I'd thoroughly enjoyed myself by sitting on her head and making her lick out the generous handful of the stuff that she had managed to shove down the gusset of my own knickers and up my pussy.

Last year, she hadn't made the final, losing out to a huge fat girl called Annabelle – Topsy, to most of us. Melody hadn't realised how much muscle it takes to hold up twenty stone or so of flesh and had made the mistake of trying to grapple. Topsy had simply sat on her and stripped her at leisure, to Melody's absolute fury. I'd laughed myself silly watching, but had been glad when my friend Amber had put Topsy out in the next round. Amber's trick had simply been to keep running until poor Topsy was exhausted, then dart in and pull the big girl's clothing off bit by bit without ever really coming to grips. I'd beaten Amber in the final, dressed in camisoles by mutual agreement, and wrestling in lard and eggs because we'd both refused to give Morris Rathwell his customary bribe – a cock-sucking session.

It was bigger this year, with twenty-five girls in competition in a contest spread out over four clubs and a special for the final. First off, there were eliminators between the smaller and weaker girls, partly to get the crowd's interest, and partly to get us down to a convenient sixteen competitors. Despite being second seed I volunteered, just to get the feel of it back before the serious stuff started.

The pairings were decided by lottery, and in true Rathwell style he had the balls pulled out of a girl's pussy. It did look cute, to be fair, with Harmony tied upside down to a frame while her pussy was stuffed with numbered balls. Melody did the draw, cheerfully dipping her hand into her sister's honey-pot and calling out the numbers until Harmony was squirming with pleasure. I got paired up with little Sophie Cherwell, which was great because I adore cute blondes, and she's ever so sweet and ever so dirty.

There were nine eliminators in all, and Sophie and I were on last, so Anderson and I sought her out and sat with her to watch. She was with her friend Cindy, who is the most realistic trannie I know, and claims to have had his cock sucked by Morris Rathwell, although I'm not sure I can believe that. We had a great evening, and were all fairly tipsy by the time Sophie and I were called up.

Sophie was a walk-over, as I had known she would be. In fact, she had only entered for the fun of being stripped and rolled about in filth. She got her wish, too, because Rathwell had chosen bubble-and-squeak with sausages to wrestle. We were in maids' outfits, and I took my time, stripping her slowly in a variety of holds and finishing by sliding a sausage up her pussy. The crowd enjoyed this almost as much as she did and she came home with us afterwards to round off an excellent night.

That put me safely in the main sixteen and I was thoroughly looking forward to the following month's club. The eight seeds were now placed, and I could see what my progress was likely to be. Assuming everything went to form, I would get a drawer, then Trisha, then Amber, and Melody in the final. Trisha and Amber I felt fairly confident in being able to handle. Melody was different. She had put in a lot of exercise over the year and her body, always muscular, looked fit and hard. In addition to that, she'd gone in for this sort of African queen look, with her skin oiled and big copper bracelets on her arms but not a stitch besides. Just looking at her heavy black breasts and powerful buttocks had my heart fluttering, but the look of haughty certainty on her face made me want to grovel at her feet, which was not a good sign.

Rathwell did the draw himself, only with some girl I didn't know stark naked and upside down because Harmony was one of the competitors. I got paired with Karen, a bubbly young woman I'd met a few times but never had the chance to play with. She was a good deal shorter than me, but fairly well built, and I could see the match would be no pushover.

Nor was it. Our outfits were little white sailor suits and frillies, which may have looked sexy to Rathwell but made me feel ridiculous. The medium was vegetable oil, which was horribly slippery and got everywhere. It also made it impossible to stay upright or stop ourselves getting in some really ludicrous poses, and the audience was in stitches before either of us so much as had our breasts bare.

Eventually I managed to get her top open and jam her arms by pulling it down her back. She was stuck and knew it, but I slipped, and the next thing I knew she was on top of me. She got me in a head-lock and pulled my frillies down to give everyone a good look at my bum, but she couldn't get them off and I spent the rest of the fight with them around my thighs. I must have struck some pretty rude poses, and the audience were laughing fit to burst, but I managed to get her suit off and then sit on her back. I had my knickers down and one tit peeping out, that was all, so not a bad win. After peeling down Karen's frillies at my leisure I gave her a gentle spanking to seal my victory and that was that. On to round two.

We'd been on second last, and the only upset had been Harmony beating Trisha. Harmony has all of her sister's power and grace but is really too submissive to make a good wrestler. This time, though, she had a bee in her bonnet about something and, although she ended up in just her badly torn frillies, Trisha was starkers and red-bottomed.

That left Melody, who'd drawn Carrie Gibson. Carrie is a close friend of Amber and Ginny, a slim, long-legged redhead and pretty sporty. Pretty attractive, too, with her cheeky ways and pert looks, certainly with her bum hugged in the ridiculous frilly knickers once Melody had stripped her topless within about ten seconds of the bell. The frillies lasted about ten more seconds. It looked great, with Carrie's long legs kicking and her little round bum wriggling as Melody finished her off with a sound spanking. It was worrying, too, because Carrie's fit and Melody's victory had looked pretty effortless.

I spent as much time as possible over the next month working out, because Harmony might be submissive, but she was no weakling. Some of this was done in places like the gym and playing for our local netball team, but more often than not, Anderson would take me out to remote woods and harness me up as a pony-girl. Pulling a twelve-stone man up a hill while being whipped across the bare buttocks with a riding crop certainly builds the stamina, and by the time the next club came around I felt ready for a dozen Harmonys.

The club was in an old generating station out on the estuary, hardly an erotic venue, but the old turbines were still in place and I felt that the air of industrial decay was rather suitable. Rathwell obviously thought so as well, because he had ordained boiler suits as the kit and sump oil as the wrestling medium. When I pointed out to him what diesel does to the skin, he told me not to be silly and that it was actually dilute molasses. This wasn't altogether reassuring, especially as I'd managed to grow my hair just down to the top of my bum and could imagine what the molasses would do to it.

When he opened a barrel, I got the sticky sweet smell right up my nose, but as it oozed out into a viscous pool I had to admit that it at least looked like diesel oil. Being a disgusting old bastard, Rathwell threw in several old cloths and some wood-shavings painted silver to look like swarf. The resultant mess looked truly revolting, but at least it wasn't real.

I got into my boiler suit, along with knickers, T-shirt and heavy boots. It was not going to be an easy outfit to strip someone out of, especially with a big, active girl like Harmony. She has perhaps a stone on me, which I could see being to her advantage, but then I know her and was pretty confident.

The first bout was between Amber and Topsy and didn't go to form. The sticky molasses slowed them both equally and Topsy was able to bring her weight to bear. Amber put up a good fight, and managed to snap the shoulder catches on Topsy's boiler suit and pull her boobs out. That was all, but Amber was still clutching her knickers in a desperate attempt to keep them up when Topsy sat on her back. Amber failed and was quickly naked. Her stripping had taken less than ten minutes.

When Amber dominates other girls, she likes to sit on our faces and have her bumhole tongued. That's what Topsy made her do herself, right in front of everybody. It was nice seeing Amber made to lick, for a change. She's always doing it to me, and she did look sweet in the nude with twenty stone of seriously curvy female sat on her face. The prospect of meeting Topsy in the next round wasn't so cheerful.

Ginny Scott and a tall, dark-haired girl called Naomi went next. It looked a fairly even match, but I didn't know Naomi well enough to judge her form. Ginny's all curves but really too soft and gentle, yet she did well enough and fairly quickly had Naomi down to T-shirt and knickers while both of them were liberally covered in molasses. Naomi fought back and soon they were both in nothing more than torn knickers. Ginny had most of her bum showing and looked the worse off, but she managed to get a good grip and all of a sudden Naomi was sitting there starkers with a look of surprise on her face. Ginny was pretty good about winning, contenting herself with making Naomi kiss her boobs and bum-cheeks. They ended up cuddling and walked out of the ring arm in arm, doubtless to play together in the showers.

Harmony and I were on next, and I felt my pulse quicken as Rathwell made the announcement. A fresh barrel of molasses was poured out into the sunken area that was the ring and we were on. Anderson gave me a firm slap on my bottom as I climbed over the ropes and then I was in the ring, facing Harmony across a pool of muck. She looked confident, with her dark skin slick with oil and her big breasts straining her T-shirt against the straps of her boiler suit. A tell-tale outline showed that she was sporting a strap-on under her boiler suit, which showed what was going to happen to me if I lost.

She smiled at me and I stuck my tongue out in retort, then we closed. We grappled and went down, landing with a sticky thud in the sea of molasses. I was on top, but she had my hair and pulled, loosening it and dragging me off. I sat down hard in the mess and felt the moisture penetrate my knickers. Even as she tried to get me in a head-hold, I had tweaked open one of her boiler suit catches. With a quick jerk at her T-shirt I had a breast out, only for her to roll on top of me. For an instant, my mouth was full of molasses-smeared nipple and then I had cocked a leg up and rolled her over in turn.

Harmony struggled away and tried to stand, but ended up on her knees. She was breathing hard, her hair and face filthy with brown goo, one large, dark breast peeping out over the top of her boiler suit. She made to reach for the catch and I dived at her, knocking her back and scrabbling for the second catch. A moment later, both her boobs were out and her T-shirt was up over her head, rendering her pretty well helpless. She pulled loose with a violent effort, leaving the T-shirt in my hand and her topless with the boiler suit in a tangle around her waist.

I dived after her, only to slip and go head first into the muck. Before I could rise, Harmony had grappled me and I felt her naked breasts against my neck. For a moment she was on top of me, and I felt the rubbery shaft of the dildo push between my bum-cheeks. She gave a little shove, as if to mimic buggering me. The idea of taking a dildo up the bum in front of several hundred people gave me a kick of submissive pleasure, but I shrugged it off, determined not to get too turned on. If anybody was going to play that game, it was me.

She put her hands under me, trying to get at my boiler suit clips. I gave a despairing groan and sagged down, only to turn suddenly and hard beneath her. Down she went, but one of my catches was loose. Closing quickly, I stuffed my hand down the front of her boiler suit. I found the dildo and discovered that the harness was on over her knickers. This was cheating, but it was no time to argue. Forcing my hand down the front of her knickers, I found her pussy and applied my finger to her clit.

Harmony gave an angry grunt and tried to push me off, but I had an arm round her back. She pushed hard, kicking out as I frigged her. We both knew what would happen and she fought desperately, thrashing and writhing. She couldn't do it: I was too strong for her and the pleasure I was giving her was too much to resist. Her grunts became moans, her struggles subsided and then she was limp in my arms, breathing hard. I kissed her, her mouth opening under mine after only the briefest resistance. My hand went down her back, stroking the sticky skin, running my nails down her spine, finding the waistband of her knickers and the catch of the dildo harness.

It came loose in my hand and I felt the pressure come off. Still keeping a hold, I began to ease her boiler suit down, exposing her hips and the filthy seat of her knickers. She made a last, feeble effort to resist, but I pulled the front of her knickers down and buried my face in her pussy. I began to lick, curling one hand around her bottom and using the other to finish stripping her. Her pussy was clean and tasted of girl, not molasses. I was beginning to get into her for more than just the sake of victory.

I finished her off anyway, fiddling with her boots and peeling her boiler suit off one-handed while I licked her pussy and fondled her bottom. She put up a bit of resistance when the time came to have her knickers pulled off, but not much. Then she was naked and I'd won.

It wasn't over. The crowd had been cheering wildly but they were no more than background noise. I had a beautiful black girl naked and willing – also covered in sweat and molasses, but I didn't care. I stripped to my knickers and put on the dildo. It was huge, a great fat thing made of black rubber with an immense scrotum. The crowd went quiet as they realised what I was going to do, then began to chant, demanding that I fuck her.

I had no intention of disappointing them. Harmony was on her back. She was playing with her breasts, the big, black nipples hard between her fingers. Her eyes were locked on the dildo sprouting from my crotch. She licked her lips, the pink tip of her tongue running fast, back and forth. Then she spread her thighs and offered me the damp pink heart of her sex. I mounted her and her legs spread further under my weight. The dildo was in my hand, nudging her pussy, finding the hole.

Harmony gave a long sigh of pleasure as the dildo slid up her and we started to fuck. For a while I had her as most men like to fuck me, on top with my thighs spread to accommodate them. Then I knelt up, improving my view and allowing her to masturbate. She looked gorgeous, her fine dark body spread out beneath me, her breasts high, her nipples stiff, her belly slick with moisture.

I took hold of her ankles, pushed the dildo back up and began to fuck her again. I knew she'd do it, and sure enough before too long she had one hand on her pussy and another feeling a breast. I sped up and she began to frig, spreading her pussy lips with two fingers and rubbing at her clit with a third. The crowd were howling with pleasure, then clapping in time to my pushes. When Harmony came, we got a standing ovation.

That was that. I was on such a dominant high that I didn't even frig myself off in front of the crowd, but let Harmony lick me in the showers. We had a cuddle after I'd come, and fell to discussing the competition.

Melody was up against Cassie Smith, another coloured girl and the number eight seed, but really not in Melody's class. By the time I emerged from the showers, it was just about over, with Cassie in a pair of very dirty knickers and Melody without a stitch out of place and not even all that badly soiled. Less than a minute later, Cassie was upside down with her knickers being peeled up her legs. Never one to be magnanimous in victory, Melody stuffed Cassie's mouth with the ruined knickers and dished out a spanking that had the crowd clapping in time and catcalling for more. Melody gave it, spreading Cassie out in the pool of molasses and ordering her to frig off. Cassie did it, and came too, which I thought was pretty game of her.

That was that, all to form except for the elimination of Amber. I could see the way Rathwell was playing it – give Topsy her weight advantage in the quarters and semis, then go for something easier to move in and light clothing for the final. That way, Melody would beat Topsy through sheer pace and agility. Unfortunately, it left me as the semi-final sacrifice.

I had no intention of going out so easily. It was time to bribe Morris Rathwell.

* * *

If I didn't get off on sexual humiliation, I really couldn't take sex with Morris Rathwell. As it is, just now and then I let the poor old boy play a little. He likes to bugger girls, which is more than I really like to take – from him, anyway – and so I visited him at his office, where there would be no chance of anything so messy or protracted.

Harmony was in the outside office, as always, and gave me the dirtiest of smiles as I went in. Rathwell – who's nobody's fool and knew exactly what I was after – was seated behind his desk with his hands folded in his lap and a self-satisfied look on his face.

'Come to bargain, Victoria, my dear?' he asked as I took a chair.

'I'll put this straight,' I replied. 'I'll give you a nice slow suck, naked if you like. In return you put Annabelle and me in cheap lingerie and we wrestle in something that lets me keep moving.'

'Victoria, Victoria,' he chided. 'Surely you're not suggesting I fix the match for you?'

'No,' I answered, 'just that you don't fix it for Annabelle.'

'As if I would,' he answered. 'Having said that, she dropped round to see me the other day, at home. Very obliging girl, young Annabelle, and there's something strangely appealing about having a really big girl grovelling to me. Big fat bottoms are fun to cane, too – plenty of target.'

'She let you cane her?'

'That and a rub between her tits. It's not every day I get a chance to come off over a pair of forty-eight G tits, so you'll have to do better than your striptease and blow-job. She had some ideas about full Victorian dress and honey which I thought highly imaginative. Do you fancy lunch, by the way?'

'Lunch?'

'Yes, there's a little club off Ludgate Hill: very exclusive. They do private rooms.'

They did, so I ended up serving him and Harmony. They made me strip and stuck a carrot up my bottom, which amused them no end. Afterwards, I had to lick Harmony while Rathwell buggered me and smoked a cigar at the same time, if you please! They even made me eat my lunch off a plate on the floor and finished the session with twelve of his belt across my bare bum. I felt shamefully good afterwards. My sole regret was that nobody had caught us. I'd have loved to be caught like that. Rathwell would have been thrown out of the club. Whether it had been worth it tactically was debatable. He had guaranteed me fair play, no more.

I spent the rest of the month training hard. Pony-carting, wrestling with girlfriends and even wrestling with Ginny's brother Matthew, who's well over six foot and weighs sixteen stone or so. He beat me, but he was sweating hard by the end. By the night of the match, I was as fit as I ever have been, but still a sight less confident than I had been before meeting Harmony.

Topsy is fat by any standards, but she's no lard tub. I stand a fraction under six foot, but I only have an inch or so on her. Her breasts are vast, like footballs, and if they seem remarkably buoyant, it's because she has enormous shoulder muscles to support them. Despite several plump, pink rolls on her middle, she goes in at the waist and her bottom is very much girl-shaped, but twice as large as it has any right to be. Her legs are long and exaggeratedly female, bulging at hip and thigh and surprisingly slim at the ankle. Overall, the impression is of a very sexy girl who's been fed on cream cakes for years – soft, plump and yielding. It's false. I'd seen her wrestle and knew she could hold Melody down with one arm.

Rathwell had compromised, which I suppose was only fair. We were to wrestle in Victorian underwear – combinations, corsets and knee stockings – and six-inch-deep mud. The underwear was really rather sweet, fine linen with lots of lace and frills, while the corsets were fully boned with fastenings at the front and lacing at the rear. I'll say one thing for Morris, he's not mean. The corsets alone must have cost close on a hundred pounds each and if there was anything left after the match, we were welcome to have them. Actually I think he claws it all back from his tax, but it's still nice to be bought pretty clothes.

We were back in the warehouse where the first round had been held, and the ring was a pool that could have been used to keep penguins. The mud was dark brown and glutinous. Just to look at it made me feel cold and slimy.

Melody and Ginny were on first. For size and weight, they looked an even match but, even in her fancy underwear, Melody looked the stronger. Besides, like Harmony, Ginny is really too soppy, and too much the slut. Sure enough, it went Melody's way, but not as easily as she might have liked. The problem was that, with the fiddly Victorian underwear, it was next to impossible to strip an opponent without leaving oneself open. Melody kept trying to get Ginny face-down and mounted, but she couldn't hold the position. I could imagine myself helpless with Topsy sat on my bottom and determined to avoid the position at all costs.

Melody took every opportunity to smack bottom and squeeze pussy until Ginny was too horny to fight properly. Both girls had open chemise tops and bare breasts and, when Melody managed to get her lips to one of Ginny's nipples, I thought it was all over. Ginny went down, slowly, allowing Melody to mount her. Two swift tugs had Ginny's corset open and chemise down. With her boobs entirely bare, she lay back, spreading herself submissively in the mud. Melody turned her body, intending to sit on Ginny's chest while she finished stripping her. Suddenly, Ginny jerked up, sending Melody sprawling face first in the muck.

After that it turned into a real catfight, both girls tearing at each other's clothes and well as slapping and pulling hair. In the end, Melody's sheer ferocity pulled her through, and Ginny was left naked and beaten, face-down in the mud. Melody had one stocking left and a scrap of torn linen around her waist: nothing more.

Ginny got spanked, then was made to kneel and lick Melody to orgasm. She looked good, on her knees with her lovely plump white curves naked and muddy while she applied her tongue to her powerful black conqueror's pussy. Unfortunately, her eagerness rather spoilt the image of victor and vanquished.

As soon as a new barrel of mud had been poured into the ring, Rathwell announced Topsy and me. Victorian clothing suits big girls, and Topsy really looked the part in her corset and frillies. She also looked ominously large and powerful, and gave me a seriously disconcerting smile as she climbed into the ring.

We faced off, ankle-deep in the mud, which was thick, sticky and probably favoured her. She was cautious, while I had no intention of rushing in blindly, and the crowd had begun to jeer and whoop before we touched. When we did, it was a simple clasp of hands, gauging each other's strength. She pulled and leant back, drawing me forward with her weight but with her arm gradually straightening from the force I was applying. Suddenly she tugged, but I wrenched my hand away and she went backward, tottered for an instant and then fell back, with her face set in alarm.

She went down hard, right on her bottom in the centre of the ring. Mud splashed, soiling my legs. I stood back, aware that it might be a trick to get me to grapple. Topsy smiled and turned, coming on to all fours to rise. Suddenly, the bow that closed her corset was uppermost, too tempting to resist. I dived forward and caught a lace in my hands, slippery with mud. I pulled, but she was rising. The bow gave and I tore at the laces, only to have her suddenly twist and send me sprawling into the mud.

A hand grabbed my ankle and I felt her weight on my legs. I kicked but met flesh, soft but immobile. My legs were pinned; then she was astride me, humping her body on top of mine until I was flat on my back.

Her full weight was across my hips, pressing me down hard on to the canvas. I could feel the mud squeezing up between my bum-cheeks and into my pussy: slimy and cold. Her huge breasts were in my face, smothering me and bringing me a strange, urgent need for a spanking.

Fighting down the urge to submit, I threw my arms around her back and hugged her to me, protecting my own clothing but allowing me to get at her corset laces. The bow was loose, and a quick tug had it open. She gave a grunt of annoyance and rolled sideways, bringing me with her. I threw myself backward, escaping the clinch. For a moment, we were face to face. I grabbed at the front of her corset and felt the catches slip, even as she grabbed my wrists. She pulled my wrists apart but my fingers were locked in her corset and the catches came open. If I held on, she would have me on my back, but her corset would be off.

I did it, allowing her to mount me at the expense of her corset, which fell back as she settled her weight on my belly. She forced my arms out, spread-eagling me in the mud as I kicked her corset away. Tucking my legs beneath me I tried to lift, only for her to bounce on my tummy and slam me back down in the muck. Struggling was useless, so I stopped, leaving her seated triumphantly on top of me, pinned beneath her weight.

'Submit, Vicky,' she panted.

'No.'

'Ever licked a big girl?'

'Yes,' I answered, which rather took the sting out of her.

She paused, catching her breath and then flipped herself around with a speed that caught me completely unawares. I tried to roll but too late as her weight settled on my chest. Her legs were on my arms, which hurt and I cried out in protest as she lifted her body, up and back.

'Now, I'm going to strip you, then you can lick me out,' she crowed.

I said nothing. Her enormous bottom was over my face. The seat of her combinations was sodden with mud and clinging to her skin. Her buttocks were like two medicine balls in a sack, huge and resilient. All I could do was stare at her massive backside as she started to strip me. My stockings went first, peeled off my legs despite my best efforts to kick against her grip. Then it was my corset, popped open at the front and left lying open beneath me. My chemise followed, unlaced at the front to bare my breasts and rolled slowly down my body, over my tummy, to the line of my pubic hair . . .

I began to panic, wriggling helplessly beneath her weight. Once my combinations were off, I'd be made to kiss her bumhole, just as Amber had done. That would be the end of me, defeated, and not even in the final. I was writhing, but it was no good. She leant forward, taking a firm grip on my combinations in order to deliver the *coup de grâce* in style and stretching her own taut across the plump lips of her pussy. I felt my bottom lift and then drop into the mud, bare. The crowd yelled in delight at my exposure . . .

And I sank my teeth into Topsy's pussy-lips.

As her scream cut through the noise of the crowd, I was already hurling myself to the side. Her weight was still on me, but not evenly. She fell, landing heavily in the mud as I rolled and danced upright, grabbing at my combinations. Two twists and they were fastened around my hips, low and baggy, like a huge nappy.

She was rising, as before, going on to all fours. The slit of her combinations was half open, displaying a great slice of creamy bum-cheek, while one huge, mud-smeared breast hung free of the top. A tear showed where the garment had proved unequal to the strain of Topsy's body. She looked at me, her smile replaced by angry disbelief.

I rushed in, dizzy with the thrill of fighting. Our bodies closed, hot, wet flesh smacking against my naked breasts. My arms were under hers, stopping her getting at what remained of my clothes. My fingers scrabbled at her, finding purchase, tearing . . .

Topsy's chemise burst and her huge breasts spilt out. There was cloth in my hand and I hurled myself backward. I heard a rip and a savage yell from the crowd. Topsy stood naked above me, her combinations a soiled rag around her ankles. She dropped, almost on me as I rolled away. A leg brushed my side. I grabbed it. Her foot was in my hand, the stocking toe loose. My combinations were wrenched down, exposing my bum. Topsy's stocking came off in my hand as I locked my legs. A leg was thrown over my back, her foot pulling free of her ruined combinations. I grabbed her leg as her hands closed on my ankle and wrist. Her stocking was in my hand, loose, peeling down even as my other arm was twisted cruelly into the small of my back. I kicked, hard, my breath coming out in a rush as her bottom slammed me down. My face was in the mud, my mouth full. Blinded, choking, I gave a last desperate jerk. Her stocking came free, then off as my knees gave way and my combinations were torn up my calves. I kicked with all my strength, only to feel my ankle come free and hear her yell of triumph.

Somewhere, a thousand miles away, a whistle sounded. I lay prone and helpless, my eyes tight shut, my mouth full of foul-tasting mud, pinned beneath Topsy with the heat of her naked pussy on my spine. In one hand, I held a muddy rag, her stocking, her final garment. Something was caught around my ankle: my combinations, down but not fully off.

I'd done it. It felt as if I'd been on a rack – and I should know – but I'd done it.

The bout with Topsy left me bruised and sore, so I was extremely glad of the break before the final. For a week I rested, allowing Anderson to pamper me.

As often happens after a good tussle, I had developed an interest in Topsy and she in me. I mainly wanted to explore the feelings I had received with her breasts smothering me – a powerful urge to be spanked and then cuddled. We arranged a date and I got my wish. She put me over her knee and stripped my bum, then spanked me until I was howling and near to tears. Only then did she put me to her breasts, allowing me to cuddle and take a nipple in my mouth. The pain and helplessness of the spanking made a beautiful contrast with the tenderness of being suckled, and I let her masturbate me to the most wonderful orgasm, with her teat still in my mouth. In return she wanted to be caned, which surprised me as, at the clubs, she preferred to dominate. I gave her twelve and made her kiss my bumhole, just for Amber's sake. She became deeply submissive afterwards and we spent a pleasant night in bed together.

Sex with Topsy put me back on form. I started training again and trying to figure out how to beat Melody. She seemed stronger than the previous year and also supremely confident. Meanwhile, I had certainly had the harder route to the final. Of one thing I could be certain: Rathwell would give her all the breaks.

For one thing, she would know the clothes and medium in advance, and that was where Topsy came in handy. I persuaded her to feign annoyance at my rough handling of my pussy and to visit Rathwell. This was the final and, with two thousand pounds at stake, there could be no playing around. She succeeded, too, not from Rathwell – who is far too shrewd – but from Harmony, who not only talks too much but has an innate sense of fair play.

Rathwell had decided on the purist option – baked beans. It was to be the best of three strips, too: bikinis, school-girl and full leather gear, which made for one hell of a competition.

I could see Rathwell's logic. Bikinis were fair, so was school uniform. Domination gear was not, because she would have her own customised kit while I would have to make do with what he gave me. Sure it would look fair, but I knew Rathwell, and I knew it wouldn't be.

On the night, my adrenalin was pumping even before we reached the club. Going inside was like walking into a wall of sound: loud music with the bass turned high, Rathwell's voice blaring out over the PA, the clamour of a thousand people. I could feel my pulse hammering as I walked out to the centre of the warehouse. Rathwell announced my presence and the crowd gave a roar of approval as I threw my coat off to leave myself naked.

I've always liked to exhibit myself, but that was one of the most glorious moments of all. Over a thousand people were staring at me as I walked across the floor. I was naked, not covered by so much as a stitch, and every one of them wanted me. The feeling lasted all the way across the hall, until I arrived underneath Rathwell's commentator's box and demanded with seeming innocence what the details of the bout were to be.

My question was picked up on the mike and boomed out across the hall. In response Rathwell went into his act, declaring a contest of three strips, in baked beans, wearing bikinis, school uniform and domination gear respectively. I gave a curt nod in response and turned to face the ring, incidentally flashing my breasts and pussy to the entire hall. The ring was raised and roped – like a proper wrestling ring – and at the centre stood my opponent.

Melody looked magnificent, oiled and powerful in a miniscule turquoise bikini that left next to nothing to the imagination. There was a catlike grace about her that was frankly scary, and just to look at her was to want to be dominated. I played it as coolly as I could, catching the scarlet bikini handed down by Rathwell, sticking my nose in the air and walking to where Anderson and Amber had seats reserved.

As I pulled the bikini on, I discovered Rathwell's first trick. It was too big for me. In fact it probably belonged to one of his girls, who have a good deal more hip and bust than I. Amber knotted the sides for me, but this did nothing for my rapidly declining confidence. To make matters worse, Sophie came bouncing over to us to say how wonderful Melody looked and that she'd never seen a woman looking so strong and in control. Even putting Sophie across my knee for a round fifty spanks didn't entirely restore my confidence, and I began the walk down to the ring with a hard lump in my throat and a queasy feeling in my stomach.

Melody was waiting for me, her hands on her hips and a sneer of contempt on her face. She likes me, really – or, at least, she likes sex with me – so I stuck my tongue out in response and climbed into the ring. She was against the ropes in one corner, and I took up the opposite position, leaving us facing each other across a glistening sea of baked beans. The music stopped and the roar of the crowd fell to a low rumble. Melody's full lips curved up into a knowing smile and Rathwell sounded the bell.

I was determined to test my strength against hers and came out fast, only to discover that the canvas was not flat but sagged down beneath the weight of the baked beans. Down I went, full length, to land face-down in the middle of the ring. I went under, floundering desperately in about two feet of beans and sauce. Even as I found bottom and tried desperately to sit up, I felt Melody's hands on my bikini top.

There were beans in my mouth and in my eyes, caking my hair and down my cleavage. It felt disgusting, but it was not time to be prissy. I felt my breasts spill out of the bikini cups and lashed out determined that, if I was to sacrifice my top, then so would she. I got lucky, finding a breast and locking my fingers in her cup. She grunted with effort and my bikini top was wrenched off, but I had hers too. She grappled on to me but her boobs were out, pressed bare against my own in a welter of slimy tomato sauce.

It was impossible. I couldn't see and I couldn't get any purchase. Melody grabbed my hair and pushed my face under the beans, forcing me to let go of her. I tried to crawl away but she grabbed my bikini pants. Down they came and I felt the clammy muck on my bottom and pussy. I grabbed them and tried to stop her pulling them off, but I couldn't breathe and was forced to let go.

That was it. With a soggy sound, my bikini pants came off my ankles, leaving me stark naked and defeated. Even as the whistle went to signal Melody's victory, the crowd had started to cheer, joining my victor's yells of triumph as she paraded my sauce-sodden pants around the ring. All I could do was crawl out of the deep part and slump down into the mess, thoroughly beaten and too exhausted to rise. Wiping the sauce from my eyes, I drew in a deep breath of air laden with the scent of baked bean, pussy and sweat, and waited. It just remained for Melody to finish me off, probably with a good spanking to get me back for my treatment of her twin sister.

The roar of the crowd took on a new urgency. I opened my eyes to find Melody standing over me with her bikini pants pulled aside to expose the rich, black hair of her pussy with the pink centre spread wide. I realised her intention immediately, and felt a strange sensation of despair mixed with strongly submissive pleasure. I'd been beaten: now I was to be urinated on.

I watched, fascinated, as a jet of pale liquid erupted from her pee-hole. It landed on my belly, splashing my breasts before she adjusted the set of her hips to spray my pubic hair and down between my legs. Her urine felt hot on my skin, and her scent was thick in my nostrils as she sprayed my body, slowly, methodically, making sure I was really able to appreciate what was being done to me.

The crowd went wild as they watched Melody piss on me: clapping, screaming out encouragement and even suggesting she do it in my face. Their delight at my degradation put the final touch to my feeling of utter defeat, and I simply lay back and allowed Melody to soil my body. Even when she responded to their demands and peed in my face, I only shut my eyes and let her warm urine splatter against my lips and cheeks. She finished off on my breasts, leaving me soaked in her piss and filthy with baked beans and sauce, naked and beaten in front of a thousand or more onlookers.

It was only the first round, but I'd been pissed on and was high on submission, giving Melody a big advantage. All I could do was run to the loos and masturbate over the experience, but that only went so far in restoring my will to win.

Pissing on a beaten girl is pretty heavy stuff, and really the sort of thing I'd have expected to be done to me if I'd lost the whole match, not just the round. Clearly, Melody had reserved an even greater humiliation for me if she won, which was a pretty alarming thought.

Once more pink, but still naked, I rejoined Anderson and Amber. They did their best to restore my confidence, pointing out that the sagging canvas and overlarge bikini had been pretty mean tricks. Amber was sympathetic, but Anderson – who has a knack with my feelings – managed to make me angry. I was hardly brimming with enthusiasm when Harmony came over with my school uniform, but at least I no longer felt like grovelling at Melody's feet.

The 'school uniform' was typical Rathwell, and like nothing any real schoolgirl ever wore. The skirt barely covered my bum, for one thing, although it was pleated. Nor do I remember fishnets and six-inch heels at my school. The knickers, at least, were authentic: big, navy ones that wouldn't have raised even my ex-housemistress's eyebrows. The blouse and tie would also have passed, although with our knots pulled tight and half our buttons undone, we hardly looked ready for chapel.

I dressed and stood to show off, drawing an appreciative leer from Anderson and a pat on my bottom from Amber. Down in the ring, they were adding fresh beans, while Melody was already in her corner. It's hard not to look cute in school uniform, and Melody is an exceptionally pretty girl, for all her hard airs and muscle. Now she was trying to look stern, but only succeeded in looking sulky. The image of a girl's face after a spanking came to my mind, and with it a boost of confidence.

That sparked a new thought as I climbed into the ring. The last time I'd been in school uniform had been at Amber's. She has a mirror system, so a girl who's being spanked can see her own face and bottom while it's done. I'd looked pretty sulky myself at the time, just like Melody, but it was because Amber had lifted me across her shoulder and spanked me. I'm stronger than her, but I'd been pretty well helpless and it occurred to me that Melody might benefit from a similar treatment.

When the bell went I came forward slowly, determined not to repeat my mistake of the first round. Melody did the same, coming in poised and ready, her arms spread to catch me. As we closed I ducked, feinted to the side and then came in fast, catching her tummy with my shoulder. Her breath came out in a sharp gasp and she squealed as I rose, lifting her clear of the beans, even as my hand went up the back of her school skirt. I had a grip on her knickers before she could recover herself and began to pull them down as I sank to my knees with her full weight on my shoulder.

Melody's school pants came down under her skirt and

off her legs, despite her kicks. She was writhing like an eel, kicking and scratching me, swearing in fury and spraying beans everywhere. I grabbed for her skirt button, trying to ignore the distracting feeling of her bare, muscular buttocks wriggling against my arm. The button popped and I wrenched her skirt down, revealing her naked bottom to the crowd. They yelled approval and she gave a snarl of fury. Her nails dug hard into my back, but I pulled out one of her suspender straps and let it snap back, drawing another snarl of protest. Her feet were kicking frantically but I clutched for them, only to lose control of her. I felt my balance go and the next instant was deep in the baked beans but with one shoe in my hand.

I struggled quickly to my feet to find Melody also rising. She was side on to me and looked a little dazed, with her stocking-clad foot slipping in the beans as she tried to gain purchase. Her bum was too tempting to ignore and, as I came forward, I planted a hard smack full across her cheeks. She yelped and pulled hard away, which was exactly what I'd intended. I shoved hard, sending her sprawling and then I was on her back and had her blouse in my hands. It came up, but not off, instead catching on her wrists. It couldn't have been better. Had the blouse come away, her arms would have been free and we'd have grappled on even terms. As it was, a few rapid turns had her wrists strapped together and she was helpless.

After that, it was easy. She kicked and swore and tried to bite me, but I peeled her stockings off while the crowd laughed and cheered. They seemed to enjoy seeing her helpless even more than they'd enjoyed seeing us really fight, so I made a big display of unclipping her suspender belt. Her tie came next and I used it to tie her ankles with a bow, leaving her unable to rise when I undid her wrists. Everyone was egging me on, so I took a big handful of beans and squashed them up her pussy. She gave a wonderful groan of defeat and so I gave her clit a quick rub and smacked her thighs before finishing her strip. She hadn't given up because, when her blouse came loose, she clawed at me, but I simply tugged the bow at her feet and she was naked.

I'd won, and also thoroughly humiliated Melody, much to the crowd's delight. The temptation was to piss on her, and she clearly expected me to, because she was lying in the beans with her lower lip trembling and a genuinely sulky look on her face. Well, it had to be done, so I pulled aside the gusset of my school knickers and positioned my pussy right over her face. She looked up, trembling so hard that her breasts were wobbling like huge chocolate custards. I strained, trying to pee, feeling the pressure build, knowing I could do it. Then the little slut opened her mouth and I pissed in it. The crowd gave a wild cheer as they watched us, my urine bubbling out of the sides of Melody's mouth and running down on to her breasts and belly. I let every last drop fall on her, then leant down and calmly shut her jaw, making her swallow her last mouthful. It's a beautiful way to take a victory, especially when it's revenge.

Her submissive ecstasy didn't last long. In the showers, she came into my cubicle, to tell me that I'd been lucky and generally to try and exert her dominance over me. I told her to give it a rest and offered to help get the baked beans out of her pussy, which might have got interesting had Rathwell not appeared at that moment.

'Hi, girls: nice fight,' he greeted us. 'Cute arse, Vicky.'

He slapped my wet bottom, so I responded by putting the bar of soap into the breast pocket of his suit.

'How's the betting?' Melody asked as he stood back out of my range.

'Great, great,' he replied. 'After the first, you went up to ten to nine on. Now it's down to three to two, but the good money's still on you. Say, you don't want to throw it, do you? We'd make a killing.'

'No, I don't!' she snapped. 'I aim to take this little tart and fuck her, just like she fucked Harmony – only up her arse.'

'What with?' I demanded.

'You ain't seen my dom gear, girl,' she answered.

'Girls, girls: not out of the ring,' Rathwell interrupted. 'But, on the subject of gear for the final, are there any objections to a free choice of clothing?'

'None,' I answered and, for an instant, one corner of his mouth twitched up into a sly smile.

'You're going to lose, girl,' Melody drawled. 'But that's what you want, deep down, and don't pretend it ain't.'

I slapped her bottom, but she kept trying to needle me until we'd finished showering. Rathwell watched us, all the while absently stroking his crotch, and then told us we'd got twenty minutes' break before Sophie performed a striptease in the beans. After that we'd be on.

Melody and I towelled ourselves down and applied powder and a touch of war-paint. Only when she left to get kitted up did I allow myself to appear anything other than calm and then I ran to the back room where I had agreed to meet Anderson and Amber. They were already there, with a great pile of leather gear for me to chose from. Thanks to Topsy, I would be properly armoured and with luck would be giving Melody Rathwell more than she bargained for.

Anderson and Amber worked feverishly on my leather, our ears straining for Sophie's striptease music. It started and I knew we had five minutes, yet only seconds seemed to have passed when it finished with an abrupt crescendo. Then Rathwell's voice sounded, announcing the fight. I swallowed hard as Amber made a final adjustment to my leather shorts, then stood, as ready as I would ever be.

I knew that a naked, baked bean-smeared Sophie would draw the crowd's attention, and so waited until she was clear before making my entrance. The crowd were having a great time and cheered me to the echo, while there was a loud under-chorus of prices being offered and bets taken. The big board showed me at four to one, and the last thing that caught my attention before I climbed into the ring was Anderson feverishly trying to get some notes out of his wallet.

Melody was there before me, and I was impressed. She had gone for her warrior queen look. Not so much the African type, this time, as something out of a science fantasy film. Her breasts, buttocks and face were bare, but that was about it. A studded leather corset protected her midriff, while a heavy collar, high boots, metal arm rings, gauntlets, greaves and a helmet covered most of the rest. All of it was buckled on and strapped tight. I could see it would be hell to get off. In her hand she held a coiled bull-whip, a vicious thing of plaited leather, but most daunting of all was her pussy protection, which consisted of a sort of demented codpiece from which sprouted a good twelve inches of thick black rubber dildo.

It was as thick as a cucumber and I felt a weak fluttering in my stomach at the memory of her threat to bugger me if I won. She would do it, too, and my bumhole clenched in painful anticipation. My alarm must have shown in my eyes, because Melody gave me a really wicked grin. Then she turned, still looking back, and stuck out her bottom.

As her bum was bare, I thought this was just a rude gesture, a demand that I kiss her anus in submission even before the fight had begun. It was more than that, as I realised when I stopped staring at her bottom and looked up a little. Her corset fastened with padlocks. I swallowed hard, once more imagining that cucumber-thick strap-on up my bum. Rathwell's voice boomed out over the PA, the bell went and we were on.

Melody came forward, sliding her feet carefully into the baked beans as she shook her whip lose. I braced my left arm, ready to take a blow on my gauntlet. Our eyes met and she bared her teeth in a catlike snarl, then struck. I ducked, parrying the thong as it lashed at my legs. It caught my arm and smacked against my thigh, leaving a stinging weal as she drew it back.

I stayed in a crouch, shuffling forward with my gauntletted forearm held out. Melody raised the whip high, then suddenly switched hands and brought it lashing down at my right side. It caught my leg, tracing a line of fire from my knee to my hip, but I had the thong clenched in my fist. I jerked hard and was rewarded with a look of panic on her face as she slipped and came down face-first in the backed beans – and the whip was loose in my fist.

Really, I should have mounted her, but the weals on my thighs burnt with pain and her big black bottom was sticking up from the baked beans. Anyway, my temper was rising. I hastily doubled the whipcord and lashed out, laying it across her buttocks with all my force just as her face emerged from the mess. She yelled in pain and snatched at me, grabbing my wrist.

I pitched into her and we went down in the baked beans, grappling furiously. She found my hair and shoved my face into the mess. I couldn't breathe but still had the doubled whip lash in my hand and was slashing frantically at her back and buttocks. My other hand found her hair and I pulled, hard. She snatched at my bra and I felt one boob come free, and then she took me by the neck. My head was under the baked beans and her grip made me open my mouth; then I was choking.

In all honesty, I swear I don't remember the next few minutes. I remember the awful feeling of not being able to breathe and Melody's grip on my head. I remember the swell of panic and trying to scream. That's all.

My next clear memory is of sitting on Melody's bottom and tearing at the leather of her corset with my teeth. She was babbling apologies and pleas for mercy, while Anderson was calling my name and telling me to calm down. He was outside the ring, but his face and chest were covered in baked beans.

It might have worked, had it not been for the baying of the crowd in the background. There was an insane glee to it, a berserk quality, a bloodlust that might have belonged more in a Roman colosseum. I was the object of that lust, the girl gladiator about to finish off her victim. I should have stood and walked away, shown them that for all my fiery reputation I am a civilised woman at heart. I didn't; I sat myself squarely on Melody's muscular buttocks and began to rip at her corset with my bare hands. The leather tore, slowly, leaving my nails broken and my fingers bruised, but it did tear, all the way, until I could jerk it out from beneath her and hold its ruined bulk up to the screaming crowd.

Melody made no move to resist, but simply lay there, whimpering softly and blowing bubbles in what was left of the baked beans. I stripped her slowly, making a show of each piece of her armour, until all she had left was her dildo harness. I shifted my seat and tugged the rear strap out from between her bum-cheeks. As I snipped the catch, she lifted her bottom, as meek a gesture of submission as I could have wanted. Off it came, and I was holding it in my hand, a great turgid rubber cock, crafted with every vein and wrinkle of a real cock, but of a grotesque size. Beneath the shaft there was a grossly wrinkled scrotum, heavy with fluid.

The crowd was yelling and chanting my name, cheering my victory, demanding that I fuck Melody. Her lovely bottom was in front of me, lifted, the cheeks open to hint at the dark meat of her pussy, her anus showing as a knot of glistening black flesh. I got to my feet and held the dildo aloft, drawing a yet wilder scream from the crowd. Melody lay beneath me: beautiful black Melody. Melody who had been going to bugger me: now beaten, wet with sweat and baked bean juice, her armour scattered around her, naked, and at my mercy. She turned her torso, looking back at me. Her eyes were shining, looking straight at me. The she spoke, quietly, softly: not a demand, but a plea.

'Do me, Vicky.'

The crowd were screaming – 'Fuck her! Fuck her!' – a chant of insensate lust. They needn't have bothered. I undid my shorts and let them fall to the canvas, displaying my bare sex. My pussy felt hot and ready as I fixed the monstrous strap-on into place. Melody gave a whimper and put her face in the mess of crushed baked beans, then stuck her bottom up. I knelt and stroked the shaft between her bum-cheeks, then pulled the full, dark hemispheres apart to get at her anus. Her crease was wet with sauce and sweat. Her bumhole showed pink in the centre, a tiny hole, then a wet, open blossom as she relaxed it. I put the rubber knob to her hole, a great black prick-end, impossibly large against her girly little bumhole.

I pushed, and saw her anus open, her hole growing around the rubber until it was stretched to a taut pink ring. She gave a grunt and the head popped suddenly up her.

Slowly I pushed it up, until the gross balls of the thing were hard against her pussy. Then I began to bugger her as the crowd cheered and clapped and screamed for more.

She made a real fuss, grunting and panting and wriggling her bottom on the shaft. I was high on victory and sheer dominance, but not only that. There was a protrusion right in against my clit, a bumpy rubber bulge designed to rub the wearer while she fucked her playmate. This was working its magic on me and I knew that, if I just kept going, I could come while up Melody's bottom. It was the same with her, because with every push up her rectum, the scrotum jammed on to her open pussy.

The screaming crowd became no more than background noise as my pleasure rose. I'd beaten Melody and my dildo was up her bum, showing her firmly who was boss. She was squirming on it, rubbing herself, kicking her feet, beating her fists in the mess of beans. I started to come, feeling my clit hard on the bumpy rubber, the centre of everything. We were screaming, coming together as I crushed the balls against her pussy. Something burst and I felt the dildo jerk. Suddenly the rubber scrotum was flaccid, empty, and I realised that I'd emptied whatever had been in it up Melody's bottom. She gave a gasp of shock and some thick, white substance spurted out around the shaft of the dildo as it abruptly lost its pressure. As the muck dribbled out over my pussy-hair and down her thighs I came again, out of rapture for the sheer filthiness of what I was doing.

With that orgasm, my strength seemed suddenly to go and I was sagging back. The dildo came free of Melody's anus with a sticky pop, leaving the hole to close slowly as it oozed creamy stuff down on to her pussy. My head was spinning and, for a moment, I thought I was going to faint, only for Rathwell's harsh tones to break through to me.

Then he had my wrist and was pulling me to my feet, declaring me the winner, to the sound of thunderous applause. The cup was shoved into my hands, then a wad of notes into my one remaining bra cup. Dizzy, half-conscious, I felt a wave of wonderful happiness. Rathwell called out my name once more and the crowd roared in answer, even as I heard his low whisper in my right ear.

'Nice win, Vicky, love. How about a blow-job in the showers, then?'

. . . and let's hope she didn't give it to him. Personally I'd have taken one look at Melody and surrendered, but that's just me.

The setting of the next story is very far from the London sex scene, in rural Devon. I met Helen Dale shortly after receiving my doctorate and her story precedes that time by a few months. By then, I had come to think of myself not just as sexually experienced, but as pretty well unshockable. My meeting with Helen – described in Bad Penny *– proved that I was wrong. Helen is like nobody else – really like nobody else . . .*

Puppy Days – Helen Dale

Monday March 6

I have chosen this day to begin a personal record of my progress. Since I joined Dr Richard Hetherington at Chericombe, the formal record of our research has been all that was needed. This is no longer the case as, from this day onward, I myself become part of the experiment.

I will not record the more technical side of the experiment in detail, nor will I discuss the moral implications of what Richard and I have achieved. I am a scientist and believe in knowledge for the sake of knowledge, and I doubt that I would be able to change those judgements that our critics are sure to make. Instead, I will seek to set down my emotions and private behaviour without reservation.

Following the publication of a crucial paper on gene sequencing by a Dr Birch, Richard and I have successfully broken the code to the location sequence that will enable his initial work on Chordate Interspecific Gene Transfer to be applied to specific physiological loci. Our initial experiments show that the system works and, as Richard has shown such courage in applying the initial developmental experiment to himself, I have chosen to be the subject for the altered location sequence.

We have chosen to restrict our gene exchanges to within the Mammalia, and indeed within the Eutheria. Beyond that, Richard has allowed me a free choice. This was a far easier decision for me than my initial acceptance of becoming a subject. Ever since I was a little girl, I have loved dogs and always felt close to our pets. The change is also best restricted to secondary sexual characteristics, as these are more subject to adult change that the rest of the primary genotype. Therefore I have chosen to have my mammary location sequence altered to a canid model.

To put it anther way – I'm going to have six titties and I'm going to be the world's first puppy girl!

Thursday March 9

Today, I gave myself the injection. Rather than allow Richard to do this, I did it myself, thus removing all doubt as to my own acceptance of the act. I was extremely tense, and more than a little scared, as I watched the serum flow into my vein. As expected, I felt no physical change, yet there are undoubtedly powerful psychological side effects to the process. We estimate that a period of some three months will elapse before any change in my morphology becomes evident, yet within hours of injecting the serum, I have begun to feel a compulsion towards canid behavioural patterns. On a rational level I am aware that this is entirely psychological, yet my sudden need to view Richard as master rather than senior cannot be denied.

Saturday May 20

My new nipples show! Below each of my breasts, I can see two faint circles of pigmentation, perfectly symmetrical and of even size. It is no more than a trace of melanin-rich tissue that is visible, but it means that the location sequence was perfect. I feel elated, triumphant, strong and scared at the same time, but above all, proud. This is a first, an achievement that marks a milestone second only to Richard's initial success!

I went to show him immediately and he was delighted. He was in his front room at the time, and I think someone may have seen me holding my top up for him to inspect my chest! They must have thought we made a fine pair: forty years' difference and the girl holding her top up, like a schoolgirl giving her first boyfriend a peep!

Sunday June 25

For the last month, my body has been undergoing its most radical changes since puberty. My supplementary breasts have started to swell and now form bulges of similar form to my original pair early on in puberty. The nipples are now close to the size and colour of their genotype and have increased in sensitivity.

Although my overwhelming feelings are of triumph and pride, these changes are not entirely easy to accept. For a start, I have to wear loose clothing in public and can only dare a swimsuit in the garden behind the lab. More importantly, my desire for puppy-like behaviour has increased.

Firstly, I feel a strong urge to go naked. This is new to me, as I have never even been keen on skimpy clothing, preferring the security and practicality of full, unisex clothes. Linked to this is a desire to be free to express myself physically, even to pee when and where the urge takes me.

More disturbingly, my needs to be controlled within a sexual relationship and to be physically beaten on my bottom have increased markedly. These are not new feelings for me, but I have always kept them carefully in check and never allowed either need to become more than a fantasy.

My desire for puppy-like behaviour is not a reflection of genuine canid ethology, but purely a psychological development of my own fantasies with respect to the changes of my body. Thus, I have no desire to sniff bottoms or be mated with real dogs, which are genuine facets of dog behaviour but no part of my fantasy. Yet I do want to go naked and to pee freely without thought for the consequences, which are facets both of dog behaviour and of my fantasy. Meanwhile, my desires for being put on a lead and to have my bottom beaten come only from my fantasy, yet are related to a purely anthropomorphic view of dog behaviour.

There is also a strengthening of my maternal instinct, which is manifested in a need to have my breasts suckled.

This, at least, can be explained as a result of my body's altered hormonal balances.

Monday July 24

Today we conducted an experiment on the sensitivity of my supplementary breasts. These are approaching full development and, while the body of all four still needs to fill out a little, the nipples appear to conform exactly to the genotype.

To test their sensitivity, each was given a series of identical touches and the time taken for them to become erect was recorded. The times fell within a five per cent margin of error, and there was no significant statistical difference between the new and the original ones. Nor can I detect any difference myself, while the feelings of arousal and vulnerability that normally come with the exposure of my breasts are notably stronger.

Richard remained entirely detached throughout the experiment, despite having me sitting topless in front of him and then touching my breasts himself. Since I volunteered for the main experiment, he has treated me with deep respect, even awe. I can understand this feeling as it is mirrored in my own attitude to him. He, after all, underwent the first test. I have, of course, seen his Percheron carthorse-inspired penis. In scientific terms, it is an extraordinary achievement. As a woman, it simultaneously makes me want to run away and attempt to accept it in my vagina.

I did not need to be told that Richard had become aroused by the sensitivity experiment. His penis formed a ridge down one leg of his trousers, reaching almost to his knee. With a great deal of embarrassment, he explained the reason for this.

The level of testosterone produced by his developmentally adjusted testes is appropriate not to a human male but to the horse from which we took the original sample. This horse is the property of a local farmer and can be seen grazing placidly from the lab windows. At a rough estimate, I would say that his body mass is some five times that of Richard's. Tests show Richard's testosterone levels to be far above the average for his age and weight, so it not surprising that he is experiencing difficulty controlling his aggression and sexual urge.

I responded to his problem as sympathetically as possible, although I confess to a strong urge to laugh. He thanked me for my understanding and confessed to considerable discomfort, so I suggested unfastening his trousers. Declining my suggestion, he explained to me that were he to bare his penis, the urge to touch it would be overwhelming and that he had no desire to shock me. He then went on to explain further: despite masturbating as often as four times nightly and two to three times in the course of the day, he was finding a growing need for sexual contact. The masturbation satisfied him on a physical level, but not on a mental one.

I suggested obtaining the services of a prostitute, either in Exeter or Bristol, but he pointed out that a man with a penis some fifteen inches long and notably thicker than most girls' wrists would hardly pass without comment in even the most depraved of brothels. Striking up a relationship with one of the women in the village was even less practical, as it would inevitably lead to the premature exposure of our work.

The solution was clear, although he was far too polite to suggest it first. For the sake of his mental stability and the continued smooth progress of the experiment, I would have to help him with his problem. Not only that, but as I myself am struggling with the psychological and physiological implications of the changes in my body, and will doubtless need his support, it is only reasonable that I offer him support in turn.

When I asked if being masturbated by me would help, he agreed with enthusiasm. I took him into the toilet and he freed his cock, which I masturbated in what I hope was a brisk and methodical manner. Nevertheless, it was difficult to remain detached. For one thing, the sheer size and vitality of his penis is nothing short of magnificent. My fingers do not meet around the shaft, and it is easily twice the length of any other male I have handled. Unlike ordinary human penes, it tapers somewhat from a thick base and the head shows greater elongation. When flaccid, this is entirely hidden within the prepuce, but it emerges fully during erection. There is also an intensely male, even animal, aroma to it.

I have never been good at giving male friends sexual relief purely as a favour. I simply find it too easy to become intimate. My nipples had been erect and my vulva moist after the sensitivity tests but, by the time he came, I was aroused, to say the least. The volume of semen was extraordinary, and a good deal of it ran down over my hand as I squeezed it out with a last few good tugs. It felt hot and thick, while the aroused male smell had become overpowering.

He thanked me politely, and I could sense the immense amount of tension that my little act of service had drained. After washing my hands, all I could do was stand there, feeling excited and awkward, wishing desperately for my own orgasm. Realising my predicament, he suggested that I might appreciate a few minutes alone in the loo. I thanked him for being so understanding, but my reserve was gone and I did it in front of him, seated on the loo with my skirt pulled up and my knickers at knee level. I felt deeply embarrassed afterwards, but nothing was said and we continued work as before.

Saturday August 5

Today I masturbated. I have been trying to put off this moment for some weeks, but my sexual need has finally broken through my feelings of guilt and insecurity. Rationally, I know that there is no reason why I should not take sexual pleasure in the new responses of my body. Yet the conditioning of my upbringing refuses to allow me such a logical choice. Just as masturbation used to fill me with guilt as a teenager, the thought of allowing myself to explore the full possibilities of stimulating my breasts produces an immediate reaction of shock. I am surprised to feel exactly the same emotions as I did during those earlier explorations of my body's adult responses. Although I feel that my new breasts are beautiful and sensual, touching them in a sexual way brings me a crushing awareness of the potential disapproval of society. Once I used to picture myself lying on my bed in the nude with my thighs spread apart and a finger in my pussy as my mother – or, worse, my grandmother – walked in, unannounced. Now I picture myself in the lab with my top off, testing the sensitivity of my breasts and becoming gradually aroused when a whole group of government officials burst in to arrest Richard and me.

I had intended to apply the same technique of deliberately naughty behaviour that I did as a teenager but, having put it off, I felt intensely guilty for having allowed Richard to watch me come after the sensitivity experiment. Afterwards, I resolved to hold myself back until my mind was clearer and I had not masturbated since. I have, however, been frequently aroused. This is because we have established a routine to relieve Richard of the aggression and tension of his unnaturally high testosterone levels. After work finishes, he and I will go into the lab toilet. He will produce his cock and I will masturbate him into the lavatory, then clean up the results of any inaccuracy before going home. It is done quite formally and without the emotion that characterised the sensitivity experiment, yet I cannot deny that it is arousing. Indeed, the knowledge that at half-past five each day I will be masturbating Richard's monstrous cock is enough to maintain a permanent background of sexual tension.

My resolve finally broke in the bath this morning. All four of my supplementary breasts are now fully developed, each one a full handful of soft, sensitive flesh. My nipples come to erection perfectly, so perfectly that if I perform the same sequence of touches to each of the six, they will take the same time to pop out. That was what I was doing when I began to masturbate: just marvelling at my chest and idly tweaking the nipples to erection one by one. I hadn't intended to masturbate and caught myself by surprise. I had all six nipples erect, and the desire to touch my pussy was so strong that I stopped playing with myself and started to soap my body. This only made me feel naughtier and guilty, which in turn brought back memories of breaking my sexual guilt as a teenager.

I overcame my teenage guilt by taking a deliberate pleasure in the naughtiness of what my parents referred to as 'self-abuse'. I would be pointedly rude about it, choosing to masturbate on the toilet or in the kitchen while alone in the house, rather than in the guilt-ridden darkness of my own bedroom. The technique worked, allowing me the pleasure of guilt-free masturbation and subsequent guilt-free sex.

Knowing that I was going to masturbate anyway, I did the same. My first rude act was to pee in the bath. I needed to go quite badly anyway, and that gave me an ideal opportunity to be dirty. Lifting my pussy above the water, I held myself briefly, thinking how rude I was being. Then I let myself go, sending an arc of pee down the bath and over the end to splash on the floor. Knowing that I had made a puddle on the floor made me feel even more naughty, and I began to wish that there was somebody there to beat me for it. From there, I progressed to wishing someone would beat me for having given myself extra breasts. Feeling even more lewd, I let some more pee out, this time into my cupped hands. I rubbed it over my breasts and into my nipples.

Cocking one leg over the edge of the bath so that my pussy was open and pulling the bath plug with my toe, I settled down to bring myself to orgasm. When the water had drained out I let go the rest of my pee, into the bath, all over the floor and into my hands to be rubbed on my breasts. The last of it trickled down between my bum-cheeks, leaving my bottom in a hot pool of pee.

I began to flick at my clitoris, touching around it, then on it, as I massaged my pee into my breasts. One by one I touched them, exploring their lovely gentle curves as my abdominal muscles began to tense. Then I began to rub my forearm over them, feeling all six. It was so good that it was hard to know what to come over. I had peed on the floor and over myself, especially over my breasts, but I also wanted to be turned over and beaten, or put in a pillory and made a public exhibition of: naked and with my six titties showing to a huge crowd. That was it for me, and I was imagining myself being stripped in public, humiliated and then beaten, as I came.

Afterwards I felt guilty, but it wasn't the burning guilt that used to make me never want to be so rude again. I will do it again, and when I do it may be ruder still.

Friday August 11

It is becoming harder to deny my feelings towards Richard. Not only has my need for subservience to him become stronger, but the act of holding that gigantic penis in my hand each afternoon is creating more than a professional bond of intimacy between us. He tries to remain detached while I masturbate him, treating it as a necessary act which I am under no obligation to enjoy. But today, after work, he placed a hand on my bottom at the moment of ejaculation. I made no move to stop him. Indeed, I would have been more than happy to accept a more intimate exploration. On Sunday, we are to take a picnic to the site of an Iron Age fort near Kentisbeare, but I expect that he will behave with his normal professional politeness and detachment.

My desire to behave and be treated like a puppy has also continued to grow, and I now realise that I have been taking on these characteristics subconsciously. I now prefer to go naked in my flat and feel uncomfortable with any clothes on, even a short nightie or a pair of loose knickers. This is a great change for me. Previously I never felt truly secure at night without an ankle-length nightie and a pair of big, demure knickers. Even on the hottest nights, I would keep on a T-shirt and a pair of knickers. Now I cannot bare to be other than naked.

I masturbated again, in a deeply rude act that helped spur my feelings about clothing. Taking all my most dowdy undies, I made a pile in the middle of the bathroom floor, and played with myself while squatting over them.

After feeling my titties and pussy for a while, I let out a little pee, which gave me a gloriously rude feeling of release. Putting my left arm under my lowest pair of breasts, I began to rub my pussy, fingering my vagina and touching the drips of pee that were hanging from my pussy-lips and bottom-cheeks. I did more, letting it trickle down my hand and on to my underwear, soiling it thoroughly. I touched my bottom-hole, tickling the sensitive ring and feeling the way it pouted. Clutching a big pair of pee-soaked knickers, I started to rub myself up and down the whole length of my sex. As I started to come, I transferred the knickers to my breasts and took up a bra to rub with. The nylon lace was rough on my clitoris and took me right to the edge.

I just let go, letting my pee squirt out through the bra to soak my thighs. My bottom-hole opened as I started to come and, well, I just did it.

Monday August 14

Yesterday was one of the most exciting and extraordinary days of my life! On the way to Kentisbeare, I explained to Richard my desire to be naked, and he suggested that, if we could find a suitably lonely place, I might play naked while he kept an eye out for me. The Iron Age fort, which we had hoped might be good, proved too popular with tourists so we drove on. That part of the country is full of little, round-topped hills, and it didn't take long before we found one with fields on the slopes and a small area of rough land at the summit. This proved perfect, with sparse gorse bushes screening areas of short grass, and a triangulation post from which Richard could keep watch.

Feeling grateful for his help, I undressed in front of him. My excitement rose with each scrap of clothing that I peeled off. Not that there was much of it, and Richard was moved to note that under my long, loose jumper I wore only baggy cotton trousers and knickers. I told him about destroying my old clothes, but without going into the dirty details.

From the moment I hung my knickers on a convenient

gorse bush, I felt the most extraordinary sense of liberation. It wasn't just the delightfully naughty feeling of showing off a bit in the open, but something stronger by far. Not that I knew much about outdoor nudity, because I'd never gone without a top even on the beach. I have once or twice flipped my top and bra up, or quickly bared my bum outdoors, just for the flush of daring it gives but this was far more than that. I was fully naked and showing off six perfect little breasts: quite a sight, if anybody did catch me!

I ran and played among the gorse for ages, simply enjoying my nudity. When I needed a pee, I squatted in a depression and made a puddle on the ground. When it all got too much and I needed to come, I just lay on my back on the sun-drenched grass and brought myself off with my fingers on my pussy and titties. It was lovely, and produced only a *slight* pang of guilt. After all, I had been naughtier by far on Friday night!

Only when I'd come did I begin to feel bad about Richard, who had been patiently acting as lookout for all the time I'd been playing. He made light of it, but I reminded him that I was due to masturbate him and that the hilltop was a better place to do it than the car. He agreed, and I took him down among the gorse bushes. I was still nude, and found it impossible to remain detached while I pulled at his huge cock with one hand and held his great, heavy balls in my other. He was admiring my breasts while I masturbated him, and I said he could touch.

He declined, politely, saying it would just lead to more and that he didn't want to force himself on to me. At that instant, he could have tried to put the monstrous thing up my bottom and I wouldn't have resisted, but I didn't push the issue. Instead I moved to his front, so that when he climaxed the semen went all over my breasts. As always, there was lots of it, and it felt wonderfully hot and sticky, running down over my nipples and into all the little valleys and grooves of my chest and belly.

I did it, right there in front of him, rubbing his come into my breasts and pussy, tasting it on my hands, rubbing it on my thighs and down between my bum-cheeks, smearing it in my face, then back to my pussy until I came with a second orgasm even more blindingly lovely than the first.

When I came, I called him 'Master', which is what I now want him to be.

Thursday August 17

Today was set aside for further experimentation on my psychological need for puppy-like behaviour. In the morning we agreed, quite rationally, to test two facets of that need: my need to pee freely, and my need to be put on a lead.

The question was whether these desires were entirely psychological or if they were psychosomatic and in some way related to the alteration of my genotype. While both Richard and I are fully aware that these behavioural investigations are not strictly necessary to what is essentially a genetic transfer experiment, both of us are keen to conduct them. Since last Sunday, there has been an ever increasing risqué element to our relationship, which is not only sensually and emotionally satisfying to me, but has done a great deal to calm my feelings. The evening masturbation sessions in particular are more intimate, with me naked and Richard usually coming on my breasts or bottom.

We began with the peeing experiments, which were designed to test whether I got greater pleasure for more puppy-like behaviour. For the first test, I drank two litres of water and was let naked into the garden behind the lab. I stayed on all fours and played fetch for Master with a rubber bone he had brought. This gave me a great deal of pleasure, especially from the feelings of achievement and happiness every time I laid the bone at his feet and he patted my head. I was soon wagging my bottom and begging for the bone with my hands curled up under my chin, and had forgotten all about being expected to pee. When my bladder eventually began to feel strained, it was the most natural thing in the world simply to squat down on the grass and let it all go, allowing my pee to run out in a great gush in full view of Richard. He watched indulgently and then gave me a pat on my bottom. Once back as the respectable Helen Dale, MSc, and no longer Helen the puppy-girl, my verdict was that the experience had felt more natural than naughty, and more pleasant than exciting.

After some discussion we decided that a control for the experiment would be for me to dress as I used to before my supplementary breasts grew. I would then wet myself deliberately and compare the feelings with those in my puppy guise. I had come in to the lab in a baggy jumper and loose skirt, with neither knickers nor a bra. I never wear bras nowadays, as a two-cup one looks ridiculous and I can hardly have a six-cup one made without giving everything away. I went back to my flat and put on one of my remaining pairs of knickers and an old pair of slacks.

To enhance my humiliation, I was sent out on the footpath that runs along the brook with two litres of water inside me. There was soon a genuine urgency in my bladder, but it proved no easy task to break my conditioning. Peeing is something that is done in a seated or squatting position and with the vulva open to the air. Doing it in one's knickers is simply too great a break with accepted behaviour to be easy. In the end, I had to make myself, closing my eyes and squeezing my bladder until I let go. My knickers quickly filled and it trickled down my thighs and soaked into the crotch and seat of my slacks. It felt wonderful: physically pleasant and extremely naughty. I let it all out, enjoying the warm, wet feeling and the deliciously dirty knowledge that I was peeing my knickers, until I had squeezed out the last dribble into my soaking gusset. That left me about a mile from the safety of the lab with a big stain on my bottom and crotch and all down my legs. Walking back was an agony of embarrassment and excitement. I wasn't seen but, by the time I got to safety, I was breathing hard and was seriously turned on. I had to come, and took my wet slacks down as soon as I got through the door. I masturbated through my pee-soaked knickers in front of Richard, and had a great orgasm.

Watching me gave him a hard cock and I obliged by going down on my knees and, for the first time, taking it in my mouth. It filled my whole oral cavity, an impossibly large mouthful of flesh which I mouthed on until he suddenly jerked and sent his come down my throat. I pulled back because I was gagging, and got the second lot in my face and down my jumper. I had to come again after that and put a handful of it down my wet knickers to rub into my pussy until I reached a climax even more intense than the first. Conclusion: less natural, but far more erotically stimulating. Peeing as a puppy-girl is what I feel I should do. Peeing my knickers in public is quite definitely naughty.

We tried the collar experiment after lunch. Richard had purchased a spiked collar and a good thick lead, not exactly feminine but appropriate for a dog of my weight. He put me on this stripped and it felt absolutely perfect and absolutely right. I was his puppy, on a lead at his feet, loyal and obedient. It was true bliss, an ecstasy at least partly erotic, as it gave me a strong need to be mounted and mated by my Master. The feeling that it was proper for me to be naked also reached a new peak of intensity. We repeated the process with me in my skirt, which felt completely wrong. It was still nice to feel the soft weight of my six breasts dangling from my chest as I crawled behind him, but the skirt felt entirely out of place. The rest of my clothes were soaking in a basin, but they weren't actually needed. Conclusion: yes, being on a collar and lead excites me and it excites me most when I am naked. It also makes me more servile to my Master, and more desperate to please him.

At the end, I told him he could mate me if he wanted to, but he just gave me an enigmatic smile.

Sunday August 20

Today we tested my need to have my buttocks beaten. We had intended to do this next week, but circumstances overtook us. It was a glorious day, and I badly wanted to be outside and play in the nude. Richard readily agreed and we drove over to Dartmoor, choosing a lonely wood on the north-east flank of the moor. Here I stripped and went down on all fours in the soft leaf mold.

I played for a while, scampering through the pale light of the wood, while my Master kept a careful eye out for other people. None came, and I began to feel bolder, and actually quite keen to be seen playing naked as a puppy. It was a wonderfully naughty thought, and not one I could resist for long, so I escaped Richard and ran up to where the open moor starts above the wood.

My feeling of naughtiness increased dramatically as I stepped out of the shelter of the woods. The ground was short cropped turf, with clumps of heather, gorse and bracken, an ideal place for a puppy to play. I could hear my Master calling but took no notice, instead venturing further on to the moor, my excitement growing with every moment.

I scrambled all the way to the brow of the hill, which gave on to a low dip of open land, with a higher slope rising to a tor beyond. There were people on the tor, a group of walkers, two of them standing on the top of the exposed granite height. I had to do it. They were a long way away, far enough for me to escape easily in the unlikely event of their being so offended they gave chase. What they would see was a naked girl on all fours, a girl whose chest supported not two but six breasts. It was wrong of me, and I shouldn't have done it, but they were too far away to be sure of what they could see, so I did.

From the moment I crawled out from cover, I experienced a powerful thrill of exhibitionism. For several minutes, I crawled around on the grass, until a sudden change in the way the distant walkers stood showed that I had been seen. They were watching me, watching me crawl naked with my titties swinging from my chest and my bum quite open enough to hint at the dark of my pussy fur.

I knew they'd be wondering what I was doing, and discussing it. Presumably they'd think I didn't know they could see, and presumably they'd think I was on all fours to reduce the risk of being seen myself. One of the possibilities that they considered had to be that I'd stripped to avoid the risk of soiling my clothes while I went to the loo. With that thought, I knew I had to do it, and the pressure in my belly told me it would be easy.

With my pulse hammering, I turned my bottom towards them and sank into a squat that left both my pussy and bottom-hole bare and sticking out towards them. I tensed my bladder and then just let go. My pee came gushing out, splashing on the heather under my bottom and trickling down the insides of my thighs. I took my time, enjoying the feeling of my bladder emptying and imagining them watching, amused or shocked, excited or horrified.

There was worse to come. My bumhole was everted and straining, holding my load in while I wondered if I could actually be that rude. I could. It was coming out, bit by bit, on to the ground beneath me, in full view of my watchers. With each piece, my overwhelming sense of naughtiness grew until the last of my resolve broke. I snatched at my pussy and began to rub frantically as, once more, my bumhole opened and a large piece began to come out. I came like that, imagining how disgusted they'd be watching me do it on the ground, yet secretly delighted at the intimacy of my exposure.

My courage went with my orgasm, but I had to finish and did so in an agony of shame and embarrassment. Then I ran, all the way back to the shelter of the wood and the safety of my Master's company. He was still calling for me, and when I found him and told him what I'd done he was extremely cross, genuinely so.

He told me to get on the ground; that he was going to whip me. I did as I was told, knowing I deserved it but trembling at the thought. He picked a long holly sucker, from which he stripped the leaves while I waited at his feet. When the sucker was bare, it formed a four-foot whip of springy wood, just the sight of which sent a shiver down my spine. I was about to be beaten for the first time in my life.

It would have been wrong to protest. I'd been bad and, if he had decided I needed to be beaten, then it had to be right. I put my front down in the damp leaves of the woodland floor and lifted my haunches. I was whimpering with expectation and then the stick came down and my bottom exploded with pain. I yelped aloud but he didn't pause, applying the second plumb across my poor, naked behind.

Each stroke of the stick hurt more, a stinging, fiery pain that seemed to fill my whole bottom. Yet I knew I deserved the beating and kept my haunches high, offering my Master my bare flesh to punish as he saw fit. Twelve times he brought that agonising switch down across my bottom, and twelve times I jumped and yelped. All the times I had fantasised over beatings, I had never realised it hurt so much, nor how hard it is to stay controlled during a whipping. I didn't even try, but kicked and squirmed and made a proper exhibition of myself, until he finally declared that I should have had enough to teach me my lesson.

The moment he stopped was ecstasy. I had been whipped in the nude and I'd deserved it. My bottom hurt furiously, but that was what I got for my bad behaviour – fairness, pure and simple.

I was left face down in the dirt, my bottom raised and my knees apart. I could feel every stinging welt on my buttocks and it was pure bliss. Each one represented my Master's ownership of me, his right to beat me, his right to have me grovelling naked at his feet with my pussy open and expectant of his monstrous cock.

He did me, as he should have done long before: perhaps on that first day when I took up my place as his assistant. First I was made to suck, gagging on the huge, meaty glans of his penis until I thought I would choke. Then I was put to it.

With my knees cocked well apart and my back pulled in, I offered him my sex as openly as possible. He moved behind me, cock in hand, and I felt it touch my vulva. A boyfriend once tried to put a cricket ball up me and this felt the same: a huge, round thing, impossibly big for my little pussy. But he pushed and I began to open. It was filling me to produce the most miraculous sensation. He only managed to get the glans and the meat of the foreskin inside me, but I felt as if my entire body was bursting with cock.

He fondled my beaten bottom as he fucked me, bumping his cock around inside me and stroking the hot, raw welts that decorated my buttocks. I put my face right down in the dirt, which felt right, and played with my breasts while he did me. My clitoris felt thrust out by the sheer size of what was inside me and, before long, I began to touch myself. I came once while he was inside me, feeling my pussy squeeze hard on his cock again and again. That was too much for his self-control, and he did it in me, overflowing my pussy and smearing the crease of my bottom and my vulva with come. I took some and put it on my breasts and in my mouth, then came again to the delicious feeling of being smothered in my Master's sperm. I felt totally owned by him, at that point: the adoring, servile, loyal puppy to the man who had me naked on the ground and had beaten me so thoroughly.

The beating really added to my pleasure and, in future, I want to be beaten regularly. No, it's more than that; I *need* to be beaten regularly. It is part of who I am.

Saturday August 26

I have moved in with Richard, my Master. I am to sleep naked in a dog basket at the foot of his bed and will only be permitted on to it when he wants to mate me. When that happens will be his choice, not mine, but I dearly hope that it is often and that he makes full use of my body. I adore him absolutely and would do anything to please him.

He mates me regularly now, always with me kneeling as a puppy-girl should. I am more used to the extraordinary strained feeling of having his cock inside me and have managed to take more than half its length. I would also like him to bugger me, but this is sadly impractical. Instead, I have to be content with him ejaculating into the crease of my bottom, which is in itself an exquisite experience.

I also know that he takes genuine pleasure in my puppy-girl behaviour. Previously, I had thought he had done it simply to satisfy my urges, but then he told me that his sacking from his first research post was not for unethical practices, but because he was caught walking a naked undergraduate on a lead. Perhaps he guessed at the true nature of my sexuality when he originally interviewed me. The salary is generous, thanks to our funding, and several of the candidates were better qualified. What he needed was devotion as much as skill, and that I gave him.

Never did I imagine that a relationship could feel so perfectly right. It is bliss to be owned, to be played with and to be punished, all as my Master dictates. Richard alone really knows me, and only he could achieve what we have done. I love him with an intensity far stronger than anything I have known before; my whole existence is focused on him, as his is on me.

Thursday August 31

Last Monday, we began the final test on my supplementary breasts. This was to bring me into lactation and was triggered with a simple hormonal injection.

The experiment is a success. I awoke this morning with a distinct feeling of heaviness in all six of my breasts. For a little while, I lay on my back in the basket, exploring this sensation and feeling increasingly naughty and pleased with myself. In the end, I woke my Master by crawling up on to his bed and dangling my breasts in his face. This earned me an impromptu spanking, held down across his chest, but he was delighted when he learnt the reason for my excitement.

In the lab, I stripped naked as usual and began massaging each breast in turn. After a little over six minutes, drops of milk began to form on my areolae. It is a pleasant sensation, although it currently requires effort. Nevertheless, I managed to provide samples for testing from all six breasts and make enough to toast our success with cups of warm girl-milk.

Sunday September 3

Today, I gave in to my urge to play with my milk. Never having been pregnant, I had no idea how painful unrelieved breasts are for a woman during lactation. All six of my breasts feel swollen and heavy. They swing in an odd way, too, and I am constantly aware of them. The only way to reduce this sensation is to milk myself. I have been doing this since Friday, kneeling in the bath each morning and evening and draining each breast in turn. The feeling as they empty is delicious. I can only compare it with the relief that comes with emptying my bladder when in absolute desperation for a pee. Yet it is a deeper, more fulfilling sensation, and more sexually stimulating.

I masturbated on Saturday morning, kneeling in a puddle of my own breast-milk. As when I first played with my new breasts as a part of masturbation, having milk to play with brought me feelings of guilt. These were light, but I knew I had to do it again, and in a ruder, more open context. I needed to be the puppy-girl and I needed to take at least some risk.

I told Master what I intended to do and he insisted on coming with me, to check that the coast was clear. He is also determined that there will be no more showing off in the nude.

We drove over to the wood where he first beat me and I stripped and lay down in the leaf mold. It took a moment to compose myself and then I began to stroke myself, using my fingertips on my breasts, belly and thighs. I thought of how rude I'd been, the last time we'd been in the wood, and of how I'd been beaten for my filthy behaviour. I suggested to him that a whipping might be appropriate for me and he agreed, adding that he would use a holly switch again.

Alone, I began to squeeze my breasts, gently, so that little drops of milk grew on the areolae. It felt beautiful, so good, so naughty, and I knew that what was coming was going to be special.

Master soon came back, bearing a switch to beat me with. By then, the milk was pooling between my breasts and running in warm rivulets down into the concavities of my neck, armpits and belly. My face was wet with it and my mouth full of my own sharp-sweet taste. I fed myself more, letting him watch, and then emptied my bladder on to the ground so that my bottom was in a warm, wet puddle of mud and leaves.

I held back from touching my pussy for as long as I could and then put a hand on it and rolled my legs up, offering Master my buttocks and thighs. He began to whip me, gently at first, but harder as my pleasure built. I was squeezing my breasts one by one, sending up little fountains of milk over my body and face, but most especially into my mouth.

Soon my mouth was full and the welts on my thighs and bottom had began to burn, a hot, urgent pain in strange contrast to the sweet, milky sensation on my upper body and the warm, soggy pee underneath me. As I started to come, I swallowed my mouthful of milk, tasting myself and rubbing hard at my clitoris as my orgasm rose and rose. A tall fountain of milk burst from the breast I was squeezing and splashed in my face. The switch came down hard, landing across my cheeks over my anus and I screamed, then again as it all came together in an orgasm that left me panting and whimpering with satisfaction on the ground.

Before I had recovered, Master had rolled me over and pulled me up on to my knees. He entered me and came up me while I was still dizzy with orgasm and finished by feeding me a handful of sperm from my pussy. I came again, twice, under my own fingers while I rolled the sticky mixture of come and girl-milk around in my mouth. The second was too much and I blacked out for a few seconds, slumped into the pool of mud and mess beneath me.

I am writing this in my dog basket, remembering how lovely it felt to be beaten and soiled in the woods. Yet, best of all, I know that it is an experience I can have again and again, as often as my body can take it.

Sunday September 10

Before today I thought I had fully explored the exquisite pleasures that my role as Richard's puppy-girl allowed. I was wrong.

When I went into the village this morning, it was to discover that some unspeakable bastard had left a sack with six live puppies in it at the side of the A30. Mrs Cottle at the store was seething with indignation, in which I joined. The thought of six puppies also excited me to a point where I could barely control myself and I demanded to see them. They were in the back of her shop: six of the sweetest, plumpest little bundles of fur imaginable. They are Labrador but with a little of something that is definitely not pedigree. I suppose a mongrel must have got at a show bitch.

I immediately volunteered to care for them and Mrs Cottle readily agreed. My heart was absolutely hammering as I carried the basket back to Richard's and I knew exactly what I was going to do. He was a little surprised but as indulgent as ever and suggested I took them into the living room and fed them. He didn't mean with cow's milk, either.

They were hungry, and I didn't hesitate. Pulling my jumper up, I exposed my breasts and crawled over to the basket. They latched on immediately and, from the first instant I felt those soft little snouts close on my nipples, I was quite simply in heaven. Lying down on my side, I let them struggle for position, and then helped the runt to fasten on to my bottom right breast.

I just lay there, feeding all six and stroking their soft, furry backs as they suckled me and frantically wagged their stumpy little tails. I knew it was going to happen because it felt so good, but I was still taken aback when my first orgasm came without even touching my clitoris. I put a hand down between my legs for the second, but it wasn't actually necessary.

For half an hour I just lay there, with all six puppies suckling as I came again and again and again. Twice I fainted, only to come around again as yet another orgasm hit me. It didn't stop until the puppies were finally full and, as my last orgasm drained slowly away, I knew that I had truly found myself.

. . . Helen is the softest, sweetest woman I know: also about the naughtiest and, underneath, maybe the strongest.

Certainly the most headstrong girl I know is Natasha Linnet, from Brat, *in which we followed her exploration of the more submissive and dirtier parts of her sexuality. Percy Ottershaw is the rotund and debauched gourmand from the same story. As Natasha found, he is an uninhibited sensualist whose depravity is matched only by his imagination . . .*

Fille Farci à la Mode d'Epineuil – Percy Ottershaw

One of the most delightful culinary adventures of my life occurred in a small *auberge* near the town of Tonerre. I was motoring down with young Charles Carlisle and his girlfriend, Sophie, who was later to become his wife. Our intention was to visit Chablis, where I would introduce the couple to some of the *vignerons* whom I number among my friends and acquaintances. Sadly, Charles's rather elderly Humber had proved unequal to the task and finally expired just outside the village of Epineuil shortly after one in the morning.

Charles had been driving, while Sophie and I had been enjoying a couple of bottles of champagne that we had picked up in Château Thierry. Being petite, she was a touch tipsy – well, absolutely pickled, to be truthful. It was a cold night, and we seemed to be in rather a spot, but I volunteered to scout ahead. By good fortune, there proved to be a small *auberge* less than a quarter mile further on.

With a few stones and a little diplomacy, we managed to awaken the *hôtelier* and occupy the only remaining room. All three of us were ravenous, but it was the middle of the night, and the *hôtelier*, despite being well meaning, could offer nothing more satisfying than cold *andouillette*, a moderate cheese board and the run of his cellar. To this, we could only add honey and a *pâté au Champagne*, both of which we had picked up at a farm to the south of Soissons.

We visited the cellar and chose a local rosé, Chablis of both ordinary and first-growth quality and a Sauvignon from the St Bris vineyards. We had some of the rosé with the cheese and discussed how to make the best of what remained. Now, Sophie is usually rather a cold fish, but the champagne had loosened her up a great deal and the long drive down from Calais had softened what had always been rather formal relations between her and me – to a remarkable extent, as it proved.

By the time we'd finished the cheese she was seated cross-legged in front of the fire in just her knickers and slip, with one titty peeping out and not a great deal hiding what appeared to be a deliciously plump young pussy. She was also becoming increasingly amorous with Charles and, by the time we had finished the second bottle, she had both breasts naked and was watching my reaction while he kissed a dribble of wine away from their upper slopes.

Fortune favours the bold, so I made a joke about the wine and suggested that she would make a very fine plate for our meal. I expected the answer to be at best a pleased giggle and at worst a slap in the face, but to my surprise she allowed us to tease her into stripping naked and let me watch while Charles licked the last of the *Amour de Nuits* from her breasts. That left her very excited indeed, and she made no resistance to having the larger of the *andouillettes* pushed into her vagina.

From then on, we could do no wrong. We filled her mouth with pâté and smeared it on to her breasts and belly. We shaved her pubes and coated her delightful pussy in pâté and honey. We even held her thighs wide and lifted her bottom to apply pâté to the charming little hole in between her fleshy young cheeks. Far from objecting, she reached down and held her own bottom open to allow the insertion of the next largest *andouillette* into her anus.

Dinner was then served, starting with the pâté in her mouth and finishing with the *andouillette* that had occupied her anal passage. I recall the flavours: strong and distinctly feminine. Of the wines, the two Chablis were over-subtle for the dish, and the Sauvignon was the best match.

By the end, she was quite desperate for sex. We obliged, with Charles underneath her and in her vagina, while I mounted behind and had the use of her anus. She had already come while the pâté was being licked from her vulva, and did so several more times before first Charles and then I finished inside her.

It was a glorious session, although sadly not to be repeated. Indeed, since Sophie married Charles within the year, her behaviour to me has never been more than formally polite from that day to this. I have, however, relived the experience twice since that marvellous night. Once was with a young whore in Auxerre, who enjoyed the experience but giggled incessantly and then charged me some three times her standard rate. The other was with Natasha Linnet, a wine writer to whom I described the experience with sufficient lascivious detail to make her want to try it herself.

Here then is the full recipe. Take one girl, full-figured but firm of flesh; strip her, wash and depilate her body. Truss her wrists into the small of her back; spread her thighs, and truss her ankles, running a short line between wrist and ankle trusses. Lay her on a suitable surface, ideally of a colour to suit her hair and complexion.

Select two large *andouillettes*, a firm honey and a rich pâté. For wine, choose Sauvignon de St Bris, or another intense but not over-subtle dry white. For the sake of both the digestion and hygiene, take a small glass of *Marc de Champagne* after the meal.

Insert the larger of the *andouillettes* into the girl's vagina and the smaller into her anus, in each case using a little pâté to ease her passages. Ensure that the end of each *andouillette* remains protruding.

Coat her pubic mound with the pâté, recreating the shape of her pubic bush. Fill her belly button and mouth with a generous quantity of the pâté, and use it to top her nipples, building them up to a good, but not disproportionate, size.

Spread the honey on to those areas of her body that offer a sufficiently horizontal surface and also sensitive areas. These should include her neck, breasts, belly, pubic area and parts of her thighs.

For perhaps five minutes work both *andouillettes* gently in and out of their respective orifices, warming the girl and improving the flavour of the dish.

Consume the delicacy directly from the girl's body, working downward from the mouth and finishing with the anal area. If there are two diners, remember to share the *andouillettes*, as each will have acquired its own distinctive flavour. Once finished, thank the girl for her indulgence and enjoy her body in those orifices from which the meal has been partaken.

. . . I must try it sometime, although it does seem a bit unfair on the girl. After all, she doesn't get any of the lovely grub!

From a quite different social setting comes Linda White, who appeared briefly in Bad Penny. *I have known her since my earliest childhood, as she lived in the Channel Islands, where we would holiday every summer. Only many years later, after we had shared no less than five men on a memorable and drunken evening, did I really get to know her. I had played with her as well, enjoying her firm, well-formed body in what was only my second experience of sex with other girls. Her story comes from immediately after that incident . . .*

Getting in Trouble – Linda White

Men are terrible hypocrites. I mean, if Carl or one of his mates had had five girls at the same time, he would never have shut up about it. Not only that, but all the lads would have thought he was the greatest. Let a girl do the same, and she's a slag. Unfortunately, I had done it.

It had been too good to resist. Little Penny Birch had turned up on the island for the first time in years: only she wasn't so little any more. I'd always thought of her as quiet and mousy, with her long black hair and shy smile. Now she looked really pretty and stylish and, not surprisingly, Carl and his friends hit on her right away. I knew what they were after, because it wasn't the first time. They wanted to take her out by the lighthouse and gang-bang her.

I warned her, but she didn't care. Then she invited me to join in! Well, I was pissed and I'd always fancied Carl a lot, and Pete and Saul a bit. Lewis was OK, too, just a bit fat. My brother Gary was with them, so I knew they wouldn't do anything really nasty. So I went.

They stripped us, fucked us, made us wank them and suck their cocks until I didn't know if I was coming or going. I think even Gary put his in my mouth, but it was too dark to tell, with only the lighthouse beam to see by. I was too randy to care much, anyway. When they'd finished with us, Penny jumped me, and she was worse than the guys. I'd never been with a girl before, but the guys hadn't made me come and she obviously wanted to, so I let her. She frigged me off and even touched my bumhole!

That was when the guys decided it would be funny to leave us there, starkers, and covered in their mess. We had to walk back to town naked, and hide in the hedge every time a car came past. Fortunately, Gary was back at home and let us in the kitchen window. The last thing I remember of that night is Penny giving him a lecture while she struggled to pull up her knickers.

The next day, I woke up feeling awful. Gary had put my knickers and nightie on and put me to bed, so Mum and Dad never knew anything was wrong. When I went out to work, I was sure everyone was giving me funny looks, but nobody said anything. Nothing was said when I got home, either. I met Penny that evening and, after a bit of embarrassment, we had a really good chat, which ended with her suggesting I come and visit her on the mainland. I took her address and phone number and we parted with a hug and a kiss that left me tingly and feeling ashamed of myself. The next day, she left the island.

I was sure that the story was going to get out, and I felt really bad about it. Only after two whole days did I begin to wonder if I had got away with it. Nobody seemed to have seen Penny and me leaving the Barn, where we had been drinking before it happened. The guys were silent too, oddly silent.

The next day I found out why. Carl and Pete gave me a simple choice. I kept them happy and they kept quiet about what they had done with me. Otherwise, everyone on the island got to know, including the bit with Penny.

I made a big fuss, calling then bastards and perverts, but only to save face, because they were the sexiest guys around and, since they'd had me, I hadn't been able to get the experience out of my mind. Then, if they did tell, my life was going to be unbearable. The island is too small to hide, and I knew what happened to the reputations of girls who got too carried away. Eventually I agreed, and from then on it was sex with everything.

They used to take me out to the old German bunkers

and have me relieve them. The routine was simple. I'd go into a room and they'd come in to me one by one while the others stood watch. Each was different, and I quickly learnt the ways they liked it.

Carl was always first and was really bold. He knew I liked it. At least, he knew I liked it with him: he was that sure of himself that he thought, after having him, I'd hate doing it with the others. Sure, he was the best-looking, but he was a real pig with me. First he would make me take my top and bra off, then get hard in my mouth while he groped my tits. Once he was really stiff, he'd pull back and tell me to suck on the end of his cock like it was a lollipop. Then he'd wank in my mouth, and stuff his thing right down my throat when he came, keeping it in to make me swallow his spunk.

Pete was usually second. He was crazy on my tits and would put his thing between them and tell me to jiggle them about. I think he saved it up, because he'd always come really quickly, and when he did, his mess would go all over my tits. At the end, he'd take hold of them himself and rub them around so that his mess was smeared all over – and he'd always laugh as he zipped himself up. I've never minded swallowing, but that made me feel really dirty.

Saul liked a hand-job and then a suck. The first time we did it, he pulled out of my mouth at the last instant and did it in my face, all over my nose and my eyes, which I only just shut in time. It felt really slimy and I had to ask him to get a tissue out of my bag. After that, I made sure he kept it in to the end, and then I'd swallow it quickly.

Lewis was shyer than the others, and nearly always went last. He was always dodgy about it as well, and was the only one who seemed bothered by how they'd got me to do it. That didn't stop him having a good time with me. The deal stopped at fucking, but he was really into hair and liked my bush. I'd pull down the front of my knickers to show it to him while he wanked himself up, then let him frig me while I tossed him. Sometimes he'd come in my hand; sometimes he'd demand a suck when he got close.

He was clumsy, but with his fingers on my bump I'd usually come, too, although I never let him know that.

Gary would stand outside while all this was going on, and I could tell he got really jealous. He wasn't with anyone, and obviously needed it badly, but he couldn't very well demand a blow job from his own sister, so that was that. If he remembered what I was sure we'd done by the lighthouse, then he wasn't saying anything.

So it went on, four times, until we had to take a break. This wasn't because they had started to feel bad about what they were doing, or because I tried to stop it. It was because people had started to wonder what was going on. Everything gets around on the island, and while there was no reason that I shouldn't be going around with Gary's friends, it did look a bit suspicious that we disappeared together so often. All the guys except Gary and Saul had girlfriends, and what they'd have done to me if they found out the truth didn't bear thinking about.

After a week, Carl came up with an idea to get me to themselves. He was sort of engaged to his girlfriend, Sammy, and had suggested to her that it was time they had their stag and hen parties. She had been dead keen, as it was not only an excuse for a fun night but brought their marriage a step closer to reality. The first I knew about this was when I got the invitation to her party, only to be told by Gary that I had to refuse it as I was coming to Carl's – as the entertainment!

I felt really bad. Sammy was quite a close friend, and while everyone cheats with each other's boyfriends from time to time, this was different. But there was no way out without completely ruining my reputation, and, besides, I had the memory of how I'd been used before and how this time it would last all night. Feeling a bitch, but a very randy bitch, I accepted.

On the night, I told Sammy I was ill and sneaked out the back, to be taken to a house at the lonely east end of the island in Lewis' car. When I went inside, I found that they had it all worked out. They were going to get drunk and watch a dirty video, while I was the live entertainment.

I was sat on the sofa between Carl and Paul, who quickly pulled my tits out and began to fondle one each, making my nipples hard. They put the video on, some American thing starring a black guy with a huge cock and two girls. They were supposed to be secretaries while he was a window cleaner, but it didn't matter, because they were all next to nude within five minutes of the start. The guys were laughing and making dirty jokes as the girls in the film stripped off, but I could tell they were turned on by the attention paid to my tits.

'Tell you what,' Pete laughed. 'Whatever they do, Linda's got to do it, yeah?'

Everyone agreed and I more or less had to go along with it, only asking them not to do anything really perverted. First I had to strip to my knickers and shoes, which was all the girls had on. Then one of the girls went down on the black guy and they all started arguing over who I was going to have to suck off. Carl won, of course, by which time the black guy was jerking his cock over the girl's open mouth.

'Yeah, right in it!' Saul called out.

The black guy's cock spurted up, sending a jet of white muck right into the girl's face. Most of it went in her mouth, but there were blobs on her lips and nose and a long strand remained behind, joining the tip of his thing with her tongue. She stuck it out and I could see that it was covered in spunk. He was still wanking, and a second smaller spurt came out, landing right on her tongue, to leave her with two long, sticky strands running between mouth and cock.

The other girl came up, crawling with her big tits swinging under her chest. She kissed the man's cock and licked his balls. Then the two girls kissed and pulled apart, leaving long streamers of the man's muck hanging between their faces.

'Oh yeah, gross!' Pete said.

'Shame we haven't got another tart,' Saul added. 'We could make Linda do that!'

The idea was greeted with whoops of delight while I

found myself blushing and thinking of how Penny and I had kissed with our mouths full of the taste of what we'd swallowed. It looked really disgusting as I watched the bubbly white filth trickle out around the girls' mouths on the screen, but I was desperately hoping that they'd make me do it.

'Yeah, great,' Carl answered him. 'But right now, she needs her mouth spunking in. Get on the floor, Linda.'

The others gathered round to watch as I slid to the floor and knelt between his feet. He had moved to the edge of the sofa, and his big white cock was sticking out right at my face.

'Suck it 'til I say, then I'll do it in your mouth,' he ordered.

I leant forward, gaping wide to take it in. It was hot and rubbery in my mouth, tasting all lovely and male as I began to suck. He groaned and put his hands down to my tits, which were still out of my top. It felt so nice with his big cock in my mouth and all of them watching me suck him. My pussy ached with the need to come, and I decided to diddle myself in front of them, whatever they thought of me. I parted my knees and put my hands down the front of my knickers, finding my pussy soaking with juice and my bump all nice and hard between my lips.

'She's wanking!' someone said behind me.

He sounded delighted, but also a little disgusted. I paused, suddenly less sure of myself. At that instant, Carl whipped his cock out of my mouth and pulled my head back by the hair. I gaped, as I knew it was supposed to go in my mouth. The end of his thing was jiggling about in front of my face, purple and glossy with my spit. Then it jerked and a thick wad of spunk shot out, going right into my mouth, then another, catching my nose and chin. His hand tightened against the back of my head as he forced his cock back into me. He was still coming and I could feel my mouth filling with salty slime and the others cheered and clapped. Then he was pulling out, leaving a trail of muck hanging between his cock and my lip, just like the girl in the film.

'Go on, Lindy, eat it up!' someone jeered.

I began to chew on my mouthful as they cheered me on and made noises of disgust and amazement. A blob of spunk was hanging from my nose and I could feel it wet on my cheek. I didn't mind at all; it was lovely, and I really had to come, then and there. I started to bubble Carl's muck up around my lips and let it dribble down my chin as I began to rub myself once more. I was in heaven, almost coming, opening my filth-filled mouth in the hope of another cock being put in it, crying out, only to be silenced as I got my wish.

Saul had stuffed his cock in my mouth just as I was coming, and I gagged on it as my pleasure exploded in my head. There was no getting away from it, though. He had me by the head and was fucking my mouth, even as I felt strong hands take me by the hips and something bump against the seat of my knickers. The next moment they were torn down and it was bumping first against my bare bum-cheeks, then between them, and then at the entrance to my pussy.

I felt myself fill and then, whoever it was, started to slam into me, smacking his front hard against my bum with each push. From then on I was lost, in heaven while I was used repeatedly, in my mouth, up my pussy, between my tits, even along the crease of my bum. I was made to suck cocks that had been in my pussy, and lick spunk from fingers that had been everywhere. My tits were squeezed until they were sore, and my bottom rubbed and groped until I felt like I'd been whacked. When the big black guy in the film put his balls in a girl's mouth, I was given the same treatment. Fortunately, when a girl got fucked up her bottom, they decided it had gone too far, and I was spared the pain and indignity of having a cock forced up my behind.

Only when the film finished did they finally stop, and even then I had to beg for a break to get Lewis off my tits. After a while, we started again: more gently and without the least inhibition. I had lost my knickers and top, and stayed nude for the rest of the evening, only occasionally breaking off from sex for a beer. Eventually, I was too exhausted to move and could only lie on the floor with my legs apart while Carl fucked me yet again and finished off triumphantly over my bush.

That was it for me. It was all I could do to crawl to the bathroom, with them laughing at the display I was making of my bottom and the state they had put me in. All I knew was that I had never come so many times in my life, and that I badly needed a bath.

While the bath ran, I used the bathroom mirror to try and get the worst of the mess out of my hair. I could see the window behind myself in the reflection and thought I saw a movement outside. Just as I had decided that I was dreaming, it came again, and this time there was no mistake. It was there at the window – a head, red-haired and freckly, the eyes staring crazily at my naked body. I screamed in shock and surprise even as I realised who it was – Ryan, the local creep.

That really put the dampers on the party. Carl and Pete went outside, but couldn't find him. Afterwards, we had another beer, but the mood was broken and I just wanted to go home. Gary agreed and the two of us went, even though it was miles and the lighthouse fog warning had started to go.

Outside was really creepy, with a thick fog that our torch could hardly get through. The lighthouse beam only made it worse, blinding us repeatedly. There was also the thought that Ryan was out there somewhere, and I put my arm around Gary for comfort. The poor guy had had to sit and watch me have sex all evening, and kept talking about what I'd done and what had been on the video as we went. I felt sorry for him, and was wishing I could do something. When we reached the railway crossing, we decided to follow the tracks. We were silent for a while, concentrating on stepping from sleeper to sleeper, then Gary suddenly spoke.

'Jesus, Lindy, I feel randy.'

'Gary! Have a wank, then,' I answered, feeling shocked but with a helpless naughtiness underneath. If he asked, I knew I'd do it.

'Do it for me, Lindy: just your hand,' he said, really pleading.

'Gary!' I protested, thrilled and also disgusted, especially by the implication that I might have been willing to use my mouth – or worse.

'Look, Lindy, I've got it out,' he replied.

I turned the torch on him. His cock was sticking out from his trousers like a little flagpole: well, quite a big flagpole, actually. Nobody could call my brother under-endowed. I hesitated, wanting to help but feeling really bad about it. Sober, I would never have dared, but I was far from sober. With a huge lump in my throat, I reached my hand out and touched his cock. He sighed aloud as my hand folded round it and I began to tug on the thick shaft. I was full of guilt and shame, but he was hard and hot in my hand and it felt lovely, and really exciting, more so than any of the much ruder things I had done that evening.

There, shielded from the world by the dark fog and the banks of the railway cutting, I took my own brother's cock in my hand and brought him off. When he spurted, he said my name and then thanked me, after which we remained silent all the way back home.

The next day, my feelings were really mixed up. I felt guilty for all I'd done, and unsure of myself as well. Also, the whole thing seemed to be getting out of control. Not only was I in so deep that there seemed no way out, but Ryan now knew, which meant the secret was no longer with just the guilty ones.

I couldn't deny my pleasure: just the memory of having sucked all those lovely cocks was enough to make me shiver, never mind having been entered and fondled by four hunky men! As for what I'd done with Gary, I told myself it had been no big deal. Just a favour for a very sweet brother – just something I'd done because he needed it so badly and no harm had been done by it.

The guys were well pleased with themselves and seemed to think the whole thing was one big joke. They had also latched on to the idea of me doing it with another girl, which really turned me on but made my guilty feelings even worse. To them it was just funny, in particular the idea of me going down on her, which for some reason they seemed to find hilarious.

I knew they were talking about it, and I knew what was going to happen. You see, Penny and I weren't the first girls they had gang-banged. They had caught my friend Becky the same way, a few weeks earlier, offering her a lift home and then taking turns with her in the back of Lewis' car. She'd told me how it had been, with her tits pulled out of her top and her jeans and knickers around her ankles while they had her one by one, blow-jobs at first and then fucking. She had giggled a lot when telling me, but had come to regret it when rumours had started to get out. But not everybody knew, and I could just see them trying to persuade us into giving them a girlie show.

I am not a lesbian, but Becky did have a nice body. She was taller than me, with bigger boobs and bum, which the guys really went for. We were close as well, and used to cuddle occasionally, but never anything rude. I remembered how it had felt with Penny, and could well see myself letting go.

Which is just what I did. The guys kept talking but did nothing until I happened to mention it to Pete and Saul. They were in the pub where I work, and teasing me about going with Penny. I was the one who brought up Becky's name and, by closing time, I had agreed to do it if she would.

She agreed.

That Sunday, they took us out to the old fort on Ray Island. The causeway out to it gets cut off so, for as long as the tide was high, we would have complete peace. Nobody could get to us; nobody could even see us. Part of the fort was overlooked by the fort on top of Sussex Hill. This had been made into flats but, as long as we kept close to the walls, even that was invisible. We could also see the very top of a big German observation tower called the Palace, because it looked like an old-fashioned cinema. Neither really bothered me. There was actually a little thrill from knowing that we could be seen, but weren't likely to be.

They made us start with a striptease, undressing each over while they egged us on to expose more, and to touch each other. I was feeling giggly and shy, but Becky was a lot bolder and really played to the crowd. She seemed to want to be in control, too, and quickly had me down to my knickers while she still had most of her clothes on. She made to take my knickers down, but I at least wanted her topless before I went nude. As she knelt down to take hold of my knickers, I suddenly jerked her top up. Her bra came with it and her big tits flopped out, all bare. The guys cheered and clapped. Then my knickers had been jerked down and I was showing off my bare bum and bush.

That started a game of chase, with me trying to get Becky's knickers off. We ran all over the fort, heedless of the chance of being seen, and I finally managed to catch her and pull down her knickers. She struggled while I stripped her, and then she was bare and my arms were going round her as if it was the most natural thing in the world. The guys had caught up and cheered to see us cuddling, then started to make suggestions as to what we should do with each other.

It wasn't like we were lesbians or anything, because we were doing it to turn the guys on. It was nice, though, and from the moment I cuddled Becky into my arms, I knew we would go all the way. She kissed me and I put my hands on her bottom and squeezed. It felt very different from a man's bum, softer and fuller, but it was sexy.

We had a good cuddle and a snog, feeling each other's tits and bums to show off for the boys, who soon got turned on. Sure enough, just as I was really starting to get into Becky's body, Carl said that it was time for their fun. All five of them converged on us at his word, Saul and Gary already with their erect cocks sticking out of their trousers.

Becky and I were made to do everything: wank them, suck their cocks and balls, take them between our tits and up the creases of our bums and, of course, fuck. They made us kneel side by side for the fucking, starkers with our bums up and our arms around each other's shoulders.

Lewis had me first, and came up me with his fat belly resting on my bottom while Carl did Becky.

Lewis came all over my bottom almost before he'd got a rhythm going, but Saul had rolled me over and mounted me as I was still catching my breath. He took longer, fucking until I was dizzy with pleasure and then spunking up all over my bush. Carl was still in Becky, and Gary was behind him, his erection held out like a pole. For a moment, I thought Gary was going to mount me, and I'm not sure I'd have stopped him, but instead he put his cock in Becky's mouth.

Pete had already come between my tits, but had managed to get hard again and mounted me as Carl finished off up Becky. She was moaning and her face was set in a look of total bliss as Gary pulled his cock free of her mouth and mounted her from the rear. Pete came up me even as I heard Gary grunt and knew he'd shot his load up Becky.

Without really thinking about it, Becky and I crawled into a sixty-nine and began to lick at each other. The guys were watching, fascinated but also a bit disgusted, because now our passion for each other was real. Becky's pussy was right in my mouth and I was licking her clit hard while her hands were cupping my bum and her tongue was doing marvellous things to me. I didn't care about the guys; all I wanted was the lovely soft flesh of the girl who was taking me to heaven.

Pretty quickly, Becky started having her orgasm. Each time her hole shut, a little wad of come would squirt into my face, and with that, I started to come myself. It was blinding, one of the best, with our faces buried in each other's pussies and our hands gripping each other's bums, licking and licking until everything was spent.

The next day, I was at a loose end. It was a glorious day, and everyone else was at the beach or working, but I found myself drawn to Sussex Hill. I wanted to know just how much of Ray Island fort was visible, and in how much detail, or at least that was what I told myself. Deep down, I just wanted to be alone and to try and come to terms with just how much I had enjoyed sex with Becky.

Like most of the island, the top of Sussex Hill is covered with old German fortifications, and I had soon found one that let me eat blackberries while I stared out over the sea and thought. I could see France in the distance, with a big ferry moving up the choppy water in between, while Ray Island looked as if I could have dropped a stone down into it. The place where Becky and I had got it on was invisible, but it might have been possible to glimpse us while we were playing chase.

My eyes turned back to the ferry, and my thoughts to Penny. When I'd known her before, she had been such a timid girl, shy and quiet. I could hardly believe how she had changed, breezing into the island on a plane from France and breezing out again, as free as the wind. She'd told me that she'd hitch-hiked through France, alone. She'd also had sex with a trucker and a couple from Cherbourg, acts so wild, so crazy that they seemed totally beyond my horizons. Suddenly the island – which had always been my life – seemed a dull, restrictive place, and the French coast was no longer just a piece of scenery, but a place I yearned to be.

I was feeling jealous and was wondering if I dared just chuck it all in and take up her offer, when I was interrupted by a voice calling my name. Feeling cross at whoever it was, I turned my head to find a bald, middle-aged man coming towards me through the gorse and bramble. It was Mr Blundel, a regular at the pub where I worked, one of the people from the flats in Fort Sussex, and about the last person I wanted to see. I didn't like him anyway, but was immediately concerned that he might have seen Becky and me. The bit where we had been playing catch was certainly in view from his windows. We'd been mostly in the nude, but it was a long way off, so he couldn't have seen anything really rude, but still . . .

He said nothing dodgy, but asked if I could help him search for his glasses: which seemed reasonable, until he claimed to have dropped them into a pond that had formed at the bottom of an old concrete tank-like thing. The idea was that I wade in and search with my toes, which meant taking off my shoes, socks and – surprise, surprise – my jeans.

I knew his game. His glasses probably weren't even in the pond; the dirty old bastard just wanted to see my knickers. It was difficult, because he was one of the best customers at the pub where I worked and I couldn't just tell him to fuck off. Instead, I refused as politely as I could, only for the look on his face to turn from a sort of false friendliness to annoyance.

'For goodness sake,' he sneered. 'Don't be silly. Do you think you really need to worry about a man of my age seeing you in your pants? I'm old enough to be your father. Now come along and take off your trousers. In fact, it would be sensible if you took off your pants, as well; I think it's quite deep in the middle.'

His voice was commanding, as if he were trying to order me to do it. For a moment, I felt that he was right – I was being silly, worrying about him seeing me bare. Then he laughed, as if to make my reluctance to strip off seem ridiculous, but with a nervous edge that showed him up for the dirty old sod he really was.

'No, Mr Blundel,' I answered firmly. 'I don't think that's a very good idea.'

'Honestly, Linda,' he went on, still trying to sound firm. 'Do you know something? I think you'd benefit from a good spanking!'

'Mr Blundel!'

'Come now, let's have those trousers and pants down now, or I shall have to take them down and then you'll get a red bottom for your trouble!'

'No, I won't!'

He was red-faced and I could see the lump in his trousers. He didn't just want to smack my bottom, he was going to get off on it!

'Let me put it another way, then,' he snapped. 'Either you do as I say, or your parents will hear about what you got up to down on Ray Island yesterday; and your employers, too, perhaps.'

The angry put-down I had been about to use died on my

lips. He knew! But he couldn't, or at least not more than that Becky and I had been running around in the nude; he really couldn't know the rude bits! But I was blushing hot and knew he had seen something, because the angry look on his face had turned to a wicked grin. I hesitated, trying to find a way out.

'Come on, love,' he continued, wheedling now. 'It's not much to ask. Just a nice show of your bare bottom and perhaps a little feel and a light spanking. Then you can take my cock in your hand and it'll soon be over . . .'

'OK, OK,' I answered hastily, as the picture of him fondling my bum while I jerked him off rose up in my mind. 'But . . . but not today. It's . . . you know . . . that time of the month.'

'But you'll do it?'

'I'll do it, but not now. I'll dress sexy, too, in a mini skirt; I've got a leather one . . .'

'A summer dress,' he said decisively. 'That yellow one you wear when you go down to the beach, with white knickers underneath and no bra. When will you be ready?'

'The day after tomorrow: no, the one after that, and please don't tell.'

'Oh, don't worry about that, but you had better not be trying to fool me. Now, how about a flash of that lovely bottom to show me you mean it?'

I turned, popped my jeans button and, as briefly as I could, pulled down my trousers. My knickers went with them, and for a moment I was showing him my bare bum. Then I was covered again and making a hasty departure down the track.

My mind was in whirl as I walked back to town. I had put him off, but that was all. In just three days' time, I was going to have to do as he said or that was my reputation blown sky-high. It would have been pretty unbearable for people to know that I'd let myself go with Carl and the guys, but to be known as a lesbian would be worse, far worse! The thought of Mr Blundel's hands crawling all over my bottom – and doubtless my boobs and pussy too – was awful, but not that awful. If he'd wanted to fuck me,

I'd have let him tell and then set Carl on him afterward, but as it was I knew I was going to have to do it.

All the way back I thought about it. He'd make me lift my summer dress and pull down my knickers. He'd feel my bum up and probably touch my hole. He'd pull my tits out and put a finger up my pussy. He'd take his dirty old cock out and make me wank him while he felt me. I'd probably be in the nude by then, and maybe with a stingy bottom if he'd decided I needed spanking.

It was awful, thinking of making myself a sex toy for a dirty old man. He'd always leched over me, but now I was going to have to do it, and all because I'd let myself get carried away. When I got home and changed for work, I found that the gusset of my knickers was soaking with juice, which was even worse.

On the way to work I felt that I had reached the depths of confusion and shame. I'd done some things that I'd always been taught to believe were really bad, and I was faced with the prospect of having to do worse. But I'd enjoyed it all, and I had the awful feeling that if I let Mr Blundel have me, it would turn me on. I wouldn't enjoy it, but it would turn me on. I felt terrible, thoroughly ashamed of myself and excited at the same time, a condition that I couldn't imagine getting any worse until I came on duty behind the bar.

Ryan was there, as smug and slimy as ever, sitting in a window seat with his Walkman on and looking at me with his creepy grin. I knew he was after me. I mean, what else would he be doing there? He had chosen his night carefully as well, because there was a big beach party going on down at the east end of the island and all the younger people would be there.

I tried to phone Gary to collect me after work, but he had left the house. After two more frantic calls, I managed to get Lewis, who promised to pass my message on. All I could do was hope, and I spent the rest of the evening feeling really nervous and drinking far more vodka than was good for me. Ryan stayed in his seat, sipping a pint and occasionally looking at me in a way that made my flesh crawl. Finally closing time came and he left, giving me a last look as he went out of the door.

It would have been easy to get a lift home, but I've always been stubborn and I didn't see why Ryan should stop me going to the beach party. Telling myself that he was just a lech and wouldn't actually dare to do anything, I declined my boss's offer of a lift.

In the square outside, the night was warm and quiet, eerily quiet. I had goosebumps and a horrid, shivery feeling in the back of my neck, as if someone was watching me. Immediately, my stubbornness seemed very silly. I was sure Ryan was watching me, probably from the shadows of one of the little lanes that join the square.

I wanted to run, but made myself walk, starting at every shadow as I made for the busier part of town. A light at the end of the street made a puddle of welcoming yellow glow, but it was dark between it and me. I hurried on, then stopped at a noise to one side: a step, then another, then a dark, tall figure stepped out from the end of a lane.

My heart went into my throat, and I felt myself start to panic as thoughts of rape came up in my mind. Then I realised it was not Ryan, but Gary. He saw the state I was in and immediately put his arms round me, cuddling me into his broad, hard chest. Immediately I wasn't scared of Ryan any more. In fact I was hoping he'd see, just so the creep would feel jealous that someone else was getting what he could never have. In the near blackness, he would never realise that it was my own brother. As Gary held me close, I whispered into his ear, suggesting that he put his arm round me as we walked.

It was done half in devilment and half for comfort, because although I no longer felt threatened by Ryan, it is a long way out to the east end, and the lights are a long way apart. I was sure Ryan would follow, far enough back to run if he had to, but never too far to lose sight each time we passed under a light. He'd be there, watching jealously, and wishing he had me. I wanted to tease, to get back at him for scaring me, but there was something else as well – the memory of Gary's cock, stiff in my hand on the railway track ...

'Ryan's watching,' I said suddenly. 'Feel my bum, like you were my boyfriend.'

It was an excuse, and I think he knew it, too. I was randy and I wanted my bum felt, and . . . oh, who cares if it was my brother, Gary began to explore my bottom and all I could do was giggle. He was making a real show of it for Ryan, squeezing my cheeks and stroking me as if my bum was his property. It felt lovely, and when he slid a hand between my legs and stroked the material over my pussy, it was just too much.

'Why don't you put your hand down my jeans?' I suggested.

He said nothing, but his hand left the cheeks of my bum and rose to the waistband. It wouldn't go, and I had to undo my belt and popper. Once his hand was in, he gave up pretending and he soon had it down my knickers, feeling my bare cheeks and even teasing a little way between them. I didn't want to stop him; in fact, I was wondering if he'd like to go around to my front. As we came under another patch of light, he said something that showed he was thinking much the same thing.

'My cock's hard, Lindy.'

'I bet it is,' I giggled back.

'Would you wank me off again?'

I nodded my head, trembling at the thought of his cock in my hand.

'What about Ryan?' I asked.

'Let's lose him.'

He ran, pulling his hand from my knickers to catch hold of mine and pull me behind him. I was stumbling and laughing as we went, dashing blindly down the road towards the next light. As we rounded a gentle bend, Gary suddenly pulled me off the road, up a bank and in among a thick stand of pine trees.

We waited, crouched down among the dark trees with the scent of resin strong in the air. Gary's hand was over my mouth to stop me giggling. I could hear a car in the distance but as the engine noise faded, I heard footsteps, brisk at first, then slower. It was Ryan, I just knew it.

It felt great, watching silently as he came closer. For a moment he was visible, and sure enough, it was Ryan, gawky and creepy as ever, sneaking slowly along and imagining he was following us. He probably thought I was with one of the other guys and was hoping to watch me have my tits felt up or something, because the expression on his face was really dirty.

I put my arm back around Gary, feeling a little scared by the way Ryan looked and the thought that all that dirtiness was directed at me. Gary's hand left my mouth, moving down, but not away, on to my chest to cup one of my boobs under my jumper. I should have stopped him, but I stayed quiet and let him feel, with my breath coming quicker as my nipple stiffened under his fingers. I felt guilty, badly guilty, but I couldn't stop myself; the feeling was just too nice. He continued to feel me as the sound of Ryan's footsteps faded away; my pleasure rose as the chance of being found decreased.

Sensing my resignation to what we were doing, he began to pull my top up and quickly had my tits out. Then it was my jeans, pulled off along with my trainers and socks as I lay on my back among the soft pine needles. My knickers came last, and with them went my last hope of retaining the slightest bit of decency. He began to explore me, feeling my body and whispering compliments – first my tits and tummy, then my hips and bum, then my pussy. He put a finger in me and began to rub me and that was it, all I could do was spread my thighs apart, and ask softly for him to take me.

He came forward, kneeling between my legs and taking my hand to put it on his cock. It was rock-hard and felt huge in my hand as I guided it towards my pussy. He followed the pressure, and then his cock touched my pussy. He was going to do it, he was actually going to fuck his own sister. I could feel the knob of his cock against my hole – round and warm. He pushed, and then I was opening and he was coming inside, filling me with lovely thick, hard meat. I heard myself groan as he slid inside me, a noise of hopeless surrender as much as of passion. Then his arms had come under my shoulders and my own had closed around his back as we began to fuck.

I thought he'd come quickly and was hoping he'd have the sense to pull out and do it over my belly, even through my ecstasy. Instead, he settled down to a good rhythm, really letting me get the feel of what we were doing. After a while, he rose and rolled me up so that my legs were against my tits and my pussy stuck right out, then he entered me again.

Somehow, that made it an even dirtier thing to be doing. What had started as raw need had become much more deliberate as he moved my body about to get the full pleasure from me. I didn't care. We stayed with my legs up for quite a while, and again I thought he was going to come, only for him to once more pull out.

'Go in doggy,' he panted.

I giggled as I rolled over and presented him with my bum. He put his cock back in me and began to hump, laughing at the grunting noises I was making as we fucked. I wanted to come, and reached back to rub my bump, only for him to pull out again and demand to have his cock sucked. Of course I did it, playing with myself while I licked and sucked at his lovely hard cock and tasted him mixed up with my own juice.

After that, we just went wild, sucking and fucking in every way we could think of, not to mention snogging and having a thoroughly good feel of each other. He put it between my tits and along my bum-slit, sucked my nipples and kissed my pussy, even put a finger in my bumhole when I asked him to do it. I came like that, with his finger up my bum and his cock in one hand while I rubbed at myself with the other. I felt a bit bad after my orgasm, but he was in no mood to stop, and he told me to get on my knees so that he could finish off with me in doggy position.

I went and he took me by the hips and began to fuck, really hard this time and clearly near to orgasm. As I'd come, I was feeling more sensible, and guilty again, but it seemed only fair to let him have me, until he started to groan and I knew he was going to come up me.

'Not in me!' I managed. 'Rub it up my bum or something!'

He gave a last few, hard shoves, then pulled out and settled his cock between the cheeks of my bottom. He began to rut between them, with his cock rubbing on my bumhole and his balls slapping on my pussy. His hands were on my bum, squeezing it and squashing his cock between my cheeks.

'Christ, you're a good fuck, Lindy,' he growled. 'Oh, yeah, I'm going to come, Lindy! I'm coming, sis, I'm coming, all up your lovely bum!'

I felt his mess splash out over my bottom, right in the crease and all over my back. Then he was rubbing his cock in it, all hot and slimy between my bum-cheeks as he finished off. Finally, he wiped his prick on my bum and it was over.

The next day I felt a lot better than I had expected to. I knew I'd done something I shouldn't have done, but it was more like sharing a naughty secret than of feeling really bad about something, like I might have done if I'd pinched money from the till at work. I suppose it's one of those things that seems dreadful until you do it, but it had been nice, really nice.

For the next two days, my only worry was the approaching meeting with Mr Blundel. I thought of a dozen ways of getting out of it; but, other than simply leaving the island, every one seemed likely to get me into more trouble than it solved. On the morning of the third day, I was really starting to worry and could only think of how his hands were going to feel groping my bum and tits, wondering whether he would spank me and how much it would hurt.

Then a letter arrived addressed to me and what was in it blew all thoughts of Mr Blundel out of my mind. It was a tape, nothing more.

It all seemed a bit weird, so I took it up to my room and listened with the head-phones on, which was just as well, because the first thing I heard was the sounds of my own passion and then Gary's voice calling me Lindy and sis, and asking me to go in doggy position. Next came Ryan's voice telling me that, unless I wanted copies of the tape circulated, I had better meet him that evening in the very same pine copse. He ended with a very clear statement of what he was going to do when we met – he wanted to fuck me up my bottom.

I sat on my bed, feeling numb, and thinking of Ryan's cock going up my bum-hole. My jeans and knickers would be peeled down and the little hole between my cheeks greased up. Then he'd push his cock up my bottom. Worse still, it would happen after my meeting with Mr Blundel, and my poor bum would be red from spanking, which Ryan would see. No, it was not going to happen. I was not going to be spanked and I was not going to be bum-fucked!

There was only one thing for it. With trembling fingers, I reached for my address book and found Penny Birch's number in England.

. . . and guess who was the first to spank her sweet little bottom! I also led indirectly to her getting buggered. That was by Henry Gresham, and is another story but not the one presented here.

Henry is Amber's Godfather and he appeared in Penny in Harness *and* A Taste of Amber. *He is big and gentle and kind, but also the most skilful male spanker of girls' bottoms I've met, not to mention an expert pony-girl master. Amber is very fond of him and occasionally lets him spank me or has me suck what is the third largest penis I've had inside me. His story is a fairy tale but also an allegory which many people would do well to take notice of . . .*

The Story of the Ice Princess – Henry Gresham

This is the story of the Ice Princess, and it is a story with a moral. It is also a dirty story.

Once upon a time, there was a knight who sought to achieve servitude to the ideal lady. To him, the lightest glance of any woman was an honour, and yet he knew that true fulfilment was only possible as the basest slave of the loftiest of all women. Many rumours had reached him of women said to be of flawless beauty, and absolute purity of soul; yet among all these the undoubted paragon was the Ice Princess.

The Ice Princess was said to live in a tower in the far north. A great wood full of wolves and bears and beasts yet more dire surrounded the tower. Beyond the wood was a pinnacle of ice a thousand feet high and as smooth as glass. At the summit of the mountain stood a castle guarded by a giant carnivorous ape, and in the topmost tower of the castle dwelt the Ice Princess.

To be accepted into her service was said to be the highest honour that a mere man could achieve, and it was this honour that the knight sought. He knew full well that to serve her meant frequent whippings, sleeping naked and bound at the foot of her bed, and treating her lightest whim as an unbreakable command. Yet all this he sought, as it was the natural order of existence for man to be slave to woman, and it was his destiny to be the perfect slave to the perfect woman.

Taking leave of his exclusively male retainers, the knight set out on his quest. He rode for a hundred leagues and set sail for a further hundred. Arriving in a port that swirled with the colours and scents of a hundred races of man, he sought out a wise man and put to him this question:

'I seek the perfect woman, whom I shall serve with absolute devotion. Do you know of the Ice Princess?'

'The Ice Princess I believe to be a fable,' replied the wise man, 'but at the edge of the desert lives the Fire Witch, who drives a chariot pulled by twelve men. Their devotion to her is as absolute as that of a drunk to his bottle, so perhaps it is she whom you seek.'

'And is she perfect?'

'She is said to be. I have not seen her. Yet, in my experience, which spans near four-score years, the beauty of woman is overrated. Moreover, great beauty is often correlated with arrogance, vanity, callousness and other vices. My advice would be to seek a plump wench, merry and of moderate looks, who is skilled in the culinary and cock-sucking arts. Beauty fades, humour and cooking skill do not; while my wife's performance at fellatio has improved notably since she lost the last of her teeth.'

Undeterred by the wise man's irreverence, the knight set forth for the desert. Towards sundown he came to a cottage, at which he sought lodging. A woman answered the door, a comely peasant wench, full-chested and round of haunch. Aware that he was in the presence of one of the higher sex, even if not an especially elevated specimen, the knight bowed low and requested the honour of lodging in her barn.

She answered that he might, but on condition that he performed three tasks: cleaning the stables, slaying a basilisk that was menacing the local community and accepting in her stead a whipping ordained by her liegelord. The knight accepted. The next morning he cleaned the stables by diverting a stream through them and killed the basilisk by using his highly polished shield as a mirror. At noon, he was whipped through the village at the tail of a cart.

Filled with a sense of having provided services to one of the higher sex and of sparing her the ignominy of being stripped, paraded in public and beaten with canes, the knight continued on his way. After some time, he came upon a beggar urchin seated by the road, soiled with grime and with her clothes no more than tatters on her body.

Filled with dismay that a woman should be in so demeaned a state, he offered to wash her, provide food for her, and give her his magnificent cloak of blue cloth. All this she accepted and, when she had bathed, eaten and wrapped herself in the cloak, she proved to be a veritable paragon of beauty. Aroused by the sight, he asked if she might not enjoy making more intimate use of his poor body. She accepted and bade him lie in the dirt. Mounting him, she spent a full two hours riding his erect penis, tearing at his clothes in her ecstasy and reaching many climaxes. When she finally dismounted, he was left soiled with grime and his clothes no more than tatters on his body.

As the day progressed, the landscape became ever more arid and finally gave way to a desert of flame-coloured sand. Here was a great structure of massive stone blocks sheltered among an oasis of palms and feathery undergrowth. Addressing himself to the door, he was greeted by a tall woman of haughty beauty whose hair matched the burning red sand of the desert. Immediately he sank to his belly and kissed the ground at her feet, then gave his rehearsed speech.

'O Fire Witch, I have travelled far for the honour of serving as your meanest slave. I humbly entreat you to accept me in the knowledge that I may be whipped, tied and used for intimate services as you dictate. Set me a task and I shall endeavour to prove myself worthy.'

'You have already proved worthy,' the Witch replied, with a smile that showed how much greater her intelligence was than his own. 'For both the peasant wench and the urchin were myself and you served both well, despite their lowly status.'

Awed by the witch's refined perception and innate sense

of justice, the knight squirmed in the sand. He was taken to the stables and the least satisfactory of the twelve slaves was dismissed. The knight was then haltered, tethered and left in the stable to await his new mistress's needs. At first he stood in a lather of anticipation, awaiting the moment when she would come and use him. He imagined that he would be first horse-whipped, then made to give her a tongue bath which would finish at her perfect vulva.

Nobody came that night, nor the next, save only the stable boy with their feed. On the third night, it became evident to him that the witch only wished to use him as a draught beast and had no need for his erotic services. This conclusion was further borne out on the fourth night when the Fire Witch entertained three local girls. All evening, shrieks of feminine laughter rang out from the witch's mansion, and before midnight these had changed to cries of abandoned ecstasy and weird climactic screams. None of the males were called upon to assist.

On the fifth day, the knight determined that he had been mistaken in assuming the Fire Witch to be the perfect lady. Clearly, she had no use for male slaves save to pull her chariot, and that seldom. His need was to give complete and unreserved service, not to spend his time chained in a stable with eleven other men.

Chewing through his halter with his teeth, he retrieved his horse and arms and fled the manse of the Fire Witch. For a day, she pursued him in her chariot, but for all her goading of the human draught beasts, she rapidly fell behind his horse.

Continuing to the north and east, the knight came into a land of open, windy skies and great expanses of rolling corn. Here he chanced upon a scythe-man plying his trade near the roadside. Impressed by the look of erudition on the old man's face, the knight put his question:

'I seek the perfect woman, whom I will serve with absolute devotion. Do you know of the Ice Princess?'

'I do not,' replied the scythe-man, 'but this is the kingdom of Gravitas, and it is unthinkable that the qualities of your Ice Princess could exceed those of Queen Narcissa.'

'And is she perfect?'

'Unquestionably. To say otherwise is to be raised on a kite one thousand feet into the air, at which point the string is cut.'

'That is a just and appropriate fate for entertaining such a spiteful doubt.'

'None who have suffered it have claimed otherwise.'

The knight thanked the scythe-man and turned his horse towards the capital city of the Kingdom of Gravitas. Here he sought out the major-domo of the palace but was informed that the queen chose her servants solely from experienced men of proven worth and undoubted loyalty. These were selected exclusively from among men already in service to the nobility of Gravitas.

Undeterred, the knight presented himself to the preceptor of the slave market and demanded to be sold at the next auction. Somewhat puzzled, the preceptor accepted the request and the knight was purchased by Leilla, the daughter of a wealthy merchant. His price was four pecks, roughly that of a sheep after its prime years.

Although her status in trade clearly made her less than perfect, the knight felt honoured to be Leilla's slave. He was kept in her private washroom, chained naked to the cistern by links plated with silver. His tasks were simple: cleaning the washroom, towelling and powdering Leilla after her ablutions, and tonguing clean the vulvas and fundaments of her and her female guests when necessary. When he was not being made use of, she paid no heed to him whatsoever.

A week after his purchase, one of the house guests was the Lady Aveline, a maid in waiting to Queen Narcissa and a person of some importance. Following the skilled purification of her anus by the knight, the Lady Aveline gaily asked Leilla if she might take him as her property. Leilla gave him away with no more concern than she was showing to the pips of the orange she was eating at the time.

Service with the Lady Aveline was to the knight a yet higher honour, she being noble and inherently more refined than Leilla. He also lived in the west wing of the palace, where he was employed as lower body servant to his mistress. Again his place was in the washroom, and again he was naked and chained by his neck to the cistern. The chain, however, was of pure silver and his services of a yet more intimate nature. It amused the Lady Aveline to use his mouth in place of her chamberpot, and this she did each evening, putting him into a state of submissive bliss. On viewing his straining erection after the first such act, she made quick use of it and then had him tongue her to a climax. This became a regular practice, and the Lady Aveline began to boast of his prowess as a toilet slave.

When word of this reached the ears of Queen Narcissa, the knight was immediately sent for. The Queen proved to be a woman of great height and proud bearing. Her face was veiled and her body covered by voluminous robes to spare her the gaze of the vulgar, yet even kneeling at the foot of her throne put the knight into hitherto unparalleled ecstasy. The Lady Aveline gave him into the custody of the Queen's major-domo with all the meekness appropriate towards one who commands life and death.

Certain that he had finally found his destiny, the knight was led to the Queen's washroom and chained to the cistern with links of pure, fine gold. All that day he trembled with excitement and his erection remained solid despite two involuntary ejaculations.

When at last the Queen came to her washroom and lifted her veil, she proved to be not only considerable older than both Leilla and the Lady Aveline, but a good deal less beautiful. Further distances from the dominant ideal were revealed when she dropped her gown to reveal breasts of uneven size, a belly notably inclined to sag and pendulous labia. As final proof of her lack of perfection, her face showed neither composure nor high intelligence, but only vanity and spite.

Realising his mistake, the knight stunned her with a chamberpot, broke the feeble gold links of the chain and made a hasty retreat. The Queen, being naked and half-conscious, was unable to follow. Stealing her robes, arms and a horse, he managed to escape the palace by impersonation. Thus he won free, and although he was followed for three days by men in balloons and on kites, he evaded capture.

Continuing to the north, the knight reached a place where the road ran between low, barren hills and stone outcrops. Here he came to find a hut built of crude rocks outside which sat a white-bearded hermit. The man's sagacity was evident in the length of his beard, so the knight put the question to him:

'I seek the perfect woman, whom I will serve with absolute devotion. Do you know of the Ice Princess?'

'I know of no Ice Princess,' replied the hermit, 'but a hundred miles to the east begins the realm of Cis-Pyridine, which is ruled over by the Empress Jhavaxan, who is said to be the daughter of the Lord of Hell himself.'

'And is she perfect?'

'She keeps ten thousand male slaves, ten of whom are culled each day and replaced with a further ten. To look on her naked body is death, yet each night all ten thousand vie to be taken to her bedchamber. Could there be a more lofty ideal of womanhood?'

Thanking the hermit, the knight went on his way, determined that in the terrible Empress he had finally found his perfect lady. True, to serve her was said to be to die, yet he was confident that his quality as a slave would trigger her undoubted sense of magnanimity.

After a long ride across a country of wooded hills and long, cold lakes he reached the capital city of Cis-Pyridine. The palace was evident, a great structure of grey granite that towered above the rest of the city. Passing through streets thronged almost entirely with women and children, he approached the massive edifice and was admitted.

On applying to the Constable of Gigolos, he was stripped and taken into the inner palace on a silver chain. There he was led into a great chamber, in which sat ninety-nine other men, each seeking the privilege of becoming one of the Empress Jhavaxan's ten-thousand gigolos. Each of the men was a model of virility, young, tall and well muscled, yet the knight knew no despair, for he had faith.

After a dinner of cold gruel served in a trough at the centre of the chamber, the constable returned to lead the men into the presence of the board of judgement. Here, the least pulchritudinous of the applicants were taken away to an unknown fate. Those who were judged bereft of adequate wit, or whose breath smelt badly, were also removed, until only twenty remained. These twenty were divided into pairs and ordered to wrestle, the winner of each bout becoming a successful applicant. The knight triumphed over his adversary and was thus admitted to serve in slavery to the Empress.

For three weeks the knight remained in the seraglio, oiling his body and performing exercises in the hope that he might eventually be allowed the ultimate honour and called upon to serve in the Empress's bedchamber. At noon of the twenty-second day, he and nine others were called and told that they were to vie for the privilege of service.

To prove himself worthy of the Empress, the knight was ordered to satisfy ten serving-girls with his tongue. He knelt before the first and lifted her skirts, revealing a cunt as plump and sweet as a ripe apricot and thatched with golden down as soft as that of a duckling. With his mind full of the honour of what he was doing, he applied his tongue to the deep furrow at the centre of her womanhood. With a skill born of long worship of the female body he brought her to a climax. Nine more times he repeated the process, each time attaining an added increment of the bliss that came only from serving the superior sex. When the last girl had come to climax, he was chained to the wall, his face still sticky with the divine female exudations. Of the ten suitors, only four succeeded in bringing the full ten serving girls to climax.

Six men were removed, and the Knight stood with the remainder as ten beautiful merchant's daughters entered the room. His penis was already a rigid pole, but at the sight of the girls it began to twitch at the prospect of further worship of the female body. Amid much giggling, all ten girls knelt in a line and threw up their skirts, exposing ten bottoms as round and firm as peaches. At the centre of each bottom was the puckered hole of the girl's anus, and it was these that the suitors were commanded to lick. By the skilful application of his tongue-tip to the interior of each girl's anal aperture, the knight succeeded in exciting all ten, either to the point of climax or to such excitement that they brought themselves to climax by hand.

Of the four contenders, only one other had managed to equal the knight's feat. Now ten ladies of the court were brought in, each as lovely as the dawn and possessed of a serenity that left the knight weak-kneed and trembling. It was commanded that under no circumstances was he to ejaculate. He and his one remaining rival were ordered to kneel in shallow tubs of zinc. With his cock feeling as if it must burst, he watched all ten ladies strip to their corsets and stockings, leaving their breasts thrust out and their bottoms and bellies framed in ruffled silk. One by one the ladies approached the men and danced, flaunting their most intimate secrets inches from the faces of the agonised suitors. Each lady would finish her performance by flooding the mouth of one man or the other with urine, until the knight was kneeling in an inch-deep pool of hot, yellow liquid and in a state of erotic rapture that he had never before known. By repeated recitation of the low man's prayer for stamina within his head, he managed to hold himself back from orgasm. Yet his rival was no less strong of will.

Both men were washed down with buckets of icy water and commanded to lie prone on the floor. Now two of the Empress's own daughters entered the room, both naked save for silken gloves. Each girl was of surpassing beauty and possessed of magnificent hauteur. The knight found himself in the final extremes of passion as one of these exquisite beings, whose toes he felt unworthy to kiss, sank into a squat over his face and took his penis in a gloved hand. Her scent was strong in his head. The beautiful puckered ring of her anus was positioned directly over his mouth. As she began to masturbate him, with her exquisite bottom wobbling just inches from his face, he strained to prevent his ejaculation. Yet he was unable to hold himself, and gave a sigh of defeat, only to hear his rival grunt and hear the other girl's squeal of disgust as her heavy chest and round belly were splashed with vile male ejaculate.

Barely able to stand, and with his penis purple with engorging blood, he was led from the room and to a pair of golden doors twenty feet high, through which he was thrust. With his head swimming with the ecstasy of his coming submission to the will of the Empress, the knight entered the Imperial bedchamber, ready to fall grovelling to the floor and beg for the kiss of his Lady's whip.

But the Empress was old, ugly and clearly mad. Her face showed none of the composed superiority he had sought, but only a deranged savagery. Here, sadly, was no ideal of the higher sex, but only a blood-crazed virago.

Seizing a ceremonial mace, the knight brained the Empress and fought his way out of the palace. Appropriating a horse, he rode for five days before outdistancing the remaining nine thousand, nine hundred and ninety-nine gigolos.

Selling the mace at a market town, the knight once more purchased suitable clothing and arms. For a further fortnight he rode north, across dark, brooding hills and sweeps of grey moorland. At last he came to the borders of a great, dark forest, beside which, in the very shadow of the trees, stood an inn. Pushing inside, he inquired of the innkeeper:

'I seek the perfect woman, whom I will serve with absolute devotion. Do you know of the Ice Princess?'

'Certainly,' replied the innkeeper. 'Our custom comes largely from adventurers seeking to achieve her.'

'At last! A marvel!' declared the Knight. 'And is she truly the quintessence of womanhood?'

'She is said to be pretty, and also winsome,' the innkeeper replied, scratching his nose, 'but she and I do not move in the same circles.'

'What of the reports of knights who have won through to the castle but failed to achieve her exalted standards?'

'None come back.'

'Tonight I will meditate in my room and so purify my thoughts,' the Knight declared. 'Tomorrow I will go forth and complete my quest or die in the attempt.'

'All payment in advance,' the innkeeper replied.

The inn had but one other customer that night, a giant of a man whose rust-stained armour was propped by the fire. Thinking to recognise a kindred spirit, the knight performed an introduction and inquired as to whether the man also sought the Ice Princess.

'Indeed I do,' the giant replied with gruff geniality. 'I am Sigismund the Black and I have travelled over a thousand leagues to have a crack at this legendary wench.'

'I too seek to worship at her feet, although I am of course unworthy,' the knight replied. 'Also I have travelled a great distance.'

'Good journey?' Sigismund demanded, taking a great draught from his mug.

'I have suffered many tribulations and avoided three great temptations, and now my heart is glad, for I near the end of my quest.'

'In Ai-Corahai I slew a sloth-demon, and at an inn by the river Uisage I enjoyed a wench with breasts like melons. Otherwise, it has been a dull journey.'

Colouring slightly at the crudity of his companion's words, the knight continued on a vein more becoming his status as a simple male.

'Given your precedence at this inn, honour demands that I allow you to leave first in the morning.'

'That is a most creditable concession,' Sigismund replied. 'In return, should I achieve the Princess, I give my word that you may bed her every third night until the marriage. The sole provision being that you enjoy her only in her rear passage.'

'Sodomise the Princess? An unthinkable act! Impossible that any of the higher sex should be subjected to such degradation!'

'Please yourself. Personally, I find that the greater number of them thoroughly appreciate a stiff penis up the bumhole.'

With a noncommittal shrug of his massive shoulders, Sigismund the Black returned to his beef bone. For a moment of hot anger, the knight thought of challenging the giant to a duel in order to avenge the insult to the Ice Princess. Yet that would risk robbing her of his servitude and so was not to be countenanced. Also, the giant's armour bore numerous dents and the head of his mace was a ball of spike-encrusted iron some two hand-spans in width.

Throughout the hours of darkness, the knight sought to cleanse his mind of impure thoughts and thus make himself worthy of acceptance as the Princess's slave. This task was rendered difficult by the presence of Sigismund the Black in a neighbouring room. Until shortly before dawn, it was impossible to achieve the state of hopeless adoration needed, owing to the grunts and squeals of delight issuing from the giant and at least two girls whom the knight guessed to be the innkeeper's older daughters.

The knight fasted that morning, while Sigismund took toasted oat cakes, smoked fish, venison, a hot infusion of herbs and a vessel of sweet wine. While the knight prayed, Sigismund teased the girls, then took the eldest roughly over a bench while her father looked on with an indulgent smile. Seeing the girl's broad white bottom bounce to the giant's thrusts and hearing her cries of pleasure, the Knight found it hard to concentrate, yet he knew in his heart that Sigismund was barely worthy to kiss the girl's sandal.

An hour later, the giant left, now fully armoured and swinging his mace, wishing the knight luck as he strode from the inn. For two hours, the knight remained in prayer to the Supreme Mother, and then followed his rival. The darkness of the trees closed about him; yet he knew no fear, for it was his destiny.

As the knight travelled through the forest, the local beasts and monsters were notable only for their absence. Indeed, the signs of them were confined to an occasional patch of blood, fur or scales among the vegetation and it became evident that there were advantages to travelling behind Sigismund the Black.

For two full days he pushed his way through the forest, and on the afternoon of the second day he became aware that what he had thought was a towering cloud was in fact a great pinnacle of ice. Immediately his heart swelled within his breast. Here was the mountain of the Ice Princess, and at its summit stood the castle in which she dwelt, the ideal of feminine superiority.

With renewed vigour he fought his way to the base of the cliff of ice. Warily, the knight considered the daunting prospect of scaling the mountain. A bit of ice struck the ground nearby and drew his eyes upward. High above was the figure of Sigismund the Black, a dark dot against the immense wall of glistening white. A brief search revealed the deep holds cut by the giant and the knight began to climb with no more than a slight sense of irritation for the lessening of his great challenge.

At length he achieved the summit of the ice cliff and stood before the castle. It was a conglomeration of towers and appeared to be built of solid pearl. At the centre stood a tower three times the height of its neighbours, and from its topmost window fluttered a handkerchief of white silk. The gate was clear, a black arch leading into the castle from the far side of a bridge that crossed the moat as a single, narrow span. At the near side of this bridge lay the body of the man-ape, its head crushed, apparently by a single mace blow.

Certain that he had at last achieved his life's purpose, the knight strode forward. In a mounting frenzy of submissive need, he made his way unopposed into the castle and to the central tower. His heart was hammering as he began to climb the spiral stairs that lined the interior of the tower. Despite the evident prowess of Sigismund the Black, the knight had no fear that it might be too late. The giant's attitude was all too evidently improper for a mere male to take when seeking servitude at the feet of the Ice Princess. Inevitably, he would be rejected.

In contrast, the knight sought only to serve the Princess's every whim. With a cool, disdainful word she would order him to his knees and then suffer him to kiss the floor at her feet. Then he would be accepted as her slave, a slave so low, so obedient that she would need no other. He would be whipped regularly, with a thonged lash, as he knelt at the foot of her bed with his hands tied to a post. He would give her tongue baths, starting with her exquisite toes and cleaning her every limb and orifice until he finished by bringing her to climax beneath his tongue. He would sleep naked at the foot of her bed, bound hand and foot and with his penis in a spiked cage to prevent improper erection. Yes, she would be his perfect Lady, his Mistress, his Princess, fulfilling his every need . . .

In a lather of submissive ecstasy, he burst through the door of the chamber. The Ice Princess lay across Sigismund's lap, her beautiful spider's-web gown lifted to her neck and her exquisite bottom naked and spanked to the colour of the setting sun. On her face was a smile of unalloyed serenity.

. . . yes, quite, it was her *need that he should have been fulfilling, and her need was a jolly good spanking, just like mine. The moral is supposed to be never to expect perfection because it is a purely human and highly subjective concept, but I prefer my version.*

My cousin Susan appears in Bad Penny *as a cheeky little girl and then a grown-up rebel. She likes to think of herself as the black sheep of the family, and I am the only one she really gets on with. The reason is simple – we are both dirty-minded little sluts. The difference is that, while I try and keep a respectable face for the outside world, she doesn't.*

She is quite tall, very slim and cultivates a deliberately outrageous look, with several tattoos, piercings and crazy hairstyles. Her big sister, Kate, gave me my first lesbian experience, but it turned out to be Susan who was the really filthy one . . .

Sulky – Susan James

'. . . and you needn't sulk about it, either!' my mother's voice carried to me as I dashed from the room.

Not sulk! I was seventeen years old and she had spanked me! Seventeen – and I had been put across her lap and had my school skirt lifted! Seventeen – and I'd had my pants pulled down to show my bottom off! Seventeen – and I'd been given a bare-bottom spanking! A spanking!

I slammed the front door behind me. My cheeks, both the ones on my face and the ones down my pants, were burning. There were tears in my eyes and a hard lump of anger in my throat.

It wasn't fair. I hadn't been naughty. I certainly hadn't been naughty enough to justify a spanking. All I had done was take a few inches off my school skirts! She'd lectured me while it was being done, as well. She'd called me a disgrace. She'd gone on about how much uniforms cost and how she'd have to buy new skirts. She'd demanded to know what the neighbours would think of me wandering around in a skirt so short that my pants showed every time I bent over.

That really capped it all. I mean, if she was so worried about people seeing my pants, then why had she taken me across her lap in the drawing room? You would have thought she'd at least have had the decency to take me up to my room, where I could be punished in private. But no, she had had to do it in the only room in the house that is visible from the road: and, worse, looks directly across to old Colonel Aimsworth's house opposite.

As I slammed the garden gate behind me, my worst fears were justified. The Colonel was in his front garden, clipping his ridiculous topiary pigeons. Normally, he either ignored me completely or gave a gruff grunt of recognition. Now he smiled, and that smile said everything. He'd seen me spanked!

I had thought I'd been blushing before. I hadn't even known the meaning of blushing. My cheeks now felt as if they were going to burst into flames. I'd been done in the armchair Dad normally likes to sit in. My bum had been towards the window – bare! I'd kicked about so hard that I'd had to have my arm twisted up into the small of my back and I certainly hadn't kept my thighs together. The Colonel would have seen everything! My bare pussy! My bumhole!

Clenching my fists in an agony of embarrassment, I ran down the lane. I had no idea where I was going, or what I intended to do: only that I needed some privacy. It was bad enough to have been spanked, worse to know that Colonel Aimsworth had seen it being done, but worse by far was the terrible realisation of what the spanking had done to me. The gusset of my pants was soaking wet – I was turned on!

I ran on. My mind was in turmoil, unsure what to do, unsure even what to think. Only when I reached the top of the hill did I stop. Here, with countryside stretching away in every direction, the futility of running came home to me. It was the same on all sides, mile after mile of nice countryside set with nice houses where nice people worried about what their neighbours might think, and whether their daughters looked respectable.

There was a gate nearby and I went to sit on it, feeling thoroughly sorry for myself. I knew I was sulking, but I didn't care. I had every right to sulk.

I wanted to be with different people, ones who didn't care what the neighbours thought, ones who didn't throw a paddy if their daughters wore short skirts – ideally, ones who didn't care if their daughters wandered about starkers. No, actually I wanted to do something really, really naughty – like streak through the village or offer old Colonel Aimsworth a blow-job for fifty pence. Then they'd know that it wasn't 'just a phase she's going through'.

The trouble was, that was exactly what they would say. I could just picture it: Mrs Harrison at the post office saying, 'Poor Elaine, Susan is such a trial, but she'll grow out of it, they always do.' Then there would be Miss Brinkley-Bomefield, who always managed to be condescending and sympathetic at the same time; and Colonel Aimsworth, muttering seriously about how he'd seen me spanked and about how it would do me good – all the while with his wrinkly old cock rock-hard down his underpants.

That was what I needed – cock. Not a wrinkly old specimen either, but a nice smooth, big one belonging to someone who thought of me as a sexy little rebel and not a recalcitrant schoolgirl. I'd suck it first, to get that lovely man-taste and feel his cock-flesh expand in my mouth. He could do it in my mouth, as well, just for the pleasure of thinking how shocked they'd all be at the idea of me with a big, fat cock in my hand and spunk dribbling down my chin. Then I'd demand a lick in return and come under his tongue . . .

I really was turned on. My experience of cock-sucking ran to a few hasty blow-jobs on holiday and I hadn't let anybody come in my mouth. As to anything within immediate reach, there was only the local lad who had persuaded me to pull his cock for him while he read a dirty magazine. I'd been quite turned on by the end, but he had been so inept – very much a boy rather than a man. What I wanted was a man, a big, muscular brute who'd make me suck his cock, and twist my hair in his hand while he did it, and stroke my neck, and laugh when he'd spunked up in my mouth and made me swallow it. It was a lovely idea, but it would be sure to get out, and then everybody would be talking about me, and . . .

I stopped, feeling rather cross with myself. I wanted to

do something rude, I really did. I wanted it to be something dirty, and sexy, and as contrary as possible to everything I'm supposed to be. Yet how was I ever going to manage it if I didn't even have the guts to contemplate asking one of the local boys if he'd like his cock sucked?

Once more I started to sulk, feeling sorry for myself – feeling anything but a rebel, feeling exactly the way my mother would expect me to feel after she'd given me a spanking.

It was at that realisation that I determined to do something – anything, just as long as I could prove to myself that I was not to be kept down. The question was: what?

I jumped down from the gate, which was a start. A puddle in a wheel rut provided a distorted and slightly rude image of me, a skinny little schoolgirl in an indecently short red tartan skirt and white pants which I knew hid the shame of pink-spanked bum-cheeks. That, then, was the first thing to change – my look. Now, for that, I knew where to go.

Billy the Neck lived in a cottage near Yatten. Many of the more adventurous girls at my school liked to go there, partly because doing so provided a thrill of the illicit, and partly to listen to his outrageous stories. He was also really easy-going, and let us tease him, and generally misbehave, without ever loosing his cool. Nor was he at all threatening: so little so, in fact, that we automatically dismissed the wilder details of his stories as sheer fantasy.

He claimed to have been a pop-star back in the seventies, but none of us believed him. Certainly his name didn't appear in any of the books we could find, but he knew his stuff and looked the part, which was all we really cared about. He was stick-thin and over six feet tall, with long bony fingers and green eyes. His manner was just so easy and, as far as we knew, he didn't do anything but loaf around his cottage. He also wore his hair in tall green spikes with the sides shaved, and kept the look fresh, which meant he had all the kit.

That was how I wanted to look, and just the thought of

it had me smiling as I started off toward Yatten. I had no doubt whatever that he would do it for me, as he always made a big deal of not caring what other people thought about him. Also, he was always teasing us about looking so prim and proper, and suggesting piercings and tattoos and so on. I didn't even worry about going there alone, in fact a rebellious little voice inside me was telling me that it was exactly what I should be doing.

It was a good two miles to his cottage, but my mood held firm all the way. I even took off the silly little bra Mummy makes me wear and threw it into a hedge. Having my titties bare under my blouse felt great, and put a new spring into my step. When I got there he was in his garden, lolling back in a deck-chair with nothing on but a pair of tatty jeans and his indispensable dark glasses.

He greeted me with his normal casual friendliness, offering a drag at his fat cigarette and throwing me a can of beer from the cooler by his side. I accepted both, and if he was at all surprised by my being alone, he didn't show it. The brief moment of ill-ease that always occurred when I visited him passed as he laughed at me for getting my blouse and tie covered in beer foam, and we settled down to talk and drink and smoke.

In no time, my chagrin at Mummy's treatment of my bottom had passed, and I was giggling over a story about how his band had been arrested after a concert for holding a competition to see who could piss the furthest on to the tracks from one of the platforms in Victoria Station. I didn't believe him, but it made me laugh and when he had finished I asked straight out if he could give me a punk make-over.

He thought it was a great idea and the next two hours were spent in his bathroom. He had loads of good stuff, and by the end I could never have imagined I would look so different, nor so good. He had shaved either side of my head, leaving a broad path that he had then divided into three. What was left he had dyed a brilliant, electric blue and teased into spikes, the tallest of which must have stuck up two feet from my head!

To complete the transformation, I kicked off my sensible shoes and took my long white socks off to go barefoot, then ripped the hem of my school skirt away to leave it even shorter and with a really cute ragged edge. He had a huge, badly torn T-shirt with 'Suzie' written on it, which replaced my white school blouse. Apparently it had been the name of some singer, but it was me now, and the black background and gold letters went with my hair. He even had some old make-up, which I put on myself, using lots of black with highlights in turquoise and gold. Strings of safety pins made impromptu punk earrings, and that was it.

That morning I had been Susan James, an innocent schoolgirl, so skinny that I could barely pass for eighteen in pubs. Now I was Suzie, a cheeky young punk, full of attitude, ready to spit at any barman with the nerve to question me – or maybe flash my knickers to show what I thought of him, even my bare bum.

Mummy was really going to throw a cow when she saw me. I'd be back over her knee with my pants down in seconds, but it would be worth it. I wouldn't say where I'd had it done, either: not if she took me out in the garden and did me in front of Colonel Aimsworth, nor even if she asked the Colonel to do the spanking!

I gave Billy a twirl, and he grinned back admiringly.

'Fuck, but that takes me back,' he said. 'You've got the look, you've really got the fucking look!'

I struck a pose, sticking one hip out and setting my mouth in what I hoped was a punkish sneer.

'Nice,' he responded. 'Yeah, you've got the look, Suzie. Fuck, do I wish you had the attitude.'

'Who says I haven't?' I answered, immediately piqued.

'Well . . .' he drawled. 'I don't want you to take this the wrong way or nothing, but you're a posh girl . . .'

'So,' I broke in, 'just because Mummy and Daddy are well off doesn't mean I'm stuck-up.'

'Yeah, yeah,' he answered, 'sure, but you've got to have the background to understand it. Like Lucy, who was our lead singer: she didn't just look the part, she lived the part.'

'And so could I!' I retorted. 'I really feel this is me, not just a pose. If I didn't have my parents on my back all the time, I bet I could be like her – wilder, maybe.'

'That's a laugh!' he answered, 'No way, girl. I mean, like, now if she wanted a piss, say, she'd just whip her knickers down – that's if she was wearing any – and she'd do it in the street. She didn't give a fuck who saw.'

'I could be like that,' I said, feeling a bit defensive as I sat down in one of his plastic bucket seats. 'I wouldn't care who saw.'

'You say that,' he went on, 'but, deep down, you know you would.'

'How do you know –'

'No, no,' he broke in, 'I mean, don't get me wrong. I'm not down on you or nothing. It's just that you ain't got the background. You couldn't do it, see? You think you could but you couldn't, because if you've even got to think about it, then you couldn't.'

'I bet I could,' I responded.

'Yeah, you say that, but when it comes down to it, you know you won't,' he continued. 'See, you'll always find an excuse not to. Like: you would, but not in front of a bloke; or you would, but only if you'd had just one more beer. The bottom line is, you couldn't do it, and I know that.'

Actually, he was wrong there, because I'd once let my friend Barbara pee on me, but I didn't feel like admitting it to him. Instead, I drained the last of my beer, slid a little further down my chair, spread my legs and pulled aside the gusset of my pants.

'Hey, not –' he said as I squeezed my bladder and just let go.

It was too late. A fountain of pee burst from my pussy.

'Not on the fucking floor!' he yelled. 'Jesus, Suzie!'

I was laughing as my pee sprayed out in a long arch of pale gold droplets. It splashed on the carpet with a gentle pattering noise, soaking everything. I could feel it running down my pussy as well, into my pants and down under my bum to form a warm, wet puddle in my chair.

'Fuck me!' Billy swore as his beer can dropped from his fingers.

His eyes were glued to my open pussy and the rude, golden stream erupting from my pee-hole. I was peeing on the floor and it felt wonderful – really dirty, really sexy and, best of all, absolutely free.

He was just staring, wide-eyed at my bare pussy. My gush turned to a trickle and then a dribble, leaving a big wet patch on the carpet. He put a hand to his crotch, adjusting the position of what was obviously an uncomfortably stiff cock. I giggled, stuck my tongue out at him and pulled open my pussy-lips to show him my hole. He swallowed and again put his hand on his cock, only this time openly.

'Wank for me, Suzie,' he asked.

'If you do it, too,' I answered.

He gave no reply, but eagerly pulled down his zip and took out a long, white penis that was very nearly erect. With his eyes focused on my pussy, he began to masturbate. I watched his cock grow stiffer, delighting in the exhibition I was making of myself and then deciding to make it ruder still.

I lifted my top, spreading my thighs wide as I did so. As my titties came on show, he began to pull at his cock with more speed. It was fully stiff as I pulled my pants aside again. He gave a grunt of appreciation at the sight of my pussy. I stuck my chest out and cocked my legs as far apart as they would go, showing him everything. It was obvious how excited he was; his cock looked fit to burst. I loved the idea of showing off for him but, as I began to rub at my pussy, I was wondering how his long, skinny, pale cock would feel in my hand, then up my pussy. My finger found my clitty and I was in heaven, willing to postpone my helping of cock at least until I had had a good play.

'That's nice,' he drawled, 'that's what I like: a posh little schoolgirl with her cunt on show, wanking off in her own piss.'

I felt myself blushing. He was so crude, so dirty, so unlike any of the boys I'd been with. My clitty was a hard bud under my finger, jiggling as I rubbed and with each jiggle sending a new flush of pleasure through me.

'Come on,' he growled, 'stick it out further. Spread that tight little fuck-hole for Billy.'

I paused in my rubbing to pull my lips open and show him the centre of my pussy, imagining how he would be able to see the dark hole disappearing into my body, with my flesh all wet and pink around it.

'Oh, you little darling,' he gasped. 'God, but I'd like to fuck you!'

'Do it, then,' I moaned.

He didn't waste time, but came forward, kneeling in my pee. I took my legs under the knees and held them up, offering myself as his thumb caught back the gusset of my pants. I felt him put the head of his cock to my pussy and then he was in, sliding up my sopping hole. He began to fuck me and I groaned out loud, lost in the delight of what we were doing and the feel of a long, stiff cock inside me.

Holding me by the thighs, he began to fuck me. His eyes were riveted on my body as he slid his cock in and out of my vagina, clearly excited as much by how I looked as by the feel of my body. Each push produced a loud squelching noise, while the warm, wet sensation around my bottom also kept the thought that I was being fucked in my own pee-puddle firmly in my mind.

As he began to go faster, I closed my eyes and focused on the picture of myself in my mind. I saw myself as I wanted to be: a young punk girl laid back in a bucket seat while a punk man pumped his penis in and out of her open pussy. My titties were bare, with a big, torn T-shirt pulled up over them. My skirt was a rag of red tartan that would have done more to tease than to conceal, even if it hadn't been lifted to show off the front to my pants. My pants were girlish enough, but they had been pulled aside, first to pee all over the floor and then to admit my lover's cock. My hair was a riot of turquoise spikes, my ears hung with safety pins. Best of all, rudest of all, my skirt and pants were sodden with my own pee, while my bottom was squelching about in a pool of it.

I had one hand on my pussy; the other was cupping a titty. My clitty was being jiggled about under a finger, while my nipple was hard under a thumb. I was going to come.

Billy got there first, suddenly whipping his cock out of me and spraying hot spunk all over my pussy and hand. It felt slimy and warm as I began to rub it over my pussy and into my pubes, and my own orgasm started with the thought of just how rude I must look with my sex smeared with come while I masturbated. He called me a slut as I came, and with that word my own orgasm exploded in my head, wiping away everything else in a great spasm of ecstasy.

If I had been feeling relaxed before, after we had fucked I was well at ease. I stripped naked, and did my washing like that, enjoying simply being in the nude. I even hung my wet clothes on the line without a stitch on, adding the thrill of the risk of being seen to the pleasure of nakedness. Back indoors, Billy opened another couple of beers and rolled a new cigarette while I spread myself out on his moth-eaten old settee, gloriously naked and unselfconscious. As we talked, my desire to be naughty began to increase once more, and I was wondering if he was ready for another fuck, when he came up with a great idea.

'How about having your cunt punked up?' he suggested.

'With the hair dyed or something?' I replied.

'Yeah, and shaved into a pattern,' he continued, 'like a diamond, or Lucy used to do hers in corporal's stripes.'

'OK, let's do it,' I answered, 'but I want sergeant's stripes, in the same blue as my hair.'

I was well up for it, and giggled crazily while he made a big show of rubbing shaving foam into my bush. Being shaved was a lovely feeling, too, both sensual and naughty. So by the time half my pubic mound was slick and bare, I was well turned on. My feeling grew stronger still as I was washed, trimmed and then dyed. My pussy was gaping, and running juice, which I knew he could see. By the end, when he was drying between my legs with a towel, I was ready to be mounted then and there on the bathroom floor. Billy's cock was half-stiff – hanging down between his legs like a long pink sausage – but rather than put it in me, he showed me how my pussy looked in a shaving mirror.

'That is cute!' I told him as I inspected my smart, electric blue sergeant's stripes.

'You're not joking,' he answered. 'Fancy another?'

'Yes, please,' I responded.

I was sat on the floor with my thighs wide apart, stark naked and ready. All he had to do was lie forward and put it in me, but instead he took hold of his cock and began to masturbate while he admired my blue pussy hair.

'Do you know what would make the best touch?' he said hoarsely.

'What?'

'A fucking great nappy pin stuck right through your cunt-lips.'

'Oh, God: do it then, go on!'

'Hang on, Suzie, it's not . . .'

'Just do it, Billy, put it through my lips.'

'Be cool, girl, it's not that easy. Just wait.'

'OK.'

I had never known such need as I sat there with my legs apart and my lower lip trembling hard. I was scared – terrified, in fact – but I badly wanted him to do it, to pin my pussy-lips together, to have my sex tarted up with a big metal pin. Working with quick eager fingers – and sometimes breaking off to tug at his cock – he went through the process of getting a pin ready for my pussy. He took one from a pack, a big, shiny thing with a pink safety head that made what he was going to do with it seem all the more rude. This was held in the flame of his lighter, and then dropped into a shot glass of high-strength vodka.

He was experienced, I could tell, which made me feel a little less nervous as I sat there with my legs open. I was still trembling, and my dirty feelings were fighting against a fear of pain, even as he finished the sterilising process by washing his hands in the vodka.

'Spread 'em and hold your cunt lips apart,' he instructed. 'It won't hurt, no more than an injection.'

Injections aren't normally given in the pussy, but it was too late to back out. I cocked my thighs open as far as they would go and stretched my outer lips wide, presenting him with the inner. He came forward, holding the terrifying great pin between two fingers, open, the point glittering in the light. I shut my eyes and clamped my teeth hard shut. His hand touched my pussy, pinching the lips, pulling them out. There was a sudden, sharp pain and then I was in ecstasy. It had been done. I had a pin through my pussy-lips, and it felt so good.

I opened my eyes to find Billy sitting back to admire his handiwork. He was grinning broadly, obviously well pleased with himself, and his cock was more stiff than not.

'Nice,' he drawled.

'Show me,' I replied.

He put the shaving mirror down between my legs, giving me a close-up view of my sex. It was lovely, and I felt the delicious rude feeling inside me become stronger still as I admired my pussy. The mound was slick and pink, decorated by the electric blue triple-V of the sergeant's stripes that he had made from my hair. Below, my pussy was glistening wet and open, the inner lips prominent at the centre – and there, joining them, stuck blatantly through that most intimate and secret part of my body, was a big, shiny nappy pin.

'Thank you, Billy, that feels so nice,' I said. 'Do you want to have me now?'

He didn't answer, but reached out for the box of smaller pins we had been using to decorate my ears.

'What we used to do,' he drawled as he spread them out on the carpet, 'was make the girls kneel and then put a chain on their cunt pins. How about it?'

'OK,' I giggled.

I sat with my legs apart, merrily showing him everything while he made a long chain of safety pins. Never in my life had I felt so natural, so relaxed, and so naughty.

'There we are,' he announced, when he had finished. 'One cunt chain. Turn over.'

I did as I was told, turning to present him my bottom and the nappy pin that held my pussy-lips together. His fingers touched me, stroking my sex-lips and then taking a gentle hold on the pin.

'Get up,' he ordered and gave the pin a tweak. 'I'm going to put your cunt lead on.'

All I could do was lift my bum, responding to the pressure of the nappy pin as he put me in an increasingly rude and vulnerable position. As I rose, I felt my bum-cheeks open and I knew I was showing off the little hole between them. My face was on the floor, my bottom stuck up high, with every rude detail open for his inspection. I felt his fingers on my pussy and heard the click as he fastened the line of pins to my pussy-pin. He pulled, forcing me to stick my bum up higher still. I was helpless, completely under his control, chained by the pussy and unable to do anything but flaunt myself as he wished me to.

'Nice cunt, Suzie,' he said from behind me. 'Nice arse, too. I like 'em lean – and your hole looks nice and tight.'

I shivered at his words, hoping he would carry on talking, because the very crudity of what he was saying was having a really powerful effect on me.

'You want fucking, you really do,' he continued. 'Your cunt's dripping like a fucking tap.'

I looked back. He was standing over me, the end of the safety-pin chain held between two fingers, his eyes glued to my stretched-out pussy-lips. In his other hand he held his cock, erect and poised over my open vagina. I gave him a pleading look, desperate for the lovely, long prick to be slid into my pussy so that I could be fucked with my lips pinned together.

'Won't go in your cunt, Suzie,' he said. 'There ain't enough room, but there's more than one way to have a girl.'

'Do you want a suck, then?' I offered.

'How about up your arse?' he responded.

'In my bum-hole?' I gasped.

'Haven't you had one up the arse before?' he asked in what seemed to be genuine surprise.

'No!' I answered.

'You posh girls, you don't know you're born!' he laughed. 'Well, there's always a first time, so how about it?'

'I'm . . . I'm not sure.'

'Come on, Suzie, or ain't you dirty enough?'

'I . . . Yes, but . . . Oh, I don't know . . .'

'Come on, love, you know what they say. One up the bum – no harm done.'

Nobody had ever said it to me before, and no one had ever done it, either. I had to admit it was tempting. I'd put fingers up my bottom, and liked the sensation. Taking a cock up it was a different matter: such a dirty act, not something that Miss Susan James would ever do – but something that Suzie the punk would do.

'Come on, Suzie,' he urged. 'I want my cock up your posh little arse.'

'I'm not sure,' I answered. 'Let me think a bit.'

'Come on, girl, you know you want it.'

I did want it, quite badly. Nothing I could imagine could be more openly rebellious to my upbringing than letting Billy have his way with me up my bum-hole. 'Don't let your pants down,' that was what Mummy always said: as if the moment a girl's pants came down, she was bound to fuck. Well, I had let my pants down, several times, but this was something else – the offer of a cock, not where nature had intended, but up my bottom.

'Some girls love it, and I bet you'll be one of them,' he continued. 'Some aren't so keen, but you can all take it, and all like it in the end. It feels good. You'll love it.'

'Okay, I'll do it,' I stammered, 'but don't hurt me.'

'Don't worry, there's a knack to shagging a girl up the arse. Hang around, I need some grease.'

He bent down and I watched him pin the end of my cunt-lead to his bathroom curtains, forcing me to keep my bum well up. That really made me feel helpless. All I could do was kneel trembling on the floor, while I waited for my bottom-hole to be greased. He was whistling to himself as he rummaged in the cupboard, and I saw him discard several types of cream or jelly before selecting a fat blue tube, a good half of which had already been used.

'This is best for arse-holes,' he said casually. 'Do you want to do it, or shall I?'

'I will,' I answered.

He watched with undisguised pleasure as I squeezed a long worm of lubricant on to my middle finger and delved back between my bum-cheeks. It felt cold on my anus, but the little hole opened easily and I felt a lovely, dirty feeling as my finger slid up my bottom.

'Wank it in and out a bit,' he said.

I didn't need telling. The feel of my finger up my bottom was lovely, and I was already looking forward to it being replaced by his cock. He was tugging at his penis while he watched me finger my bum, leaving him with a rock-hard erection, long, white and skinny, but still a great deal thicker than my finger. When my bum-hole felt good and ready I resumed my kneeling position and braced myself for buggery. Billy unfastened my cunt-chain from the curtain and squatted down behind him, laying his cock along the crease of my bum.

'Just push your arse-hole out,' he said, 'like you were on the crapper.'

'You're a dirty bastard, Billy,' I managed, but I did as I was told.

'No dirtier than you, pissing on my floor,' he answered. 'Yeah, that's right: stick it out.'

I felt the hard, rubbery end of his cock squash against my bum-hole and knew that I was about to be buggered for the first time in my life. His penis head was round and hard against my flesh, stretching me, opening my bum-hole for what surely has to be the dirtiest thing a man can do to a woman – buggery, sodomy, arse-fucking, bum-shagging: such a filthy, filthy thing for me to be doing. As my ring stretched wide, I was already imagining how the full length of his cock would feel deep inside me, filling a place so rude, so secret, that I scarcely dared explore it with my fingers. Then my anus gave a sudden, sharp twinge of pain.

'Ow! Stop, that hurts,' I gasped.

'That's all right, love, you're plugged,' he answered.

'How much is in?'

'Just the head. Do you want it out?'

'No, leave it in. Let me touch myself.'

'Yeah, good girl: come with my knob in your ring, all right?'

'OK.'

'Great, good girl. Look, I won't bugger you if it hurts, but I'm going to wank off up your arse.'

'Yes, please, and talk to me like you do. Use really naughty words, call me nasty names, call me a slut.'

Even as I reached back to find my clit, the front of his hand began to slap against my buttocks. I could feel the nappy-pin, and I touched it, caressing the hard, smooth steel peg that was thrust through the lips of my pussy. I began to masturbate, my finger touching the pin with each rub to keep me reminded of the state I was in – my hair electric blue and half-shaved, safety pins in my ears and sex-lips, the head of a man's penis in my bum-hole. His cock was jiggling around in my hole as he masturbated up me, the safety pin chain tinkling with our joint motions. Then he began to speak.

'Feels good does it?' he drawled. 'Kneeling with a cunt-chain on and my dick up your arse?'

'Yes.'

'You're just a little punk slut, aren't you?'

'Yes.'

'A filthy little tart, Suzie, a tramp who likes the feel of a dick up her snobby little butt.'

'Yes, Billy.'

'You're a fucking tease, too. This isn't your first time, is it?'

'Yes, it is.'

'Bollocks: you're too fucking eager.'

'No.'

'Yeah, sure. You've had boys up your rosebud before, haven't you, slut?'

'No, I promise, you're the first.'

'You're a fucking liar, Suzie. You've done it at that posh school of yours, haven't you? You had your panties down round behind the bike sheds, haven't you? Then some lucky kid's had his dick up your butthole, hasn't he?'

'Oh, please.'

'Or maybe it was two or three at a time, watching while they take turns up your arse?'

'Oh, yes.'

'Or maybe a teacher, someone you needed a favour from. I can just see you, holding your arse-cheeks apart to show some old pervert your brown-eye, then grunting like the little tart you are while he shags your arse.'

'Yes: more like that, Billy, more.'

'Or maybe it was the caretaker, with your la-di-da little skirt up and your knickers down so he can toss over your arse. You'd think you were doing him a favour, letting the poor old bastard wank over your bum. But you'd get turned on wouldn't you, you slut? You'd let him grease your arse, and then fuck it.'

'Yes, Billy; I'm coming, Billy!'

'And you'd come, frigging yourself while his dirty great cock was up your shitter . . . oh, yeah, fuck, Suzie, that's good . . . you fucking little whore . . . Jesus!'

I had come, and I'd felt my bum-hole contract around the head of his cock as if I was trying to squeeze his spunk up my bottom. He gave a grunt and I thought he was coming, only for him to start to speak again.

'Well, it's not the caretaker now, you little fuck dolly, it's me, now – Billy the neck – and I'm going to do a hand-shandy up your box. You've come with my knob in your hole, and now it's my turn.'

'Do it, Billy!'

'I'm going to come up your dirt-box, you little slut,' he grunted and his cock was jerked from my anus.

I squeaked and the next instant felt something warm and wet splash into my gaping bum-hole. He had come in me, up my bum, and was wanking his cock dry into the open hole, watching the thick, white droplets run inside. My anus closed and I felt some sperm ooze out, only for his cock to be rammed back in, hard, so that the juicy, receptive hole took not just the head but several inches of cock. I yelled out as it went up me, and then I was coming again, lost in ecstasy, in the slimy feeling of come on my sex, in the pain of the cock in my anus, in the sting of the pin through my pussy-lips, in the burning of my clitty under my finger.

About an hour later, after another beer and a shared roll-up, I left Billy to start home. I knew he'd used me, but I didn't care. It had been a great experience, and exactly what I'd needed.

I'd kept my look, too: all of it, even the safety pin. I was me, Suzie. I'd been buggered and my pussy-lips were fastened together with a safety pin, and it felt oh, so rude. All the way back, it was as if I was actually a different person. Old ladies who had always given me patronising smiles now eyed me with disapproval and even alarm. The men working on the gatehouse at Ildon, who had ignored me completely just hours before, now wolf-whistled and demanded I lift my top. Best of all was Miss Brinkley-Bomefield, who has known me all my life but completely failed to recognise me. She gave me a really filthy look, which turned to one of true outrage as I flashed my pants at her.

Another two hundred yards along the road was my house and, as I approached, my footsteps began to falter. Mummy would take one look at me and haul me across her knee, I was sure of it. I'd get spanked, and inevitably she'd take my pants down. If I went over too far, she'd see my pussy and then there really would be hell to pay. Still, it was too late, and so I carried on, only for my apprehension to deepen at the sight of Colonel Aimsworth still clipping away at his wretched pigeons.

He gave me a look that combined amazement and lust, and I stuck my tongue out at him in response. I went into the house, hoping to get to my room without being seen, at least to postpone my spanking or to take it where the Colonel couldn't see. Unfortunately, Mummy was coming out of the drawing room at that exact instant. Her state of frozen shock lasted little more than a second.

Exactly as I had anticipated, she grabbed my wrist and dragged me across the room to Dad's armchair. She sat down hard and I was thrown across her lap. An instant later, my skirt was up and my pants had been wrenched down, baring my bum to the air and also to Colonel Aimsworth.

The spanking was hard, accurate and delivered without a word. Slap after slap landed on my bum, each one stinging and making my cheeks bounce. I knew my bum would be going red, I knew that I was making a fine display of my pussy to the window, I knew that the harder slaps were making my bum-hole show, and I knew the Colonel could see right between my legs.

It was just like the morning's spanking – painful and delivered without a thought for my modesty – only a lot sterner. I was finally lectured, too – told how bad I was and how I deserved what was being done to me, how I ought to be spanked more often and how dreadful my hair looked. Again, by the end, my bottom was throbbing with pain and doubtless bright red. Again I got my buns slapped until her hand was too sore to go on.

Only this time, when I got up from her lap, I didn't run sniffling from the room. I showed her my pussy hair, then I laughed.

. . . and bang went the last chance of making a respectable girl out of her. Yet, for all Susan's outrageous behaviour, in some ways she's quite normal.

We met Poppaea in Black Mischief, *when Amber, Ginny and I played a very naughty trick on her. She is petite, delicate and easily recognised by the bright green hair that reaches all the way down to quite the prettiest, roundest little bottom I have ever had the privilege to kiss. In character she is sensitive, fey and filled with wonderful pagan beliefs and ideals. Her story comes from before I met her, when she was still developing the extravagant world which she has created in her own mind. The only shame is that it couldn't possibly be true . . . Oh, and don't try this at home . . .*

The Malice of Satyrs – Poppaea

On Soussans Down, three ley lines cross. A stone circle sits at their union, thirteen wind-worn uprights. At their centre the ground rises, forming a soft hummock of grass on which I lie, naked with my thighs open, as if to welcome a lover inside me.

This is the high moor, the open moor, the place where the Wish Hunt rides. It is a raw place, a masculine place, a place of hard stone and urgent winds. There is little of the Earth Mother here and much of the Horned God. That is why I have come here, to give to him: and also perhaps to take. It will not be him, but one of his that comes to take me. Then my acceptance to the mystery will be whole.

As I dwell on what I am to do, I know a trace of fear, but no more. Fear is for those who reject the old Gods, for those who deny nature, for those who pray to alien, southern deities. For me, the Wish Hunt should not be feared and Lilith has schooled me well.

To my side is a crucible of heavy bronze and in it the thick black elixir compounded to allow me to see and understand what is real but hidden. I wait, chanting and composing my mind, my naked body shivering in the cold pre-dawn. Slowly the east lightens, turning black to grey and then to dull green, ochre and purple, the colours of the high moor. I take up the crucible and, as the first arc of red-gold breasts the ridge of Hamel Down, I begin to drink.

The elixir is thick, and hard to swallow. There is the bitterness of agaric, the sweet of Banyuls, the bite of my own spice and the salt of my last lover's seed. Slowly it courses down my throat, burning a trail to the heart of my femininity as the solstice sun rises to proclaim the power of the Horned God. As the last drop touches my lip, the brilliant globe pulls free of the horizon and its warmth touches my body.

I settle myself back, once more lying supine and receptive as I begin the invocation. There is warmth now, the warmth of an embrace, and air is clear and sharp, allowing sounds to travel unhindered. I hear a raven in the far distance, and the shifting of the leaves among the trees. Beyond, on the edge of awareness, I hear the pipe, mocking as it always is, yet also calling me.

The sound seems to come from all sides, yet I am drawn towards the rising sun and down into the valley bottom. I push through thick pines, then cross open, rock-strewn moor and a mesh of gullies and sinks where men once drew metal from the ground. The stream is ahead of me, scattering the sunlight among its water, babbling to the rhythm of the pipes. Boulders break its course, heavy with yellow and grey lichens, moss of rich green. Rowan trees and dwarf willow grow on its banks, screening a strip of soft grass. As my bare toes sink into the soft ground the piping loses its haunting, gleeful tone and becomes frantic, a cacophony of sudden alarm and naked lust.

I raise my eyes and he is there, a squat satyr, horned and hirsute, his round buttocks planted on a rock of equal rotundity, his fat belly quivering with emotion. His eyes meet mine and he knows I see him. They are brown and bright, wide with surprise and desire. Abruptly he turns, planting his fat, richly furred thighs wide apart to show himself to me – grotesquely priapic.

His cock rises from a nest of hair, a thick, stubby thing with the pink tip already protruding from the dark, wrinkled flesh of the foreskin and twitching in anticipation of my body. Below hangs the leathery, hairless testicle sac, its bare, nut-brown skin moving sluggishly as the penis grows. He grabs it, and, with a sudden flurry of hard tugs, brings it to full erection.

Expecting me to run, he gives a wild laugh and clatters his hooves on the rock. I smile and his face becomes angry, then crafty, with all the lascivious cunning of his kind. My urge is to come forward, to go to him, spread my thighs in the cool water and let him take his pleasure of me. Yet I must have his seed in my womb and I know how he will ridicule my need if I go too willingly. He will throw me on my back and have me, thrusting the fatness of his member inside as he pins me down in the water with his powerful forearms. At the instant at which I anticipate fulfilment, he will pull back and, with a gust of coarse laughter, penetrate my anus and waste his seed in my bowels. To him it will be a rich jest; to me, failure.

I beckon, summoning him forward as I nod towards his rigid erection and open my mouth in a gesture intentionally lewd. He grabs his penis and gives it another flurry of tugs, but holds back. I turn, bending at the waist to display the full femininity of my bottom, a taunt that I feel sure he will be unable to resist. He rises and extends a long tongue to lick the head of his penis, keeping his eyes on the twin spheres of my rear all the while. I reach back and pull myself open, displaying the willingness of my vagina and the temptation of my anus. He licks his cock again, flicking the tip of his tongue over his glans, for pleasure and to moisten it in anticipation of the holes that lead into my body.

Now the temptation is too much and he comes forward, moving slyly, intent on my capture, yet all the while jerking at his majestic erection. I bend to touch my toes and looking back, offering myself without reserve. With a cackle of glee, he leaps forward, snatching at me . . .

I have already gone. His grunt of anger and frustration follows me as I run along the stream, scrambling and leaping to escape. Twice I have to feign a stumble to allow his stumpy legs to keep up. Then I trip and sprawl full-length on the lush grass. In a moment he is on me, grunting and chortling in triumph, his cock rubbing feverishly between my buttocks. For a moment, I think that I am to be buggered, but then hands take me by the hips and roll me over.

He is on top of me, his fat, beaming face looking into mine. His hands grip me and I am pushed down on to the dank ground. Then his cock is pushing at me, finding my hole, opening me, filling me until I can feel it throughout my body. Leaning his fat belly against my stomach, he begins to use me. I can see his face against the sky, his features set in the rapture of my enveloping flesh, the fox-brown stubble of his hair reflecting the sun.

To him, my ravishment is a thing not just of ecstasy but of high comedy. As we fuck, he laughs, occasionally breaking off to point at me with derision and delight. Only when the pleasure begins to show in my face does he let go of my arms and begin to paw my breasts, exploring their shape and the twin buds of my nipples with his blunt claws. I can only sigh and lie back, lost in a rapture that is as much mental as physical as he humps on my prostrate body. His bulbous gut is smacking against my belly, his coarse pubic hair rubbing on my clitoris, his hands clawing at my breasts, his tongue licking at my face and neck, his cock pushing ever deeper inside me . . .

I come, and hear his laughter at the helpless pleasure. Now there is a new urgency in his pushes, a need to reach his own climax now that I have given the final surrender. All thoughts of mischief forgotten in the exaltation of capturing and subduing me, he floods my womb with seed. Still he pushes, until his seed bursts out, moistening the crevices of my bottom and soaking the ground beneath me.

Now I am at his mercy, lying ravished on the ground with his seed spilling from my vagina. First it is his hands, the long fingers and blunt claws exploring me with a youthful delight and thoroughness. They stroke my breasts and belly, tickle me on my feet and beneath the curve of my buttocks, invade my mouth and vagina, probe deep into my anus. Soon I am on heat again and clutching for his cock, which he allows me to touch while he investigates me.

Slowly his touches become yet more intimate and invasive. He begins to use his lips and long tongue, then his horns and hooves. In my hand I can feel his penis squirming, filling with blood and then emptying, but becoming ever more erect. Suddenly, he pulls my hand from it and gives me a look of doubt.

It lasts only a moment and then he returns to the task of indulging himself on my body. A horn is poked into my vagina and then put to my mouth so that I must taste my own arousal. I respond, sucking the creamy sharpness from its rough, bulbous tip. This he finds amusing and gives a brief, capering dance, flaunting first his penis and then his buttocks at my face. The process is repeated with my anus, to leave him crowing with pleasure at his own cleverness.

He begins to chuckle to himself as his senses of wickedness and curiosity grow. With it his touches become ever more familiar, ever more designed to despoil me. He kisses me, only to spit in my mouth. He squats over my head and lowers his balls into my mouth, and then begins to bounce on my face so that I am forced to suck the fat plums of his testicles. His buttocks are directly over my face, two straining balls of flesh that wobble in time to his hops. Each is grown with thick, russet fur, except patches on each crest, which are bald and pink. They slap against my face like two water-filled balloons, then settle as he brings his legs up on to my chest.

His full weight is on my face, his sharp little hooves resting lightly on my breasts. My nipples are caught in the clefts of his hooves, erect and hard, stinging to malicious little kicks. I moan and sigh around my mouthful of his balls at each sharp little pain, making him chuckle and then sing out in pure glee at my helpless sensuality. For a long time he rides my face, only to abruptly tire of the sport and dismount.

I am put once more to his cock. This I know will be his final triumph, the zenith of his malicious humour. Yet I still fail to read the excited leer on his face as he slaps his long, flaccid penis against my lips. I open my mouth and take him in, starting to suck, only to receive a sudden flood of urine down my throat. At my look of dismay, he starts to cackle. I gag briefly but manage to swallow, an act he greets with unconcealed delight. Still with his penis pumping hot fluid down my throat, he begins a capering dance, hopping from one hoof to the other and all the while watching the junction of his cock and my mouth with wide eyes full of merriment. I swallow as best I can, drinking his hot, acrid urine until he has drained himself fully down my throat and my belly is swollen and round with his water.

Finished, he makes no move to remove his penis from my mouth, but strokes my chin tentatively with a horny finger. I begin to suck once more and his grin of mirth droops a fraction while his eyes takes on a glazed expression. Soon I am rewarded as his cock begins to harden in my mouth. As I suck, his pungent, male cock taste grows, mingling with the ammoniac tang of his urine. Soon my senses are swimming with pleasure and I take his balls in my hands, squeezing and caressing the fat testicles in their leather sack while he paws my breasts.

I curl my legs high, offering my vagina, should my mouth prove inadequate. Yet even as I feel the cool air on my open vulva his penis jerks and my mouth is flooded with seed. This time I swallow eagerly, gulping it down to the tune of grunting and then exclamations of pure glee as his cock is thrust to the back of my throat and I gag on the head. He pulls back, leaving me with seed dribbling from my lips. Again he begins to caper, kicking his hooves high and clutching at his penis. I follow, crawling, eager to be filled again, however he chooses.

Seeing my need, a shadow of doubt passes across his face. I stop and turn, looking back over my shoulder and presenting him with my naked buttocks. Once more his face changes, caution warring with lust as his eyes feast on the details of my rear. I allow my knees to slip apart, lowering my bottom to a level at which he can conveniently mount me. My hair is trailing down my back and over my hips, offering him reins to hold, tempting him with the prospect of riding me with his penis wedged inside my bowels.

The crafty look returns to his face and he begins to stroke his penis. His eyes flicker from my face to my bottom, gauging my heat, watching the soft, wet entrance to my vagina, judging how easy it will be to violate my anal opening. For him that will be the culminating joke of my defilement: to penetrate my anus, to bugger me and spill his seed deep in my bowels.

He comes forward, smiling slyly, his erection once more jutting out beneath his paunch. He is reaching for my hair and, once he has it, I know that there will be no escape. I will be buggered. His wild laughter will fill the air as he rides my anus and steers me by my hair, bouncing on the soft saddle of my buttocks until his cock erupts inside me.

I want it, and I know that before he is satisfied that he is done with me, his lust must have been slaked in every orifice of my body. In truth, that is not enough for me. I want the God himself to come and take me, to pull me up on to the back of his beast and mount me on his penis. Yet I must resist, and keep my faith.

He rests his penis between my open buttocks, a hot pole that tempts me strongly to surrender. I jerk my head forward, pulling my hair clear of his reaching hand, then I am on my feet and running. His howl of frustration rings loud in my ears as I once more run down the valley. Then he is coming, his fat legs pumping as he clutches his bursting erection.

Glancing back I taunt, deliberately wriggling my bottom to show what he can have, if only he can catch me. His face is purple, bloated with the hot blood of lust and anger. I feel a pang of alarm and dash on, scampering over rocks and through bog, ever further down towards the distant trees.

If he catches me, I know my fate. I will be dragged back to the high moor and subjected to buggery and then to a series of yet more depraved pleasures. To him, it will be a delightful erotic farce as I am made to perform rude tricks and adopt lewd poses. It will be hours until he is sated and leaves me spoiled and sore among the rocks. I will beg for his touch as he leaves but he will simply laugh, not deigning to further abuse my soiled body.

Yet this serves only as a spur to me. He is short, his stumpy legs quite unable to match my pace. The raw, uncontrolled carnality in his face becomes comic, no terror but a thing of amusement. Once more I begin to taunt – pausing on a rock to cup my breasts and push my tongue out towards him; throwing a cartwheel in defiance of his ability to catch me; feigning a trip and landing kneeling with my bottom spread wide to his out-thrust penis. With each mocking pose, his passions grow, until he is coming behind me in a blind rush. His face is purple with blood and the same swollen quality as the engorged head of his still-hard penis.

My sense of mischief grows at the sight and I dance ahead. Still he comes, ever more furious, ever more lustful, until it seems that he must burst. I am laughing, and pause once more to present him my bottom, posed insolently, mocking his virility as I reach back to stretch my buttocks wide and slide a finger into the tight hole he is so desperate to possess. His response is a scream of unbearable frustration, and then he has snatched his pipes into his hand and begun to play.

Before the melody was light, a mocking serenade to all that is female. Now it is harsh, an urgent summons. With a frantic glance to the trees below I run, no longer teasing, no longer goading my pursuer, but with a desperate urgency born of the fear rising in my throat. The piping breaks off and a cackle of laughter follows me down the valley, then the far-off sound of a horn. It is a mournful, bass sound, a sound that fills me with terror and longing.

Now truly afraid, I strain my ears for what I know must come, the baying of dogs. Sure enough, they answer their Master's call, sounding from far away yet seemingly on every side. It is far too late to pose as a worshipper; now I will be known for what I am – no sacrifice, but a thief.

Black patterns flicker among the rocks to my sides, running on the hillsides, streaking towards me. They seem no more substantial than the shadows of clouds, yet I have no illusions as to their reality, nor to their nature. As they close, the baying grows, rising to a crescendo that speaks of sharp fangs and eager, black-furred cocks. There is laughter, too, the high cackling of the satyr and another, deeper, cruel yet bringing a terrible compulsion.

I need to stop, to fall to the earth, to grovel and beg and plead. Then I will be taken, used with a malign ferocity that will make the playful malice of the satyr seem as the caress of my own hand. The hounds will take me first, smothering me in a mound of their hot bodies, mounting me one by one, slaking their rigid cocks in vagina and rectum, drenching my body with seed, filling my mouth, coating my breasts and belly, soaking my hair.

Then it will be the satyrs – slower, more methodical, calculating sexual malice in place of raw need for ejaculation. I will be probed, opened, filled and emptied, soiled. There is a trick that goes with the squat on a girl's face, the mere thought of which adds new power to my aching legs. It is bound to be done, yet it will not be the final insult. That will be the denial of my wish to be given to Him.

I will be chained by the neck to a stone, naked and filthy, a mere plaything. I will be taught lewd tricks – the sump and the reluctant slug . . .

They are close and my rape is coming near. He is behind me, angry, a towering figure, black, horned and angular, the essence of the male. The shadows close and thicken, their black coats glistening in the sun, their eyes red and savage. A claw brushes my calf and I stumble, striking a tree, scrabbling for a hold on a ledge of rock, finding my feet . . .

I am among trees. The light is green and soft, the air warm and mellow. Shadows dance around me, but green shadows, shadows with soft, flowing contours, feminine shadows. There is a scream of stark fury from behind me and a new call on the horn, a long, melancholy note.

My breath is coming in furious pants as I slip to the ground, sinking into the wet embrace of thick moss, spreading my thighs with no fear whatever. A hand strokes my hair, only to draw suddenly back.

A sudden crash announces the arrival of my lust-crazed

satyr. He has leapt on to the wall and is looking into the wood, his eyes glazed with the need for soft, female flesh, his penis brandished in front of him, erect and menacing. He sees me and waddles forward, aiming his weapon at my parted legs, at the wet centre of my vagina, then lower, to the tight bud of my anus, so cruelly denied him.

He laughs to see my exhaustion, his position forgotten in his insensate lechery. I lower my head, too tired to fight, offering whatever it amuses him to take, just so long as he is able. A callused hand takes each of my ankles, tipping me suddenly up to expose the sweat-oiled crease between my buttocks. His tongue flicks out, eager for a taste. His face shows glee, a raw, vindictive quality, the delight of a captor in the helpless surrender of his prey.

Abruptly, his look turns to consternation as he is pulled sharply back. Limber arms take him, dragging him down among the moss and ferns of the woodland floor. I see his panic, his anger at the knowledge that it is he and not I who is the victim. A braid closes around his neck, signalling the start of his time as a seed beast, and it is my turn to laugh.

The sound is echoed and then large eyes of limpid green are looking into my face, full of concern, of delight, of love. A dozen slight, female creatures surround me, their hair long and green like my own, their faces delicate and sensitive but ever alive and always showing a subtle undercurrent of mockery – the feminine reflection of the malice of Satyrs. They do not laugh at me, but with me, and I respond, smiling as they touch my hot, wet skin.

They cluster around me, touching, stroking, always gentle. The body of the tallest is an exact mirror of mine, slight, pert-breasted, delicate. She comes to me, smiling, and our mouths meet in a long kiss. I give her the seed in my mouth, our tongues meeting in the thick, rich fluid. Her kisses are exquisite, making my head swim and my knees go weak. When her mouth is full of seed, she pulls gently away and begins to kiss my chin, my neck, my breasts. I arch my back in dizzy pleasure as her lips travel lower, kissing my nipples with a soft, loving touch, tracing a slow line down the mid-line of my body, on my belly, among the curls of my lower belly, on my sex.

My eyes close in bliss as she begins to feed from my vagina, taking the seed from me into her mouth. As she laps at me, my climax comes: a complete, fulfilling moment stronger by far than my response to the satyr's brute probing.

She is rising, once more taking me into her arms, holding me, drawing me down, melting into me. As we become one, I curl into the shelter of a fern, hugging my knees to my chin, making myself small. As I drift towards sleep, my last thoughts are of the crazed anger of the Wish Hunt, of the malice of Satyrs and of what might have been with just a pinch more agaric.

. . . actually, there's probably a happy, hairy little farmhand somewhere on the edge of Dartmoor.

Finally, here's a cheeky little piece I just couldn't resist, another point of view on one of my own memoirs . . .

An Extract from the Memoirs of Colonel Bufton BiS (Devizes)

It was during my customary morning walk that I first noticed something out of the ordinary. There's a dammed fine patch of clover in the lower corner of the field, and I was just thinking about it when I noticed an open gate. Through I went, wondering what was up and whether that old fool Bloxham had done it on purpose.

If he had, then it was mangles to thistles that there was a ripe young thing or two around, and they were sure to be ready for a dose of the old pizzle. I wasn't in the best of humour, I confess. The old ring was giving me gyp and it had drizzled for most of the night. Still, it was nothing that a poke at a ready young cunt or two wouldn't set to rights and I pushed forward with an expectant snort.

The dammed field was empty: not so much as a bloody rabbit. A spot or two of clover, mark you, and some longish grass, so I began to browse around and kept one ear cocked for old Bloxham. There was no sign of the fellow, but I did hear noises from up near the ridge.

Thinking that some damned trespasser might be around, I stuck my neck up and had a good peer. I couldn't see much, at first, just the skyline and a few indistinct trees. Yet I know my part of the country dammed well, and things weren't quite as usual. Something was flapping about in the breeze, something of a different tone to the trees. I was suspicious at once. I mean, it was damned clearly a sign, and people don't leave signs about without a reason. Then I caught it, the smell of fresh cunt on the breeze. Something was definitely afoot.

I began to walk up the field, taking my time as befits my status, but not entirely without urgency. As I got closer I realised what the thing in the tree was: a pair of girl's knickers. I'd seen that sort of thing before, of course: girls tend to take them off to buck the boys up and as often as not they get left in a hedge.

These were high up, and damned noisy on the old eyes, which was different. Only when I came up over the rise did I discover that my little excursion had been far from wasted. There was a fine little thing tethered to the stile, her haunches raised and spread to show off a neat, pale cunt that was obviously on heat. She was in a deuced awkward position, and not one that I'm used to, but she was well tethered, and obviously in need of a jolly good seeing-to. They'd put something across her haunches, too, perhaps to make her more tempting. The old pizzle was stirring, eager for his morning cunt, but well, you know how people are about that sort of thing . . .

Then she made a noise, a pretty damned eager noise.

Well, what was a fellow to do?

I took a quick sniff and a lick to check that she actually was in season and then mounted up on her back, resting my weight on the stile. She made a few noises when I prodded the old pizzle at her rump, but it went in all right and I was soon bashing away merrily. She did quite a bit of snorting, and so did I, right to the moment when I put my load up her.

They're usually quiet afterwards, but this one wasn't. Not a bit of it: she kept on her racket while I had a sniff and a peer to make sure I'd serviced her properly. There was a goodly measure of the right stuff running out of her cunt, so I decided that it was a job well done and lumbered off, feeling deuced pleased with myself.

By jingo, I'd given her a good humping, and it's mangles to thistles there was a bun in the oven by the end of it!

. . . *fortunately, there wasn't, or I really would have some explaining to do!*

This information is correct at time of printing. For up-to-date information, please visit our website at www.nexus-books.co.uk

All books are priced at £6.99 unless another price is given.

ABANDONED ALICE	Adriana Arden 0 352 33969 1	☐
ALICE IN CHAINS	Adriana Arden 0 352 33908 X	☐
AMAZON SLAVE	Lisette Ashton 0 352 33916 0	☐
ANGEL	Lindsay Gordon 0 352 34009 6	☐
AQUA DOMINATION	William Doughty 0 352 34020 7	☐
THE ART OF CORRECTION	Tara Black 0 352 33895 4	☐
THE ART OF SURRENDER	Madeline Bastinado 0 352 34013 4	☐
AT THE END OF HER TETHER	G.C. Scott 0 352 33857 1	☐
BELINDA BARES UP	Yolanda Celbridge 0 352 33926 8	☐
BENCH MARKS	Tara Black 0 352 33797 4	☐
BIDDING TO SIN	Rosita Varón 0 352 34063 0	☐
BINDING PROMISES	G.C. Scott 0 352 34014 2	☐
THE BLACK GARTER	Lisette Ashton 0 352 33919 5	☐
THE BLACK MASQUE	Lisette Ashton 0 352 33977 2	☐
THE BLACK ROOM	Lisette Ashton 0 352 33914 4	☐
THE BLACK WIDOW	Lisette Ashton 0 352 33973 X	☐
THE BOND	Lindsay Gordon 0 352 33996 9	☐

THE BOOK OF PUNISHMENT	Cat Scarlett 0 352 33975 6	☐
BRUSH STROKES	Penny Birch 0 352 34072 X	☐
BUSTY	Tom King 0 352 34032 0	☐
CAGED [£5.99]	Yolanda Celbridge 0 352 33650 1	☐
CALLED TO THE WILD	Angel Brake 0 352 34067 3	☐
CAPTIVES OF CHEYNER CLOSE	Adriana Arden 0 352 34028 2	☐
CARNAL POSSESSION	Yvonne Strickland 0 352 34062 2	☐
CHERRI CHASTISED	Yolanda Celbridge 0 352 33707 9	☐
COLLEGE GIRLS	Cat Scarlett 0 352 33942 X	☐
COMPANY OF SLAVES	Christina Shelly 0 352 33887 3	☐
CONCEIT AND CONSEQUENCE	Aishling Morgan 0 352 33965 9	☐
CONFESSIONS OF AN ENGLISH SLAVE	Yolanda Celbridge 0 352 33861 X	☐
CORRUPTION	Virginia Crawley 0 352 34073 8	☐
DARK MISCHIEF	Lady Alice McCloud 0 352 33998 5	☐
DEPTHS OF DEPRAVATION	Ray Gordon 0 352 33995 0	☐
DERRIÈRE	Julius Culdrose 0 352 34024 X	☐
DICE WITH DOMINATION	P.S. Brett 0 352 34023 1	☐
DISCIPLINE OF THE PRIVATE HOUSE	Esme Ombreux 0 352 33709 5	☐
DOMINANT	Felix Baron 0 352 34044 4	☐
THE DOMINO ENIGMA	Cyrian Amberlake 0 352 34064 9	☐
THE DOMINO QUEEN	Cyrian Amberlake 0 352 34074 6	☐

THE DOMINO TATTOO	Cyrian Amberlake 0 352 34037 1	☐
DOMINATION DOLLS	Lindsay Gordon 0 352 33891 1	☐
EMMA ENSLAVED	Hilary James 0 352 33883 0	☐
EMMA'S HUMILIATION	Hilary James 0 352 33910 1	☐
EMMA'S SECRET DOMINATION	Hilary James 0 352 34000 2	☐
EMMA'S SUBMISSION	Hilary James 0 352 33906 3	☐
EXPOSÉ	Laura Bowen 0 352 34035 5	☐
FAIRGROUND ATTRACTION	Lisette Ashton 0 352 33927 6	☐
FORBIDDEN READING	Lisette Ashton 0 352 34022 3	☐
FRESH FLESH	Wendy Swanscombe 0 352 34041 X	☐
THE GOVERNESS ABROAD	Yolanda Celbridge 0 352 33735 4	☐
HOT PURSUIT	Lisette Ashton 0 352 33878 4	☐
THE INDECENCIES OF ISABELLE	Penny Birch (writing as Cruella) 0 352 33989 6	☐
THE INDISCRETIONS OF ISABELLE	Penny Birch (writing as Cruella) 0 352 33882 2	☐
IN HER SERVICE	Lindsay Gordon 0 352 33968 3	☐
THE INSTITUTE	Maria Del Rey 0 352 33352 9	☐
JULIA C	Laura Bowen 0 352 33852 0	☐
KNICKERS AND BOOTS	Penny Birch 0 352 33853 9	☐
LACING LISBETH	Yolanda Celbridge 0 352 33912 8	☐
LEG LOVER	L.G. Denier 0 352 34016 9	☐

LICKED CLEAN	Yolanda Celbridge 0 352 33999 3	☐
NON FICTION: LESBIAN SEX SECRETS FOR MEN	Jamie Goddard and Kurt Brungard 0 352 33724 9	☐
LESSONS IN OBEDIENCE	Lucy Golden 0 352 33892 X	☐
LOVE JUICE	Donna Exeter 0 352 33913 6	☐
MANSLAVE	J.D. Jensen 0 352 34040 1	☐
THE MASTER OF CASTLELEIGH [£5.99]	Jacqueline Bellevois 0 352 33644 7	☐
MISS RATAN'S LESSON	Yolanda Celbridge 0 352 33791 5	☐
NAUGHTY NAUGHTY	Penny Birch 0 352 33974 4	☐
NEW EROTICA 5	Various 0 352 33956 X	☐
NEW EROTICA 6	Various 0 352 33751 6	☐
THE NEXUS LETTERS	Various 0 352 33955 1	☐
NIGHTS IN WHITE COTTON	Penny Birch 0 352 34008 8	☐
NO PAIN, NO GAIN	James Baron 0 352 33966 7	☐
NURSE'S ORDERS	Penny Birch 0 352 33739 7	☐
THE OLD PERVERSITY SHOP	Aishling Morgan 0 352 34007 X	☐
ONE WEEK IN THE PRIVATE HOUSE	Esme Ombreux 0 352 33706 0	☐
ORIGINAL SINS	Lisette Ashton 0 352 33804 0	☐
OVER THE KNEE	Fiona Locke 0 352 34079 7	☐
THE PALACE OF PLEASURES	Christobel Coleridge 0 352 33801 6	☐
PALE PLEASURES	Wendy Swanscombe 0 352 33702 8	☐

PENNY PIECES [£5.99]	Penny Birch 0 352 33631 5	☐
PETTING GIRLS	Penny Birch 0 352 33957 8	☐
PET TRAINING IN THE PRIVATE HOUSE [£5.99]	Esme Ombreux 0 352 33655 2	☐
THE PLAYER	Cat Scarlett 0 352 33894 6	☐
PLAYTHING	Penny Birch 0 352 33967 5	☐
PLEASING THEM	William Doughty 0 352 34015 0	☐
PRIZE OF PAIN	Wendy Swanscombe 0 352 33890 3	☐
THE PRIESTESS	Jacqueline Bellevois 0 352 33905 5	☐
PUNISHED IN PINK	Yolanda Celbridge 0 352 34003 7	☐
THE PUNISHMENT CAMP	Jacqueline Masterson 0 352 33940 3	☐
THE PUNISHMENT CLUB	Jacqueline Masterson 0 352 33862 8	☐
RITES OF OBEDIENCE	Lindsay Gordon 0 352 34005 3	☐
SCARLET VICE	Aishling Morgan 0 352 33988 8	☐
SCHOOLED FOR SERVICE	Lady Alice McCloud 0 352 33918 7	☐
SCHOOL FOR STINGERS	Yolanda Celbridge 0 352 33994 2	☐
THE SECRET SELF	Christina Shelly 0 352 34069 X	☐
SERVING TIME	Sarah Veitch 0 352 33509 2	☐
SEXUAL HEELING	Wendy Swanscombe 0 352 33921 7	☐
SILKEN EMBRACE	Christina Shelly 0 352 34081 9	☐
SILKEN SERVITUDE	Christina Shelly 0 352 34004 5	☐
SINS APPRENTICE	Aishling Morgan 0 352 33909 8	☐

SLAVE ACTS	Jennifer Jane Pope 0 352 33665 X	☐
SLAVE GENESIS [£5.99]	Jennifer Jane Pope 0 352 33503 3	☐
SLAVE OF THE SPARTANS	Yolanda Celbridge 0 352 34078 9	☐
THE SMARTING OF SELINA	Yolanda Celbridge 0 352 33872 5	☐
STRIP GIRL	Aishling Morgan 0 352 34077 0	☐
STRIPING KAYLA	Yvonne Marshall 0 352 33881 4	☐
STRIPPED BARE	Angel Blake 0 352 33971 3	☐
THE SUBMISSION GALLERY [£5.99]	Lindsay Gordon 0 352 33370 7	☐
THE SUBMISSION OF STELLA	Yolanda Celbridge 0 352 33854 7	☐
THE TAMING OF TRUDI	Yolanda Celbridge 0 352 33673 0	☐
TASTING CANDY	Ray Gordon 0 352 33925 X	☐
TEMPTING THE GODDESS	Aishling Morgan 0 352 33972 1	☐
THAI HONEY	Kit McCann 0 352 34068 1	☐
TICKLE TORTURE	Penny Birch 0 352 33904 7	☐
TIE AND TEASE	Penny Birch 0 352 33987 X	☐
TIGHT WHITE COTTON	Penny Birch 0 352 33970 5	☐
TOKYO BOUND	Sachi 0 352 34019 3	☐
TORMENT INCORPORATED	Murilee Martin 0 352 33943 8	☐
THE TRAINING GROUNDS	Sarah Veitch 0 352 33526 2	☐
UNDER MY MASTER'S WINGS	Lauren Wissot 0 352 34042 8	☐
UNEARTHLY DESIRES	Ray Gordon 0 352 34036 3	☐

UNIFORM DOLL	Penny Birch 0 352 33698 6	☐
VELVET SKIN [£5.99]	Aishling Morgan 0 352 33660 9	☐
WENCHES WITCHES AND STRUMPETS	Aishling Morgan 0 352 33733 8	☐
WHALEBONE STRICT	Lady Alice McCloud 0 352 34082 7	☐
WHAT HAPPENS TO BAD GIRLS	Penny Birch 0 352 34031 2	☐
WHAT SUKI WANTS	Cat Scarlett 0 352 34027 6	☐
WHEN SHE WAS BAD	Penny Birch 0 352 33859 8	☐
WHIP HAND	G.C. Scott 0 352 33694 3	☐
WHIPPING GIRL	Aishling Morgan 0 352 33789 3	☐

- - - - - - ✂ -

Please send me the books I have ticked above.

Name ....

Address ....

....

....

.... Post code ....

Send to: **Virgin Books Cash Sales, Thames Wharf Studios, Rainville Road, London W6 9HA**

US customers: for prices and details of how to order books for delivery by mail, call 888-330-8477.

Please enclose a cheque or postal order, made payable to **Nexus Books Ltd**, to the value of the books you have ordered plus postage and packing costs as follows:

UK and BFPO – £1.00 for the first book, 50p for each subsequent book.

Overseas (including Republic of Ireland) – £2.00 for the first book, £1.00 for each subsequent book.

If you would prefer to pay by VISA, ACCESS/MASTERCARD, AMEX, DINERS CLUB or SWITCH, please write your card number and expiry date here:

....

Please allow up to 28 days for delivery.

Signature ....

Our privacy policy

We will not disclose information you supply us to any other parties. We will not disclose any information which identifies you personally to any person without your express consent.

From time to time we may send out information about Nexus books and special offers. Please tick here if you do *not* wish to receive Nexus information. ☐

- - - - - - ✂ -